JASPER VALE

JASPER VALE

USA TODAY BESTSELLING AUTHOR
DEVNEY PERRY

Entangled Publishing, LLC
644 Shrewsbury Commons Ave., STE 181
Shrewsbury, PA 17361
rights@entangledpublishing.com

Amara is an imprint of Entangled Publishing, LLC.
Visit our website at www.entangledpublishing.com.

Edited by Elizabeth Nover
Cover art and design by Sarah Hansen at OkayCreations
Stock art by fantom_rd and Peter Stein/Shutterstock
Interior design by Britt Marczak

ISBN 978-1-64937-699-2

Manufactured in the United States of America

First Edition May 2024

10 9 8 7 6 5 4 3 2 1

an imprint of Entangled Publishing LLC

ALSO BY DEVNEY PERRY

CHAPTER 1

ELOISE

The Bellagio fountain sprayed water high into the air as lights lit up the streams. The white hotel stood proudly in the backdrop as the water twirled and danced in time with the music, a dramatic violin concerto.

"It looks like moonbeams." I sighed, leaning my head against Lyla's shoulder. "This is magical. We should put a water fountain in The Eloise."

My sister giggled. "Good luck convincing Dad."

"Can you imagine?" I snorted. "First, he'd tell me no. Then, he'd give me that scowly face where his eyebrows come together and he tilts his head to the side."

"Whenever he gives me the scowly face, he adds the blinky eyes," she said.

"Oh, yeah. The blinky eyes. I forgot about those." Dad would blink ten or eleven or twenty times in a row, like he was trying to figure out if I was joking or serious. "You know what I think is crap? I've never seen Dad give the scowly-blinky combo to Griffin, Knox or Mateo."

"Right? He saves it for us girls."

"Unfair."

According to Dad, our brothers didn't typically cause him the same kind of stress he claimed came with daughters. Whatever that meant.

"Are you drunk?" Lyla asked.

"Yep." I nodded. "You?"

Lyla hiccupped. "That meant yes."

I looped my arms with hers, snuggling closer as a dreamy smile settled on my face.

My limbs were a little loose. My head was a little fuzzy. My heart was a little light, floating through the air like mist. Drunk and happy, like the water fountain show.

"Tonight was fun," I murmured.

"Super fun. I'm glad we came. And I'm glad Foster won his fight."

"Me too." I let go of her arm, standing tall, then I cupped my hands to my mouth. "Go Foster Madden!"

"Eloise." Lyla swatted my arm as the people clustered around us shot me glares. "Would you shut up?"

I laughed. "Oh, who cares if I'm loud? We'll never see these fun haters again."

Tomorrow, we'd fly home to Montana. We'd say goodbye to the moonbeams and hello to reality.

Lyla and I had come to Las Vegas to watch a UFC event. Foster Madden, our sister Talia's boyfriend and the reigning middleweight champion of the world, had defended his title and defeated his opponent in tonight's fight.

He'd surprised Talia by flying us down—he hadn't wanted her to sit in the arena alone. But this was just a quick trip. Lyla and I each had to get back to Quincy for work on Monday, and tomorrow's early alarm clock would be brutal.

We'd decided to party tonight anyway. To have a few drinks.

To dance. To make the most of our cute outfits. Lyla had on a navy, one-shoulder jumpsuit that brought out the blue of her eyes. I'd opted for a simple black tube top with my tightest jeans and tallest heels. It was rare that either of us dressed up these days—demanding jobs were hell on a social life.

Tonight had been a much-needed break. I only wished it weren't coming to an end.

The fountain show finale finished too soon, and the crowd beside the Bellagio's lake dispersed.

Chase, the kid assigned to hang with us tonight, was standing a few feet away, dutifully waiting for Lyla and me with his hands clasped in front of him like he was our own personal security guard. Technically, he was.

Before Foster had swept Talia away to celebrate his victory in their hotel suite, he'd insisted Chase accompany us tonight. He worked for Foster's manager as an assistant and didn't look a day older than eighteen. I suspected that the ID he'd used to get into the club tonight wasn't exactly legal.

Considering he'd been relegated to babysitting duty, he was probably at the bottom of the UFC food chain. Poor guy. He'd followed us around all night without complaint but he looked dead on his feet.

"Ready to go to the hotel?" he asked.

I leaned in close to whisper in Lyla's ear. "Think he'll cry if we say no?"

She covered her laugh with a hand. "Yep."

Chase yawned. That damn yawn was the reason we'd left the club before midnight.

"Do you think Jasper is still at the club?" Lyla asked.

I shrugged. "I dunno."

Jasper Vale was Foster's trainer and best friend. He'd told

us about the after-party at the club and invited us along. It had mostly been guys from the UFC world, acquaintances of Jasper's and Foster's from when they'd lived in Vegas. But it had been nice to know at least one face in the crowd besides Lyla's.

"Do you want to go back and find out?" *Say yes.* More dancing. More drinks. *Say yes say yes say yes.*

Chase's face fell. He gave me this pitiful, helpless plea.

Oh, damn you, Chase.

At the club, after his twentieth yawn, I'd told him he could leave, but he'd refused. And so even though we'd been having a blast, I'd told Lyla it was time to make our way back to the hotel. I hated it when other people weren't having a good time.

Chase might be young but he was clearly smart. In just hours, he'd figured out I was the bleeding heart of the Eden family. He was wielding that yawn to shoo us along for bedtime.

Boo. "Oh, never mind," I muttered. "We should go."

"Yeah, my feet are killing me in these shoes," Lyla said.

"March on, Chase." As we started for our hotel, the chill in the night air raised goose bumps on my forearms. It was cold tonight, even for the desert. In early March, after the sun set, the temperatures dropped.

"Brr. It's co—" I gasped, patting my arms. "Oh, shit. Where's my jacket?"

We'd been on our way back to the hotel from the club when we'd passed the fountain, and I'd made our group detour so we could watch the show. I spun around, scanning the spot where we'd been standing, but my jacket wasn't anywhere in sight.

"I must have forgotten it at the club." I groaned. *Stupid Eloise.* "I love that jacket."

It was my favorite black leather coat. Not too thick. Not too thin. The sleeves were even long enough for my arms, which wasn't easy for me to find.

"We can go back and get it." It was Lyla who yawned this time.

She owned a coffee shop at home in Quincy, and considering that her normal wake-up time was well before dawn, I was proud of her for staying up so late. Normally she was in bed by nine. Lyla probably wouldn't even need an alarm in the morning. Meanwhile, there was a very real chance she'd have to drag me out of bed.

"We'll go to the suite so you can go to bed," I said. "Then me and Chase will hike back to the club for my jacket."

"Are you sure?"

I nodded, linked my arm with hers and signaled to Chase. "Lead on, Crouton."

Chase's lips pursed.

"I don't think he likes my nickname," I told Lyla.

She giggled as we fell in step, our heels clicking on the sidewalk as we trudged to our hotel, stopping outside the bank of elevators. Foster had gotten us our own suite for tonight with two separate bedrooms. Thank God. Lyla was a bed hog.

"Don't go anywhere without Chase." Lyla pointed a finger at my nose.

I raised a hand in salute. "Ma'am, yes, ma'am."

"Eww." She scrunched up her nose. "Don't ma'am me."

"Madam?"

"Queen Lyla will suffice." She tried a curtsy but stumbled, too tipsy to keep her balance.

"Oh my God." I jumped to snag her hand, helping her stand upright.

"Heels are the enemy." She shot a frown at her feet, then stepped into the open elevator. "See you in a bit?"

"Be back in a flash." I waved as the doors slid closed, then gave Chase my evilest smile. "Let's do shots."

His jaw dropped.

"Kidding," I singsonged, retracing our steps through the lobby and outside.

We'd just passed the fountain again, the water dark and calm, when a familiar face appeared on the sidewalk ahead.

"Oh, hey. There's Jasper." I pointed.

Chase raised a hand.

Jasper did the same. And in his hand was my jacket.

"Yay." I clapped my hands together, stopping as Jasper joined us on the sidewalk. "You're my hero. Thank you."

"Welcome." He held out the black leather, helping me slide it onto my arms.

I smiled up at him, having to crane my neck to keep his gaze. Wow, he was tall. Why hadn't I realized how tall he was before? He was about the same height as my brothers. "You're tall. How tall?"

"Six two." His deep voice had a rasp, like he didn't use it enough so it wasn't smooth.

"You have a nice voice."

The corner of his mouth quirked. "Are you drunk?"

"Oh, yeah." Even after all the walking, my buzz was solid. Would I feel great in six hours when I had to be at the airport? Nope.

Jasper's eyes crinkled at the sides, like he thought I was funny. Not laugh-out-loud funny, obviously, but amusing funny.

Was I funny? *I* thought I was funny. "Chase, do you think

I'm funny?"

He looked at me and blinked too many times.

I frowned. "My dad does that. The scowl-blink combo. I hate it. Maybe it's a guy thing. I talk a lot when I'm drunk."

"Huh?" Chase turned to Jasper. "I didn't understand any of that."

"You can take off," Jasper said, coming to Chase's rescue.

"But Mr. Madden said I had to stay with them until they were back in their suite."

"I'll make sure she gets back." Jasper jerked his chin. "Go. Have fun."

"I'm going to sleep." Chase took a step backward. Then another. Then he turned, walking so fast it was nearly a jog.

"Bye!" I called. "Thank you for babysitting us!"

That's when Chase actually started running.

"I don't think he liked babysitting," I told Jasper. "Can we watch the fountain show again?"

"Sure." Jasper walked toward the concrete half wall that bordered the lake, finding an open space.

I squeezed in beside him, resting my forearms on the flat surface. Then I propped a foot up between the rounded columns beneath. "I like water fountains."

"Then you're in the right place." Jasper kept his eyes aimed forward, overlooking the quiet water as I stared up at his profile.

It was the nicest profile I'd ever seen. He had a perfect forehead. Not too round. Not too flat. His dark brown hair was longer on top and shorter at the sides, a few strands sticking up out of place. He had a strong chin, square at the bottom. Soft lips with a full pout. A classic nose except there was a bump on the bridge, like it had been broken before.

"Does it hurt when you break your nose?"

"Yes." He glanced down at me, his brown eyes catching the Vegas lights and giving them a sparkle.

Jasper had lived in Montana for months. There weren't a lot of single, handsome men in my small hometown, so when Jasper had arrived in Quincy, he hadn't gone unnoticed.

Or maybe he had.

Seriously, he was hot. Smoking hot. I should have been crushing on him for months.

Was this beer goggles? I'd never had them before. Except I hadn't had any beer tonight. Just those vodka tonics and the shots Lyla and I had taken before we'd left the club, but they hadn't hit me yet.

"You're extremely hot."

Okay, maybe the shots were kicking in after all.

Jasper arched an eyebrow the same dark shade as his hair.

"You're kinda grumpy and brooding too. Also hot."

"Do you always say what's on your mind?"

"Only when I'm drunk, remember? I talk a lot."

Jasper stared down at me, something flashing in his gaze, but I couldn't make it out. The fuzzy edges of my mind were beginning to get fuzzier.

"What else?" Jasper asked.

I studied his mouth as he spoke, the way he formed the words. The flex in that sharp, chiseled jaw. "What else what?"

"What else is on your mind?"

"Oh." I let my gaze trail down his chest, taking in his broad frame stretching the black T-shirt he wore with faded jeans. The shirt's cotton molded like a second skin to his biceps and shoulders but was looser against his stomach. Did he have a six-pack? I bet he had a six-pack. "I'd kill to see you without your shirt on."

Jasper barked a laugh. It was hoarse too, like he didn't laugh enough.

Sad. Should I give him a hug?

Too busy contemplating that question, I didn't realize what he was doing until it was too late.

Jasper reached a hand behind his head, fisting his shirt. *Whoosh*.

Shirt gone.

"Holy. Freaking. Abs." My jaw dropped. "Six. Definitely six."

"Eight," he corrected. "Count again."

"Whoa." I reached out to pet a muscle, just to make sure it was real. The muscles bunched beneath my fingertips.

"That tickles."

"You're ticklish? Aww. That's adorable."

He frowned. "I think I liked it better when you called me grumpy and brooding."

"Ow, ow!" A woman walking behind us did a catcall. "Sweetie, if you're not gonna drag that man to your hotel room, please send him to mine. Planet Hollywood. Room 1132."

My cheeks flamed.

Jasper was Foster's best friend. I couldn't drag him to my hotel room, right? *Right*. That could get awkward. But I really wanted him to lose those jeans too. What did his legs look like? Were his thighs as bulky as they looked? Were they dusted with the same dark hair that trailed from his navel to the waistband of his jeans? How far did that trail go, anyway?

"Eloise."

My gaze whipped up to his face. "I like how you say my name."

"You're blushing." Jasper's voice dropped to barely a whisper. Something else crossed his gaze, maybe teasing, maybe flirting, but it happened too fast for my sluggish brain to catch.

"I'm drunk," I blurted.

"So am I."

"No way." My mouth parted. "You are?"

"Yep." He leaned in closer, his eyes, slightly unfocused, drifting to my lips.

"Um, are you going to kiss me?"

Jasper hummed. "Thinking about it."

For the first time tonight, I was speechless.

He leaned in.

I lifted my chin.

But then a gurgle filled the air and beside us, the quiet pool of water erupted into those moonbeam streams.

The people around us surged forward, forcing us against the concrete barrier and breaking the moment.

Bummer. I sighed, shifting to watch the show.

Jasper tugged on his shirt, then leaned forward too, our shoulders brushing as music filled the air.

The song was different this time, an intense symphony with a fast tempo and a heavy drum beat. The timing of the music and lights and movement was synchronized flawlessly.

"It's perfect," I murmured. "How many tries do you think it took for them to get this perfect?"

"I don't know."

I leaned into his arm, my head hitting his shoulder. He didn't shift or nudge me away, so I didn't move. "I think perfect is overrated."

"Agreed."

"When I was a kid, I used to get so mad when stuff wasn't perfect. Like if I was drawing a picture and messed up, I couldn't just erase the mistake or live with it. I'd have to get a new piece of paper and start all over again."

There'd be piles of crumpled paper around me and tears dripping down my face because I couldn't get the picture just right.

"I don't know what happened or why I did it," I said. "One day I was trying to color my dad a birthday card. He loves horses, and when I asked him what he wanted for a birthday present, he told me to draw him a horse. Have you ever tried to draw a horse?"

"No."

"Well, trust me. They're hard. I couldn't do it. I kept trying and trying. I just wanted to give him that horse and make him happy. And I had this special paper that was really thick. What do they call that paper?"

"Cardstock."

"Yeah, cardstock. It's hard to crumple so I ripped my mess-ups in half instead. Anyway, I was on my last sheet and screwed up the horse. But I didn't have any more paper. So I stole Talia's box of paints from her bedroom and covered up my ugly horse. It was just random swirls of color but I covered the whole page, all the way to the edges. There was paint everywhere by the time I was done. Talia got mad because I used her brand-new paints. Mom got mad because I made a mess and splattered some on the floor. But I loved that card. Dad hung it in his office, even though it wasn't the horse he wanted. It's still there too. And he doesn't know that underneath all the pretty colors is a really ugly horse."

The fountain show began the finale, the water jets spraying

shoots as high into the air as they'd go.

"I like perfect," I murmured. "I like imperfect too. I like wild and reckless moments that you never forget."

Like tonight.

Once more, the show ended too soon, the water dark and slowly calming. But I wasn't ready for calm. There was energy bubbling in my fingertips. Humming beneath my skin. So I moved away from the barrier, spinning in a circle with my arms out at my sides. My footing faltered, but before I could trip, a strong hand clamped over my elbow, helping me keep my balance.

"Whoa." I giggled. "No more spinning for me. Drunk and heels don't mix."

"Want to head back to your hotel?"

I pouted. "Not really."

This was fun. This was the best night I'd had in years. Something about Vegas, the crowds, the energy, was freeing.

There were no responsibilities tonight. No expectations.

"Are you really drunk?" I planted my hands on my hips, studying Jasper's face. "You don't seem drunk."

He chuckled. "How should I seem if I'm drunk?"

"I don't know." I tossed out a hand. "I've never seen you drunk before. But most people...loosen up."

"I'm loose."

I rolled my eyes. "You're all stiff. We're supposed to be having fun."

"I took my shirt off for you."

"This is true. And that was fun for me." I tapped my chin. "Do something. Right now. Prove you're drunk."

Jasper's eyes crinkled again. "Like what?"

"I don't know. You're the one who used to live here. What's

something spontaneous to do in Vegas?"

A man walking by answered for Jasper. "Get married."

I scoffed. "We can't get married."

"Why not?" the guy asked, still walking, his arms raised.

"Yeah," Jasper said. "Why not?"

CHAPTER 2

JASPER

The rustle of clothes being shoved into a suitcase filled the hotel bedroom. Then came the pad of bare feet as Eloise tiptoed to the bathroom. Seconds later, she tiptoed back. Then came a muffled plop, probably her toiletry case joining her clothes. That was followed by the click of a zipper, every notch joined so slowly it was painful to hear.

My wife was sneaking out.

My wife.

I fought the urge to curse into my pillow. My head was spinning. The headache throbbing behind my temples was less from last night's alcohol and more from this morning's situation.

But I didn't dare move. I lay completely still, my breaths shallow and nearly silent.

Eloise thought I was still asleep. We'd keep it that way. For now. Until I knew how to fix this.

What the hell had I been thinking?

I'd married Eloise. *Married.*

That word had been bouncing through my brain for hours. Hours I should have spent sleeping.

Except I hadn't slept for more than a few minutes at a time

last night. Every time I'd drift off, Eloise would curl into my side or snuggle against my back. I'd spent most of last night pushing her back to the opposite side of the bed. But each time I'd shifted away, she'd followed.

A cuddler. Of course I'd marry a woman who cuddled.

I loathed cuddling.

Fuck. Fuck. Fuck.

My head pounded with each silent curse. Of all the stupid decisions I'd made in life, last night's was by far the dumbest.

Eloise padded to the bathroom again, closing herself inside before she flipped on the light.

As I cracked my eyes open, a glow escaped from beneath the door. The faucet turned on so I shifted, burying my face in the pillow, and let out a groan.

Could this be more of a disaster?

For about an hour last night, I'd contemplated sneaking out while she'd been asleep to delay the inevitable, awkward conversation about unraveling this mess. Except the damage was done. This wasn't some random woman I'd fucked last night.

This was Eloise.

So I'd stayed. I'd cuddled.

Hell. Foster was going to skin me alive. I was a dead man for marrying Talia's sister. What if I just didn't go back to Montana? If I hid out in Vegas for the next decade, would he forgive me?

Tempting. So goddamn tempting.

Just like Eloise.

The light clicked off in the bathroom. I closed my eyes, once more feigning sleep like a goddamn coward. The door swept open almost silently except for a slight creak in the hinge. Then her bare feet crossed the room once more.

Another zipper. Another rustle.

An annulment. That was the answer.

Maybe I'd get lucky and Eloise would agree to keeping this shit show between us. No one really needed to know we'd gotten married, right? We could just deal with it on the sly.

Sort of like how she was trying to sneak out.

If she wanted to disappear this morning, I was going to let her. The annulment conversation could wait until I got back to Montana.

The sound of traffic, of the city stirring, hummed in the background. Muted light crept through the windows. Too busy stripping each other naked, we'd forgotten to close the blinds when we'd stumbled into the room last night.

We'd fucked. Hard. Bare. My cock stirred to life beneath the sheets. It had been a long, long time since I'd gone without a condom, but when Eloise had told me she was on birth control and it had been a while, well... I'd broken my own rule about protection. It had been a while for me too.

Eloise had met my passion with her own. There'd been nothing soft or gentle. We'd clawed at each other, rough and wild. It was the best sex I'd had in, well... a long damn time.

Why couldn't I have just screwed her? Why had I taken her to that fucking chapel?

Too far. I'd pushed much too far.

She wouldn't want to stay married, would she? Eloise had to know that this wasn't serious. That this was a drunken mistake.

She moved again, and even with my eyes closed, I felt her come close. Her feet, barely a whisper on the hotel room carpet, stopped beside the bed. The air shifted as Eloise crouched down.

I opened my eyes.

And saw blue.

Heart-stopping blue. Exquisite blue.

Her gaze was the color of sapphires. The cobalt of dawn. The azure of the hottest flame.

I'd gotten lost in that blue last night. First beside the Bellagio fountain. Then in this very bed.

We stared at each other, the weight of what we'd done settling between us like a ton of bricks.

Eloise's beautiful face was etched with regret. She opened her mouth, about to say something, but a knock came at the door. She jerked, nearly falling to her ass.

I shot out a hand, grabbing hers to keep her upright.

Eloise's gaze locked on my grip. Her fingers tightened, for just a moment, then she shook me loose. She held up a finger and pressed it to her lips.

Shh.

So she did want to keep me a secret.

Why did that burn? Wasn't that what I wanted too—*needed* too?

"Are you about ready to go?" Lyla called from beyond the closed door.

"Be right there," Eloise answered, but she didn't make a move for the door. She stayed crouched beside me for a long heartbeat, like she was trying to figure out what to say.

That made two of us.

"We're going to be late," Lyla said.

Eloise's shoulders fell. "One sec."

Then she gave me a sad smile before she mouthed, "I'm sorry."

Like this was her fault.

Why should she be sorry? It had been my idea. I'd been the one to hail us a cab. I'd been the one to direct the driver to the chapel. I'd been the one to rush inside, just before the midnight cutoff, and ask for a marriage license.

Me.

This whole fucking catastrophe rested firmly on my shoulders.

All because Eloise had told me that story about her horse drawing.

Damn it to hell. She wasn't the one who should be apologizing. But before I could say a word, she was gone, rushing to the corner.

She pulled on a pair of tennis shoes, then swept up the carry-on suitcase she'd packed, extending the handle. Its sharp click was like a jab to the rib cage.

I shifted, lying flat on my back, quickly tugging the covers to my chin, hoping to hide from Lyla. Then I stared at the ceiling, watching the shadows shift as Eloise eased the door open just enough to slip out.

"Ready." Eloise's attempt at chipper came out forced. Too bright and too loud.

"Why are you yelling?" Lyla grumbled. "I'm hungover. Are you?"

"Um, yeah. Let's go."

The wheels of their luggage faded as they were dragged through the suite's common room. Then the exterior door slammed closed, leaving me alone.

Foster had gotten this suite for Eloise and Lyla. He'd made sure that Talia hadn't had to sit alone during last night's fight. He'd told me all about this surprise for Talia. Not once as he'd explained the logistics had I thought I'd be sleeping in the room he'd reserved for them.

"Son of a bitch." I rolled to my stomach, burying my nose in the sheets.

Eloise's perfume clung to the cotton. Vanilla with an earthy depth. Floral but spicy, almost like a man's cologne. Except it was entirely female. Entirely Eloise.

The only good thing about her sleeping so close had been that smell. That, and my bride's naked body pressed against my own.

Fuck. Fuck. Fuck.

I pushed up on my elbows, twisting to a seat. The sheet was tangled around my legs, covering me to the waist. I dragged both hands through my hair, rubbing my eyes and the ache in my skull. Then I looked to the window, to the dawn creeping over the desert.

How could I have let this happen? How could I have taken it so far? Of all the spontaneous things to do in Vegas, why marriage?

What now?

Eloise was on her way back to Montana.

I'd planned to stay in Vegas for a while. Now that Foster's fight was over, he'd take a break from training. He'd spend time with Talia and his daughter, Kadence. There was nothing waiting for me in Montana except a rented A-frame cabin and snow.

Since snow and I didn't exactly get along well, I'd thought a month in Nevada might be a welcome change. That it would give Foster some time to figure out his next move.

He'd mentioned retirement, and as much as I'd hate to lose my time with him, I wouldn't blame him for hanging it up. He'd had an incredible career with the UFC. I was honored to be a small part of that journey.

But if he did decide to stop fighting, then I had some decisions to make. Return to Vegas? Train another fighter? Try somewhere new? It was a lot easier to think when winter wasn't trying to freeze my balls off.

Except I couldn't exactly stay in Vegas for too long now, could I? Eloise and I had a problem to solve.

And I didn't even have her phone number.

"Shit." My fist hammered into the mattress at my side. How could I have been so stupid?

With a quick yank, the sheet ripped free from my legs. I stood from the bed, prowling to the bathroom. I eyed the shower, about to turn on the spray, but changed directions, returning to the bedroom to collect my clothes strewn across the floor.

Eloise's scent, still clinging to my skin, would be my punishment today. A reminder of the epic mistake I'd made last night.

I tugged on my boxers and jeans, then pulled on last night's T-shirt. The shirt I'd taken off beside the fountain all because Eloise had wanted to see me without it on.

Who took off their shirt in public? Hell, if she had asked me to strip out of my jeans, I would have done it.

There was a reason I didn't drink.

Drunk, I was a fucking idiot.

"Ugh." I rubbed my hands over my face, like that could turn back time. Erase this humiliation.

When was the last time I'd been embarrassed? *Years*. The last time I'd felt like this it had also been because of a woman.

But Eloise wasn't to blame for the icky feeling creeping beneath my skin. No, that was all on me.

I needed to get the fuck out of this hotel room.

I needed to get the hell off the strip.

I needed to never drink tequila again.

Eloise and I had both been drunk. Not blackout drunk. Not slurring, sloppy drunk. No, we'd been the dangerous kind of drunk, the kind when you thought you were still in control. When inhibitions were low and courage was high. When you were foolish enough to believe a wild, reckless idea was the challenge of a lifetime.

"Fucking tequila."

With my shoes on, I left the room, digging my wallet from my jeans pocket. Then I took the elevator down two floors, rushing to my own hotel room. The bed was made, its white sheets crisp and undisturbed from yesterday's housekeeping.

I owned a house an hour from here, but Foster had wanted us all close to the strip for the fight, so he'd reserved me a room. Maybe I should have insisted on sleeping in my own damn bed. Then I wouldn't have gone to the club last night. I wouldn't have been anywhere near Eloise Eden.

My backpack was on a chair in the corner, so I hurried to pack it up, shoving my clothes and toiletries inside. Then I slung it over a shoulder and left the hotel, walking through the lobby to the main exit.

There were cabs waiting, but I passed them, needing to walk for a while before going home. To burn off some energy. To think.

The morning air was fresh. Crisp and cool. I drew in a long breath, smelling the water they'd used this morning to hose down the entrance. The concrete was still damp in a few places untouched by the sun. Clean, for now. Someone would probably puke on it later.

Nothing ever really stayed clean.

Especially in Vegas.

That had always been part of Vegas's appeal. No matter how many sparkling, neon bulbs they added to the strip, there was always some dirt. Grit, like the sand that waited beyond the city's borders.

People here flaunted their fake. There was freedom to be gaudy and loud. Judgment was loosened, usually by alcohol.

Last night was the ultimate example of Vegas's poison. Eloise, a pure, beautiful woman, had been corrupted by Sin City. Tainted by a man whose demons had come out to play.

With my chin down, I kept my gaze locked on the sidewalk as I headed toward Las Vegas Boulevard. Left would take me to the Bellagio fountain.

I turned right.

Not a chance I could face that fountain this morning. With no destination in mind other than *away*, I walked, my hands tucked in my pockets.

Block after block, I waited for the pressure in my chest to lighten. Exercise had always been my outlet. My refuge. Except the tension in my shoulders, the pit in my stomach, seemed to grow with every step.

That's when I looked up.

And realized this path I was walking was familiar.

"For fuck's sake, Vale."

I should have taken a left and faced that fountain. Apparently my feet had developed a mind of their own. And this morning, they wanted to return to the scene of last night's crime.

The small, square building was out of place against the backdrop of sprawling casinos and massive towers. It was too charming. Too real. It belonged anywhere else.

But that was another part of Vegas's appeal. This city

welcomed all shapes and sizes. A couple could get married by Elvis beneath the glow of neon lights at a chapel that offered ninety-nine-dollar weekday specials. Or they could come here.

The Clover Chapel.

The white stucco walls were dotted with intricate, stained glass windows. Their blues and greens caught the morning light. A steeple with a brass bell sat atop the peaked roof. Vines with dainty flowers climbed the structure.

The pale wooden doors were marked with a small four-leaf clover tacked above the threshold. At my rental in Montana, there was a horseshoe in that spot instead.

Maybe if I believed in luck, maybe if I'd ever been lucky, I would have appreciated those symbols.

The chapel was closed now. Clover herself was probably at home, rolling in the cash I'd paid last night. The Clover Chapel didn't do ninety-nine-dollar specials, certainly not for last-minute walk-ins only minutes before closing.

But you paid for their ambience.

You paid for the wisteria blooms that filled the open ceiling. They charged a premium for guests wanting to get married beneath a pergola teeming with glittering twigs, fairy lights, greenery and magnolia flowers. For the aisle lined with short, wooden pews to make you feel like you weren't getting married in Las Vegas but in some quaint country church, surrounded by beloved guests.

Of all the places in the world, why would I come here again?

The ugly horse.

I'd brought Eloise here because of the story she'd told me about that ugly horse drawing.

She'd created such a vivid picture with that tale. Of her as an angry child, painting over a sketch so she could give her dad the card he wanted. I could picture her as a kid, desperate to please her father and surrounded by her shredded attempts at a birthday card. Then her again, smiling and happy, her skin marred with every shade of paint as she flipped off the idea of perfection.

That was why I'd brought her here last night.

She wasn't the only one who wanted to take something ugly, something lacking, something painful, and cover it up with something beautiful.

"Pretty chapel, isn't it?" A woman walking a chihuahua on a sparkly pink leash passed by. Her rainbow iridescent visor matched the dog's collar.

I nodded, waiting for her to leave. Then I focused on the building again.

An ugly horse.

Covered in vibrant paint.

Yeah, this was a pretty chapel. I'd thought so the last time I'd been here.

The first time I'd gotten married in Las Vegas.

CHAPTER 3

ELOISE

"**M**iss?"

I jerked at the lady's voice. Lost in my head, drawing invisible circles on the hotel's mahogany reception counter, I hadn't heard her approach.

Guests had been sneaking up on me for the last three days, ever since I'd come home from Vegas.

"Sorry." I gave her a bright smile. "Welcome to The Eloise Inn. Checking in?"

"Yes." She nodded, then gave me her name to pull up in our reservation system.

Five minutes later, I slid over two key cards tucked into a paper envelope with her room number written on its face.

"The elevator is there." I pointed toward the foyer. "You're in room 302. Take a right when you get off the elevator and your room is at the end of the hallway. Can I have anything sent up for you this afternoon?"

"No, thank you." She smiled, glancing around the lobby. "This is my first visit to Quincy. Your hotel is delightful."

"Thank you." I beamed at the compliment. "I think it's rather delightful myself. Welcome to town. Are you here visiting friends or family?"

"My sister just moved here."

"Ah." I nodded. Had I met said sister?

Quincy was a small town. When it came to the locals, there weren't many faces I didn't recognize. Though lately, that had changed. More and more people were looking to escape city life, and my hometown was a rural gem tucked into the rugged landscape of western Montana.

"Enjoy your stay," I told the guest. "Please let me know if you need anything at all."

With a wave, she headed toward the elevator.

Beside it, the walls were lined with potted evergreens. The miniature trees were still adorned with the white twinkle lights we'd added for the holidays. Taking the lights off was on my to-do list, I just hadn't gotten to it yet. Mostly because their tiny sparkles added a bit of charm to the hallway.

We were in the strange season in Montana, not quite winter, not quite spring. Beyond the glass windows that overlooked Main Street, there was a fresh skiff of snow on the sidewalks.

A wood fire crackled in the large hearth on one side of the grand room. I'd keep the fire going until the snow was gone. I liked the gentle, smoky scent it gave the hotel's lobby. And the mantel, the stone column that towered to the rafters, just looked prettier with a fire burning in its hearth.

The Eloise Inn, named after my great-great-grandmother, had been in our family for generations. She'd been my namesake. Maybe it was fate that I loved this hotel as much as I liked to imagine she'd loved it too.

My favorite vanilla candle was burning on the coffee table, its sweetness mixing with the fire's smoke. It was cozy. Warm. I wanted guests to feel like they'd been wrapped in a hug when they walked through the doors of the hotel.

My hotel. Sort of.

Technically, The Eloise belonged to my parents, even though I'd been the manager for years. Even though most people in Quincy thought it was mine.

Not quite yet. Not officially.

Mom and Dad wanted to make sure I was ready to take over. That I was mature. That I was capable of handling this level of responsibility.

A week ago, I would have volunteered to be the poster child for responsibility. Sensible might as well have been my middle name.

Except then I'd flown to Las Vegas last weekend. And gotten married on a whim.

"Oh God." Every time I thought about Saturday night, I wanted to hurl.

What the hell was wrong with me? I was never, ever drinking again. That had been the most impulsive, reckless decision of my life.

"Ugh." I dropped my face into my hands.

I was twenty-six years old. And married to a stranger.

My family was going to freak the fuck out.

Maybe Jasper and I could keep it a secret. Get it annulled before anyone learned the truth. Erase the marriage from existence. Then it could be more like a *whoopsie*. If it was null and void by the time they found out, my parents couldn't get too mad, right?

Sneaking out of the hotel on Sunday morning hadn't been the best idea. Jasper and I should have talked. At the bare minimum, we should have exchanged phone numbers.

Was Jasper back in Montana yet? He was coming back,

wasn't he? Because I was going to need some information, like his legal name and a physical address.

And I was going to need a lawyer. I didn't have a lawyer.

In normal situations, I'd call my dad. He'd tell me who to call and what to say.

Not this time.

If I wanted to keep this marriage a secret, I'd have to find an attorney outside of Quincy. Missoula was two hours away. Was that far enough to keep any rumors from spreading? Not that I didn't trust in attorney-client privilege, but I'd lived my whole life in a small town. Secrets always had a way of coming to light.

A plan. I needed a plan.

So I plucked a pen from the pen cup and flipped to a fresh page in the notebook I'd been doodling on earlier.

Step 1: Find a lawyer.

No, that wasn't step one. I scribbled over the words, blacking them out. Then started over on the next line.

Step 1: Find Jasper.

If he was back in Quincy, he'd clearly been avoiding me. Not that I'd minded. These past few days, I hadn't been ready to face him, to relive the shame of my drunken self.

Humiliation crawled down my spine, making me cringe.

I'd gotten married.

To a stranger.

In. A. Tube top.

"What is wrong with me?"

Alcohol had played a major role in the disaster that was Saturday, but it hadn't been the only motivator. I'd gotten caught up in the adventure. In the spontaneity. In the charm of that chapel.

And Jasper had been so...certain.

Not once had he wavered.

He'd walked into that chapel, his hand holding mine, with sheer determination. And when he'd asked for a marriage license in that rugged voice, it had sounded like the best idea in the world.

Standing beneath that beautiful pergola, beneath a ceiling of wisteria blooms, I'd convinced myself it was fate.

Stupid fate.

Stupid Eloise.

It was okay. I could fix this. No more avoiding Jasper. After work, I'd track down my husband.

Talia had mentioned that he'd rented a long-term cabin from the Stewarts. They had four vacation rentals in town. Only one of those was a cabin. Which meant Jasper had to be staying in the A-frame on Alderson Road.

Well, I wasn't going to call Talia and ask. If he wasn't there, I'd swing by the other rentals until I found him.

Step 2: Ask Jasper not to tell a soul. Especially Foster.

The doors opened as my pen scribbled on the paper. My heart climbed into my throat as my parents walked inside the lobby.

"Hi," I said too brightly, tucking the notepad out of sight. Then I searched their faces for any hint of irritation.

Mom was smiling. That was a good sign, right? If she'd found out about Jasper, she'd be in tears.

Dad glanced around the lobby, taking it all in. That was normal too. If he was mad at me, he'd be wearing the scowl.

Phew. Everything was fine. They didn't know. They didn't have to know.

I'd find Jasper, and we'd figure this out. This marriage would be gone in a flash. Deleted. Erased. A blip that had never happened.

"Hi, sweetheart." Mom rounded the reception desk, standing by my tall chair. She touched a lock of my hair. "Your hair looks pretty today."

"Thanks."

Sleep had been impossible the past three days. Every time I'd drift off, I'd see Jasper's face. Either I'd dream of him at the chapel, saying *I do*. Or I'd picture him in bed as he moved inside me.

Last night, I'd woken to a throb between my legs so powerful I'd climbed out of bed at three in the morning to deep clean my refrigerator. Then I'd spent an extra thirty minutes after a shower curling my hair.

Tonight, when I inevitably woke up before dawn, I was going to scrub the baseboards around my house. *Good times.*

"Hi, kiddo." Dad stopped in front of the counter, running a hand along its edge like he was searching for any raised wood that might give a guest a splinter. But as always, it was smooth and polished to a shine.

I cleaned this counter at least ten times a day to erase fingerprints.

"Hey, Dad. What are you guys up to today?"

"Oh, just running errands," he said. "I told Griffin I'd pick up a couple things at Farm and Feed for him. Save him a trip into town."

"You're not babysitting today?" I asked Mom.

"No." She pouted. Mom often watched my nephews and niece. Three kids, all under the age of two. Only she would be disappointed to have a day off. "Winn had to cover a patrol shift last weekend, so she took today off to spend with Emma and Hudson. And Memphis wanted to keep Drake home today so they could bond with the baby."

"Ah."

Memphis, my brother Knox's wife, had just given birth to a baby boy. Harrison, named after Dad.

Not only was she my sister-in-law, but she was my favorite employee. She'd moved to Quincy for a housekeeping job at The Eloise. That was how she'd met Knox.

She was the best housekeeper I'd ever had, and selfishly, I wanted her to come back after her maternity leave. But I also wasn't fooling myself. Chances were, she'd stay home with her kids.

"How are things going here?" Dad asked.

"Good. Busy." With Memphis gone, we'd had to shuffle some staff around to cover shifts. Yesterday, I'd been shorthanded, so I'd done laundry and some general cleaning in the lobby.

Whatever it took to keep this place sparkling and guests smiling.

"We were hoping you had a minute to talk." Mom shared a look with Dad.

A look that made my stomach clench.

"Okay," I drawled. This couldn't be about Jasper. Not a chance. Regardless, my heart climbed into my throat. "About?"

"Do you want to put the sign up? Head to your office?"

A closed-door conversation? *Oh hell.* "Um..."

"We can just visit here, Anne." Dad checked over his shoulder, confirming we were alone.

The air rushed from my lungs.

A discussion at the desk meant I wasn't in deep shit. Yet.

The lobby was empty, and every guest who was due to check in today had already arrived. So while we might get the occasional interruption, it would most likely be uneventful until around five. That was when the locals would come in to eat at Knox's restaurant, Knuckles.

"What's up?" I asked.

"Two things." Dad held up a couple fingers. "I had to stop in at the bank the other day and was talking to Randy."

The bank president wasn't my favorite person in town. Whenever he came into the hotel, he brought with him an air of self-importance.

"He'd like to reserve the annex for the bank's employee appreciation dinner this summer."

"Great."

When Knox had renovated the kitchen and restaurant a few years ago, my parents had bought the building next door for events. In the original projections, the annex had been slated to pay for itself five years after the purchase. But instead of just offering it up for weddings and parties, I'd advertised it with area businesses and organizations too. Just this past week, we'd had a craft show in the annex. Next weekend, the Western Montana Country Dance Club would be here for their annual dance competition.

"Just have Randy go look at the calendar and he can reserve it on the website," I told Dad.

"Well, I guess he tried and couldn't find the right spot. He's not the most tech savvy guy."

Yet he managed to run a bank? Didn't Randy have an assistant who could help?

"Would you mind printing off the calendar for him?" Dad asked.

The whole point of me putting the annex's calendar on the website was so that I could stop printing it out and chasing down payments. But whatever. "Sure. Is he going to stop by to pick it up?"

"Any chance you could run it by the bank?"

No, I didn't want to take it to the bank and make small talk with Randy all because he couldn't be bothered to use an intuitive website. But I would. "I'll do it first thing tomorrow morning."

"Thanks."

"Of course." I forced a smile, dreading whatever else they needed. "What's item number two?"

"Well, we just wanted to check in and see how the quarter was going," he said. "We just met with the accountant to review the taxes. Last year was the best year we've ever had at the hotel."

"Oh." My chest surged with pride. "Really?"

"We're proud of you." Mom patted my arm.

"Thanks." It was a relief to hear those words, especially after how hard I'd been trying to earn them.

To earn Mom and Dad's approval.

While the restaurant belonged to Knox, the hotel was incorporated as a separate entity owned wholly by my parents. The physical building, they'd split with my brother. Two businesses run independently that shared an address.

Besides the Eden family ranch, The Eloise had always been Mom and Dad's most time-consuming business venture. Dad had always been focused on the ranch, while Mom had managed the hotel. She'd worked here for years until she'd handed me the reins after I'd graduated from college.

She'd put in her time with this business. What she wanted for their retirement was to be at home, surrounded by their grandbabies. So they'd spent recent years trying to settle their affairs. Dad wanted us all standing on our own two feet and the

Eden businesses controlled by his children.

My oldest brother, Griffin, was now running the ranch. The love of Griff's life was his wife, Winn, and their two kids. But the land was a close second.

Knox was the same. Memphis and the boys came first. If he wasn't with his family, he was happiest in a kitchen, cooking for those he loved most.

Lyla had her coffee shop.

Talia had taken her inheritance to pay for medical school and buy a house. She was a doctor at Quincy Memorial.

Mateo, our youngest brother, was a pilot, flying planes in Alaska. Of us all, he seemed like the one who was still wandering. Still finding his wings.

But as sure as Griffin was about the Eden Ranch, as dedicated as Knox was to Knuckles, I was equally as committed to The Eloise.

More than anything in the world, I wanted this to be *my* hotel.

I'd gone to college because Mom and Dad had always taught us that a higher education was important. But from the time I was sixteen, working here as a housekeeper in high school, running this hotel had been my dream. Then I'd become the manager.

I'd thought the next step would be assuming ownership.

Except then they'd offered it to Knox.

Partly because he was older. Partly because he had more experience managing a business and more money to cushion hard times. Mostly because I'd gotten into a sticky situation with an ex-employee.

Apparently, I was too soft. Too gentle.

I led with my heart.

Somehow, that had become my greatest weakness. The obstacle keeping me from my dream.

Ironic, considering Mom and Dad were the people who'd taught me to be kind. Loving. Trusting. But apparently for my dream, for this hotel, my personality was all wrong.

I loved my parents. I loved my family. But that?

It had crushed my heart.

When I'd learned they wanted to give the hotel to Knox, I'd been devastated. An epic blowup had ensued. There had been tears. There had been hysterics. Both from me.

Thankfully, Knox had turned them down. He'd convinced them to give me more time to prove myself.

Did I really need to prove myself?

There was a reason Mom and Dad didn't spend much time here. *Me.* This hotel ran on autopilot because I took my job seriously.

From housekeeping to maintenance to guest services, there wasn't a single aspect of this hotel that I didn't oversee. From the plush slippers we left for guests to the twinkle lights on the elevator's potted evergreens, I lived and breathed The Eloise.

Yet for whatever reason, it still wasn't enough. My parents had such confidence in my siblings. Even Mateo. But my brothers and sisters didn't see this side of Mom and Dad. The hovering. The micromanaging.

Though it was nice to have Mom and Dad say they were proud.

"We just wanted to recognize the changes you've made lately," Dad said. "Maybe it's time to start talking about transferring ownership."

Seriously? I reached down and pinched my own leg. Was this really happening? Finally?

"When we came to you about Knox taking over the hotel, we told you that you weren't ready," Mom said.

Ouch. I didn't need the reminder. I remembered every word of that conversation.

"And now you think I am?" I asked her.

"Yes, we do."

Holy. Shit. This was happening. This was really happening.

"Any time there's been an issue with an employee, you've handled it perfectly," Dad said. "The guest count is the highest in history."

Before me, they'd never even kept track of that number. But I could tell you how many guests we'd had every day of the year for the past three years.

"And the magazines and tourist blogs we've been mentioned in lately." Mom's smile was contagious. "It's just wonderful."

"Thanks."

For tourists traveling to Glacier National Park, Quincy was a popular tourist stop. During the summer months, we were booked solid. The same was true around the holidays. So I'd worked hard to drum up press features for The Eloise that would fill rooms during our quieter months. Spring break. Hunting season. Thanksgiving. And though there were still slow times, our off-peak seasons were getting busier and busier.

"The hotel is flourishing financially," Dad said. "You've really shown us how responsible you can be."

Responsible. That word was like a knife to my heart.

Responsible, twenty-six-year-old women didn't get married in Las Vegas on a drunken whim.

Oh, no. No no no no no.

The minute they found out about Jasper, I could kiss my hotel goodbye.

Maybe I should tell them. Get it out there in the open. Apologize and promise to fix it.

"It won't happen immediately," Dad said. "But as long as this momentum continues, we're looking at stepping away, officially, by the end of the year."

I opened my mouth but couldn't speak.

"We've shocked her, Anne," Dad teased.

Mom laughed, putting her hand on my arm. "It's just so comforting to know you'll take care of this place. That you'll be responsible for it long after we're gone."

Responsible. There was that word again.

Tell them. Tell them right now.

"I need—" The words lodged in my throat so hard I coughed.

"You okay?" Mom ran her hand up and down my spine.

I nodded, swallowing hard and choking down the confession that would end my lifelong dream. "I won't let you down."

Dad smiled, his blue eyes softening. "No, I don't think you will."

My heart crumpled.

I was going to let them down. I was going to fail them completely. They were going to be so disappointed in me. Just like with the lawsuit.

"We'll get out of your hair." Mom gave me a quick hug, then rounded the counter. "I'm making potato soup for dinner tonight. Want to join us?"

Her potato soup was a favorite. "I have plans. Next time."

"Next time." She clasped Dad's hand, interlacing their fingers, then as he waved goodbye, they headed for the door.

The moment they were out of sight, I collapsed on the counter, banging my head against the surface. "How could I be so *stupid*?"

Why had I married Jasper? Why?

Sure, he'd sort of dared me. And yeah, it had been my idea to do something spontaneous. Tattoos would have been better. Why hadn't we just gotten matching tattoos? Guaranteed, I would have regretted Jasper's name on my skin less than this marriage.

"I have to fix this." I whipped up straight and scrambled off my chair, diving for my phone and purse.

A secret. That was the only solution.

If I wanted this hotel, no one in my family could find out the truth. Which meant I needed to get to Jasper. Now. Before he told Foster. Before Foster told Talia. Before Talia told Lyla and Lyla told everyone with the last name Eden about my hasty marriage.

I put out the sign on the counter we used when the desk clerk needed to take a quick break. Then I sprinted for the elevator, hitting the button for the fourth and top floor.

Brittany was cleaning rooms today, but she'd been training recently to run the desk.

I found her vacuuming the largest room, nearly done with the cleaning for today. "Hey, can I beg a favor?"

"Of course."

"I've had sort of an emergency come up. Would you mind watching the front desk for like, an hour?"

"Sure." She nodded. "Everything okay?"

Nope. "Yep," I lied. "Be back soon."

With my keys in hand, I hustled to the stairwell, too anxious to wait for the elevator. Then I jogged to the first floor, racing through the lobby to push outside and start the trek home.

Gah. Why hadn't I driven to work today? My house was only two blocks away, part of why I rented it even though the water heater was as questionable as the furnace. But the sidewalks were slick with the recent snow, forcing me to walk instead of run.

The moment I arrived, I went straight for the garage, climbing into my gray Subaru. Then I sped across town toward Alderson Road.

Alderson was on the outskirts of town, where most of the roads were unpaved. My tires crunched on the gravel as I sped past rows of towering evergreens. Beyond their trunks was a creek that eventually flowed into the Clark Fork River, which acted as a natural boundary on one side of Quincy.

The properties out here were secluded, most of the homes large and built off the road to give their owners some privacy. The turnoff to the A-frame was the last in line, and when I reached the mailbox, I slowed to roll down the narrow driveway.

A silver Yukon was parked in front of the cabin. Inside the house, the lights glowed golden behind the windows. Standing on the front porch, with his hands tucked into the pockets of his jeans, was Jasper.

My heart tumbled.

Jasper stood statue still, his dark eyes unreadable. He was as gorgeous as he had been Saturday. That ruffled dark hair. That stony jaw dusted with stubble. Soft lips and a body built for sin. The ache in my core that had woken me this morning flared to life.

Never in my life had sex been that good. He'd made me come two—no, three—times. The fact that Lyla hadn't heard us having sex on our end of the hotel suite had been a freaking miracle. Because that man had made me scream.

Heat rose in my cheeks as I parked beside his SUV. I took a fortifying breath and climbed out of my car, walking to the base of the porch's stairs.

Here goes nothing.

"Hey there, husband."

Jasper's jaw clenched. That clench had to be a good thing. A sign that Jasper didn't want to keep the title.

"So...about this marriage."

CHAPTER 4

JASPER

Marriage.

That word packed a punch.

Eloise stood at the base of the steps, looking at me with those striking blue eyes. They caught the afternoon light, making them shine as vibrant as the sky above our heads.

She was dressed in a pair of dark jeans and a sweater with a mock turtleneck. She looked warm. Comfortable, yet stylish. Beautiful.

So goddamn beautiful.

There was some resemblance between Eloise and her older sisters. The long, dark hair. The pink lips and the shape of their mouths.

But Eloise had a youthful appearance that had nothing to do with the age gap between her and her siblings. It was just… her. She had effervescence. Energy. A spark that radiated from those pretty eyes.

My wife.

I groaned. "What a fucking mess."

"My thoughts exactly," she muttered, starting up the stairs. "Should we go inside?"

"Yeah." It was cold out today. Winter had a grip on Montana and it showed no signs of loosening its hold. When I left Quincy, I wasn't going to miss these brutal temperatures.

Though when my flight had landed this afternoon in Missoula, the weather hadn't bothered me as much as I'd expected. Either I was getting used to the snow, or contemplating the stupidity of my actions had made me numb.

Eloise stopped beside me on the porch, glancing around to take it all in.

There were two levels to the A-frame. The porch stretched across the front. Above us, a balcony extended off the loft bedroom.

When I'd come to Montana in January, the owners had built up an impressive pile of chopped wood for the fireplace. The stacks had dwindled since I'd been here, but hopefully there was enough left to get me through my stay. The logs rested against the porch's railing, bracketing the center stairs.

The A-frame wasn't like most I'd seen before. There were no massive windows out front, filling the triangular frame. Instead, those windows were on the backside of the cabin, offering a view to the landscape.

The green tin roof blended with the surrounding trees. The wood-slat siding was the same color as the earthy forest floor. It would have been almost camouflaged except the front door had been painted a bold orange-red, the color of rusted metal.

That red shouldn't have fit, not that gaudy of a color, but I couldn't imagine that door being any other shade.

"Cute cabin," Eloise said. "I've never been to this place before. I've seen some of the other Stewart properties but not this one. I like it."

"How did you know where I was staying? You didn't ask

Talia, did you?" *Shit*. If Talia knew about us, then Foster knew. And that was not a conversation I was ready to have.

"No. God no." Eloise shook her head. "Talia mentioned a while ago you'd rented a cabin from the Stewarts. Their other vacation rentals are in town."

"Ah."

"Small town." She shrugged. "Privacy has a different meaning in Quincy."

"I'm learning that." Every time I went downtown to grab dinner or a pastry from Eden Coffee, someone would wave and call me by my name. Someone I hadn't met before.

It was...odd. Not necessarily bad. Not exactly good either.

"That's actually the reason I'm here." She waved a hand to the front door. "Shall we?"

"Yeah." I walked to the door, holding it open.

She breezed past me, her perfume wafting to my nose. Vanilla and spice. Floral undertones and a hint of smoke, like she'd been near a fireplace. The combination was subtle but alluring. It was the scent I hadn't been able to stop thinking about for three days.

"When did you get back?" she asked, her gaze roving around the interior.

"About fifteen minutes ago." I'd hauled in my bag and immediately gone to light a fire. After it was lit, I'd headed outside on the porch, about to haul in more wood for later, when I'd heard tires crunching on gravel.

"Oh. Good." She seemed relieved that I hadn't been back long.

I jerked my chin for her to follow me through the cabin.

The kitchen sat at the front of the house, opposite a small dining nook. I headed for the living room, toward the open ceiling and large windows that overlooked the property. The fireplace crackled, its heat slowly chasing away the chill.

The cabin had baseboard heat, but I had a fire going whenever I was home.

Eloise spun in a circle, taking it all in, from the circular, iron staircase that led to the loft to the open bathroom door beside the laundry room.

The A-frame was small. Intimate. With the loft and another small bedroom, it offered me plenty of space.

It had been built in the seventies and had a vintage vibe. The walls were covered in tongue-and-groove boards. The honey color matched the massive beams that stretched from the floors to the peaked roof. The furniture was a mix of textured upholstery and leather, some pieces newer than others.

Nothing fancy. Everything comfortable. Just right for a guy who'd needed a rental for a couple months.

Montana was only a temporary stop.

Foster had moved up here permanently, but I'd only ever planned to stay long enough to train him through the fight. Then I'd either return to Vegas. Or find somewhere new. If Foster didn't retire, I planned to travel. To bounce back and forth. If he hung it up, then I had options.

My place in Vegas was waiting. I'd return. Or I wouldn't. But first…Eloise.

The silence between us stretched. She looked everywhere but at me.

What had happened to the woman who talked too much, who voiced every thought in her head? Maybe she was as lost for what to say as I was.

"Sorry." That seemed like a good enough place to start.

"Things, um…they got a little out of hand on Saturday."

The color rose in her cheeks. "I'm sorry too."

"It's my fault."

Three days of replaying every moment from Saturday and I still couldn't figure out what exactly had happened. But I remembered every second. From the fountain to the chapel. The image of her—writhing beneath me with that hair spread out in silky strands across a white pillow, that mouth parted in ecstasy—was branded on my brain.

A surge of blood rushed to my groin. Damn it. That, too, had been a constant the past three days. It seemed I couldn't think of Eloise and not get hard. I frowned, pissed at myself, and cast my gaze to the windows.

"You do want to get this annulled, though, right?" she asked.

"Yeah." No question. "The sooner the better."

"Phew. Thank God." The air rushed from her lungs. "Just checking."

Annulment was the only option. So why did her relief bother me so much?

I shook it off, facing her with my arms crossed over my chest. "I've got a good lawyer. I can reach out to him and get the process moving."

"Okay. Obviously I've never done this before."

I wished I could have said the same.

"Should I get a lawyer of my own?" she asked.

"If that would make you feel more comfortable."

"Maybe. I don't know." She tugged her bottom lip between her teeth, thinking about it for a moment. "I'll let you know."

"'Kay." I nodded. "Better give me your phone number."

"Right." She pulled her phone from her jeans pocket, waiting until I recited my number.

A moment later, my own dinged from where it sat on the kitchen island.

"Anything else?" I asked.

"No, uh, yes." She gave me an exaggerated frown. "I have some things happening. Good things, I hope. But this was sort of, um...irresponsible. And it would be great if we could keep it a secret."

"A secret." It wasn't like that hadn't occurred to me too. But just like her relief, it burned.

"Yes, I really need this to be as quiet as possible. Especially from my family."

"So you're asking me not to tell Foster."

"Exactly." She sighed again, more of that irritating relief.

"To lie to my best friend."

A flash of panic crossed her gaze before she clasped her hands together, shaking them as she pleaded, "Please, Jasper. My family will freak out about this. And my entire future hangs in the balance here."

That was a bit melodramatic. Or it should have been, but there was nothing but sincerity on her face. And desperation. "We can't hide this forever, Eloise."

"Not forever. Just until it's annulled. I'd rather tell people that we messed up and fixed it than have an audience while we're in the process of unraveling a mess, you know?"

A muscle in my jaw flexed as my teeth clenched.

"So, is that a yes? You'll keep it a secret?"

Fuck. I really hated lying. And not telling Foster felt like a lie by omission. But maybe she was right. Maybe it would be better to at least get the annulment started before announcing this *marriage*.

Unless we couldn't get an annulment and this turned into

a complete clusterfuck. I'd save that headache for another day.

"Fine," I clipped.

"Thank you. Okay, uh…" Eloise pointed over her shoulder for the door. "I'll get out of your way. I need to get back to work. And just call me, I guess, when you hear from your lawyer."

My gaze dropped to her ass as she walked away, taking in her slender curves and the long line of those sexy-as-fuck legs.

My body's reaction was instant. Heat flooded my veins. No good would come from me fantasizing about Eloise. Yet I couldn't tear my eyes away.

She slipped out the door, the wide curls in her hair bouncing as she jogged down the stairs. The door to her car slammed closed, and moments later, the sound of her tires on the gravel disappeared, leaving me alone in silence.

"Marriage." I chewed on the word and spit it out.

A secret marriage.

Foster was going to beat my ass for this.

We'd been friends for years. Best friends. We'd met when I'd started going to the gym where he'd trained in Vegas. The two of us had clicked instantly. He'd needed a stronger trainer, someone to push him beyond his limits. In turn, he'd challenged me too.

His career had given me a purpose. His wins were mine. So were his failures.

If he did retire, it would be the end of an era for us both. What next?

"I can't do a damn thing until I get an annulment." Or a divorce.

I balled my fists, an undercurrent of frustration buzzing beneath my skin.

A fuckup. I hated fuckups.

Normally, I'd spend a few hours in the ring with Foster, throwing punches and kicks, fighting until the frustration ebbed. But if I called him, he'd want to know why I was angry. He'd want to talk.

And I'd just agreed to keep my damn mouth shut.

So I headed for the stairs, ignoring the bags that needed to be unpacked and the laundry that needed to be washed.

I changed out of my jeans and boots, swapping them for sweats and tennis shoes. Then, with my earbuds in and loud music blaring, I headed outside and started running. It was at the end of Alderson Road that my phone dinged, the chime drowning out the music.

Digging it out, I kept running as I read Foster's text. *Make it home?*

I typed out a quick reply. *Yep*

Sorry they couldn't get you on our flight

Yeah too bad

Foster and Talia had returned to Montana today too. When I'd told him I was flying back earlier than originally planned, he'd sent me their itinerary in the hopes I could join them.

Except I'd requested the later option, not wanting to see Foster yet. Not before I'd spoken to Eloise. Maybe because I'd known it would be hard to keep the truth to myself.

A secret? How was I supposed to keep this from him?

There were things Foster didn't know about me. He knew I'd been married once, but I hadn't shared those details.

No one knew what had happened.

No one but Sam.

Except this was entirely different. Eloise would be his sister-in-law before long. Of that, I had no doubt. That made us brothers by law.

My feet stopped. My heart hammered.

Not from the run, but from the reality.

Fuck, he was going to be furious. There was a chance this would end our friendship.

"Damn it." I bent, swiped up a rock from beside the road and threw it as hard as possible into the forest. It hit a tree with a loud thwack, then dropped with a muffled thud.

Foster was one of the only people in this world I trusted wholeheartedly. He'd earned it by confiding in me his ugliest truths.

He'd told me about his history with Talia. The mistakes he'd made years ago. His desperation to win back her heart. His willingness to give up everything for her love.

Talia and I didn't know each other well, but the fact that she'd been willing to let go of the past, to forgive Foster, well... not a lot of people had that strength of character.

They'd both given me their trust.

And this was how I repaid them? With a secret marriage? A secret annulment?

This was wrong.

Eloise had begged, but I shouldn't have agreed. A secret would only make it worse.

I spun around and sprinted for the A-frame. When I reached the porch, I went straight to the shower to rinse off my run. Then I swiped my keys from the kitchen counter and drove into town, parking in an empty space on Main.

There wasn't a lot to Quincy, Montana. I supposed for most, that was its appeal. I hadn't decided if I liked the simplicity of this small town, or if it was the reason I felt this constant restlessness.

Downtown had become a regular hangout spot. I'd spent

numerous afternoons walking up and down the blocks, peering through storefronts and office windows. There wasn't a restaurant I hadn't eaten in at least twice.

And in the center of it all, the tallest building in sight, stood The Eloise Inn.

I marched toward the hotel, about to open the lobby doors, when a beautiful face appeared in the glass.

"Oh." Eloise's eyes widened as she stepped outside. "Sorry. Uh, sir."

"Sir?" What the fuck?

Eloise gulped. Then before I could inform her we needed to revisit this secret idea, she ducked past me and rushed away.

She practically flew down the sidewalk, reaching the corner and looking both ways before she crossed the street.

"What the fuck?"

Was she really going to pretend like I was some nameless stranger? That I hadn't been inside her days ago?

"Hell no." I stormed away from the hotel, following her across the street.

She walked with her head down, chin tucked and her hands pulling on the hems of her sweater, using it to cover her fingers and keep them warm.

I'd forgotten a jacket. This long-sleeved tee was too thin for the cold, but my blood was an inferno, raging hotter with every step.

Eloise headed away from Main, down a street into a residential neighborhood. We reached the end of a block, and she kept on moving.

So did I.

She was supposed to erase the bad. She was supposed to be a beautiful picture over an ugly drawing. This? Not helping.

I didn't need two miserable experiences when it came to my ex-wives.

By the start of the second block, my long strides had closed the gap between us. I trailed her by three feet.

She heard me behind her and glanced over her shoulder, those blue eyes narrowing. But she didn't stop walking.

So neither did I.

"Jasper," she hissed, shooting me a glare. "People are going to see us."

"Who?" I held out my hands, looking around the deserted street. Not a soul was out in their yard. It was too fucking cold. And no one had driven by either.

She frowned, faced forward and kept on walking.

"You could at least not run away when you see me." Or call me *sir*.

"We just agreed to keep this a secret."

"So that means I'm a fucking stranger to you now?"

She huffed, her breath a billowing cloud as she turned off the main sidewalk for a walkway. She'd changed directions so fast that I'd blown past her and had to turn around to follow her to a small, single-level house with denim-blue siding and a white door.

Eloise stopped on the stoop, bending to lift up the corner of her welcome mat and pull out a key.

"Not a great place to hide your house key," I said.

"Who's hiding it?" She slid it into the lock. "That's just where I leave it."

I blinked. "You leave your house key outside your house for anyone to find? You're joking."

She didn't answer. She shoved inside the house, dropping her phone on a small table in the entryway before walking to the adjoining living room.

I closed the door behind us and followed.

She whirled, her hands flailing in the air. "Why did you follow me here?"

I was about to tell her I'd changed my mind. That I couldn't keep this from Foster. But I didn't get the chance.

"You can't just follow me." She waved a hand between us. "If people see us, they'll know. If my parents find out, I'll lose everything. They'll think I'm not responsible. They'll think I haven't changed. They'll think I can't be trusted with The Eloise. Then that's it. Poof. They already didn't want to give it to me. They already tried to give it to Knox and probably would have except he said he didn't want it because yeah, maybe I wasn't ready for it then and maybe they were right about me being too close with the employees but it's been a good year and seriously, this will ruin everything."

She gulped down some air. Then she started pacing.

The talking? Didn't stop. Apparently my wife didn't need to be drunk to ramble.

It was like being in Vegas all over again. I watched her, transfixed, and unable to look anywhere else.

Another man might have glanced around her house. Made sure a serial killer hadn't used her not-so-hidden key to break in while she'd been at work.

But I just stared.

"Why did we get married?" Her hands dove into her glossy hair. "We could have just had sex. I definitely would have had sex. A lot of sex. Because it was good sex. I mean, we could have kept having sex. But this? My family is going to—"

"Eloise." I closed the distance between us, my eyes searching hers.

Her shoulders slumped. "I have to show them I'm responsible."

Oh, how I hated that word out of her mouth. She was too free, too pure of heart, to be trapped by the expectations of others.

"Fuck responsibility."

"Jasper." She frowned. "Not helping."

I didn't like the frown. So I sealed my lips over hers and kissed it away.

She whimpered, her body stiffening.

No, that wasn't right. The best part about Saturday was the way she'd melted for me. So I backed off enough to whisper against her mouth. "Relax."

"I can't."

"You can."

It took her a moment, but her eyes drifted closed. The tension crept from her frame. When I licked the seam of her lips, she moaned. And this time when I kissed her, she sank into it, letting me slide inside.

Damn, but she tasted good. Better than Saturday. How was that possible?

Would sex be better too?

There was only one way to find out.

CHAPTER 5

ELOISE

Jasper's tongue slid against mine in a lazy swirl before he pulled away, planting a kiss on the corner of my mouth. Soft. Sweet. Then he whipped the sweater from my body fast enough to make me gasp.

He swallowed it with a plundering kiss, then devoured my mouth. His palms flattened on my skin, pressing and pushing, his movements rough and feverish.

One moment he was slow. The next, frenzied.

Jasper made my head spin. Just like he had on Saturday. He set the pace, and there was no option but to keep up. There was no predicting his next move. There was no chance for my mind to wander or to think of anything other than Jasper.

My body, my brain, was in a constant state of anticipation, hanging on the edge, waiting, wondering what he'd do next.

No man had ever commanded me so entirely during sex. Probably why no man had ever made me come as hard, as fast, as Jasper. He fucked like delivering pleasure was his sole purpose in life.

"Jasper." My fingers dove into his hair as his mouth dropped to my pulse, sucking and licking a wet trail toward the hollow of my throat. Shivers erupted on my bare skin.

He cupped my breast, the entire curve fitting into the palm of his capable hands.

It was a gentle caress. His thumb traced my nipple through the lace of my bra. Then with a lightning-quick tug, the cup was yanked down and that same thumb gave the same pebbled nipple a flick.

Then came the pinch.

"Ah." I hissed, arching into his touch.

His mouth replaced his fingers, drawing the peak of my breast past his lips. His tongue flattened. When his teeth grazed my skin, a fresh wave of desire pooled in my core.

"Yes," I moaned, my eyes fluttering closed as I leaned into the touch.

One of my hands unthreaded from his hair, trading those dark, soft strands for the smooth fabric of his shirt. I balled it into my fist, holding tight while he tortured my nipple. I held on with all my might, keeping him in place.

"More."

He bit me again, followed it with a hard suck, and released my nipple with a pop.

Then he trailed his mouth across my sternum, freeing the other breast to give it the same treatment.

The ache in my core felt like a jackhammer, the beat pulsing between my legs.

I shoved his shirt up his ribs, needing to feel his naked skin against my own. Needing to feel him inside me.

"Fuck me. Please." If he stopped here, left me suffering, I'd never forgive him for it.

Jasper growled, releasing my breast. Then he took hold of my wrist, tearing my hand free from his shirt before he reached behind his head and yanked it free.

My knees quaked. God, that was sexy. I could watch that move a million times and it would never get old.

The chiseled plane of his chest was like a magnet to my hands. I flattened my palms against his pecs, roving up, down, side to side. The dusting of black hair over his heart scraped against my skin.

I rose up on my toes, too short to reach Jasper's mouth. But it didn't matter. He slammed his lips on mine, stealing my breath.

Our tongues dueled. Our teeth clashed. It was a kiss between two people who hadn't memorized each other's mouths yet but were cramming in every detail, like there'd be a test tomorrow and we were hellbent on a crash course.

My fingers dipped into the valleys of his washboard abs before skimming over their peaks.

Jasper seemed intent on touching every inch of my torso. His touch was like a torch, leaving sparks in its wake as he unclasped my bra and ripped it free from my arms.

The heat from his chest only made my nipples harder. His arousal dug into my hip, sending a shiver down my spine.

Jasper tore his mouth away, his panting breath mingling with my own. His eyes were so dark they were nearly black. A muscle feathered in his jaw. The corded lines of his neck strained.

What was he doing? "Why are you stopping?"

His nostrils flared. "Eloise—"

"Don't stop," I whispered, taking a step away, instantly missing the heat from his large body. Then I flicked open the button on my jeans, dragging the zipper down before pushing them off my legs, shimmying them to the floor along with my panties.

His hands balled into fists. The cut muscles in his arms flexed. His cock bulged behind his jeans, long and thick, swelling against his thigh.

My mouth went dry. Jasper was big. I'd been sore after Saturday night, and hiding it from Lyla as we'd traveled home had only made the trip more miserable.

Was this really a good idea?

I shoved that thought away. Maybe it was reckless, but right now, I needed him inside me more than I cared.

"Jasper." I took another step away, silently pleading with him to follow.

My heart climbed into my throat as we stared at each other.

His indecision was as potent as the desire swimming in my veins.

I *craved* him. Only one night, and Jasper Vale had become an addiction.

But he stood unmoving, his chest barely rising as he breathed. The only signs of life were those dark eyes dragging over every inch of my naked body.

I fought the urge to cover myself. To reach for my clothes puddled on the floor. This was the boldest I'd ever been. My nerves bubbled to the surface and spewed from my mouth.

"Don't stop," I pleaded for the second time, the desperation unmistakable. "Please. I don't ever act like this. With men. My sex life is dull. The guys I've dated have been underwhelming, to say the least."

An orgasm had been nearly as rare as a phone call the next day—by me, not them. Most of my past lovers hadn't earned a second chance.

"Then Saturday... I didn't know it could be like that."

Maybe this was something Jasper could walk away from.

Maybe the sex had been just okay. A man with that body, that talented tongue, probably always had it good.

What if I was lackluster? Oh, no. It hadn't been that good for him, had it? Why hadn't that occurred to me before I'd taken my clothes off?

"You know what? Never mind. This was a bad idea. We have enough complications. You should go, and I'm going to shut up."

Then die of embarrassment, naked in my living room.

My hands lifted, about to cover my mound. Except at that exact moment, Jasper surged.

A long stride and the space between us vanished. His lips sealed over mine, and I moaned, the relief a tidal wave that crashed into my bones. Was this pity? Did I care?

No. Not as his tongue slid against mine.

My fingers fumbled with the button on his jeans until I managed to flip it free. The zipper strained to be unlocked. My hand dove into his boxers. I was desperate to feel him in my hand, to stroke that steel.

Except Jasper tore away before I could grip him, batting my hand away as he toed off his boots and wrenched his jeans free from those bulky thighs. His black boxer briefs came with the pants.

My heart skipped at the sight of him, his cock hard and heavy between us. A pearl drop glistened at the head.

Sinew and sin.

I could stare at this naked man for days and not get enough.

Jasper reached for me, taking me by the elbow to spin me around, his chest hot granite against my back. Then he pushed me toward the back of my couch, the leather cold against my belly as he bent over me.

His breath was hot against my skin as he spoke into my ear. His cock fit into the crack of my ass, his palm skating over my cheek. "The next time you talk about any other man inside this body, I'll spank your ass so red you won't sit for a week."

My breath hitched. My pussy clenched. Why did I want that?

Jasper reached around my hip, his fingertips featherlight as they traced the inside of my thigh.

My entire body trembled as he moved higher, inch by torturous inch, until finally they dipped into my drenched slit.

"This body." He nipped at the base of my neck as his finger slipped inside. "You think I didn't like fucking you, Eloise?"

Whether it was his skilled finger or the way he growled my name, I wasn't sure, but my toes curled into the carpet.

"I haven't been able to stop thinking about this pussy." His finger eased out, shifting to my clit. "What have you done to me?"

A mewl escaped my throat as he flicked my swollen bundle of nerves. "Jasper. More."

"You want my cock, angel?"

"Yes." I pressed against him, tilting my hips.

His finger circled my clit again, driving me wild. Then he lined up at my entrance and, in a single thrust, buried himself to the hilt.

I cried out, my eyes squeezing shut as I adjusted to his size, savoring that stretch as my body molded around his.

"Fuck, you feel good." His arms wrapped around my chest, trapping me in place. His hips drove him even deeper and the world faded away.

He eased out slowly, then slammed inside again. His arms loosened and he stood tall. When I shifted, trying to straighten too, his palm splayed across my spine, between my shoulders, holding me against the couch.

So I extended my arms, bracing against the back of the couch as I rose up on my toes, pushing against him. My head was already spinning, floating to the stars.

Jasper's hands gripped me by the hips, his touch bruising.

Tomorrow, I'd have little indents, blue and black, just like I had on Sunday morning. Those marks had faded too fast, and I wanted them back.

He rocked us together, over and over, the sound of slapping skin filling the quiet house.

"Oh God, Jasper. That feels so good."

A low groan came from his chest, the sound shooting straight to my core. The piston of his hips was perfect and each time he thrust forward, he hit that spot inside that made me shake.

The palm he had on my spine slid down my back, circling the dimples above my ass before trailing around my hip. The caress was so soft compared to the power behind his thrusts. I felt him everywhere, each cell in my body at his mercy.

He tickled my ribs.

It earned a half-laugh, half-cry. Jasper knew exactly where I needed those fingers but he was toying with me.

"Jasper," I panted, letting go of the couch to snag his hand, bringing it between my legs.

"You want to come?"

"Yes." My voice was a breathy plea. "Touch me."

"Touch yourself." He ripped his hand free of my grip, bringing it to a breast. He rolled my nipple between his finger and thumb, then he plucked. Hard.

"Ah." My yelp bounced around the room as my fingers slid

to my center.

He drove deep, stopping when he was rooted. "Feel us together."

I obeyed, my fingers hesitant as I reached for where we were connected. I'd never done this before. I'd watched him disappear into my body on Saturday, but this… My eyes squeezed shut, my fingers doing the seeing.

My heart thundered, my pulse roared, as I felt his shaft and the stretch of my body around his thickness. A new shiver rolled over my shoulders.

Jasper shifted, his chest pressing against my back once more as his hand abandoned my nipple. He reached for us too, his fingers finding mine. Then he rubbed at my slick folds. "You're dripping for me."

"Yes." I nodded. "Only you."

He laced his fingers with mine, bringing them to my clit. Then he eased his cock out as his hand guided mine, circling slowly at first as his hips matched the rhythm.

Fire licked my veins as the pleasure built higher and higher. My heart raced as my limbs trembled. His thrusts hit exactly where I needed him. His fingers drove me wild. He sent me flying toward the edge until I shattered.

White stars stole my vision. Pleasure captured my breath. I broke into a thousand tiny pieces as I lost myself to the ecstasy, feeling nothing but Jasper as I came, pulse after pulse, longer and harder than I'd ever come in my life.

"Fuck me." Jasper came on a roar, the sound dull compared to the blood rushing in my ears. His body shook against mine, all those honed muscles clenching and trembling as he poured inside me.

It took minutes, hours, to float back to earth. I was in a haze when I finally cracked open my eyes.

My hand was still threaded with Jasper's and touching my core. His other arm had wrapped around my shoulders, holding me against him as his heart pounded against my spine.

"Wow," I breathed.

He stood, bringing me with him and peeling me from the couch.

My hair was in my eyes. My body felt boneless, and if not for his arm, I probably would have face planted on the floor. My legs had lost all their strength.

His teeth grazed my bare shoulder as he eased out. His come leaked down my thigh, and with our hands still threaded, he touched my center.

"I'm not keeping this a secret forever," he said. "But I'll do it. For now."

That sentence sobered me instantly. My eyes popped open. "How long?"

"Figure out a way to tell them, Eloise. Or I will."

I gulped but nodded. He was right. This couldn't continue indefinitely. "Just…give me a couple weeks."

"Fine. In the meantime, don't pretend like I'm no one." He smeared our releases along the inside of my thigh, then dragged our sticky fingers to my belly, marking me there too. "Don't run away from me. Don't pretend that you don't know what it feels like when I'm fucking you."

Okay, so maybe that hadn't been my best decision earlier. In my defense, I hadn't expected to see him and I'd panicked.

Jasper tugged his hand free and stepped away, leaving me on swaying legs.

I held on to the couch, regaining my balance.

By the time I turned around, he'd already pulled on his

jeans. His shirt came next, tugged quickly over that broad chest still damp with sweat.

"You want me to fuck you for a while, fine." He stepped into his boots. "I'll give you the orgasms the losers from your past couldn't. But when I see you on the street, you look at me."

A lump formed in my throat.

I hadn't meant to hurt him. To make him feel like nothing. But I was afraid that when I looked at him, anyone around us would see. They'd see the desire. The craving. The intimacy.

"Jasper—"

He didn't let me apologize. He marched out the door, slamming it closed behind him.

He left me standing naked in my living room with his come still dripping down my leg.

"Shit." I buried my face in my hands, biting the inside of my cheek to keep from crying.

I'd messed up. Again.

Somehow, I'd managed to make Jasper feel used. Cheap.

Was that what other men thought of me? Those guys I'd dated and hadn't called again, did they feel like I'd used them?

My dating history was a train wreck. My marriage history wasn't any better.

"Oh God. I have a marriage history."

My stomach churned. Someday, I'd meet the man of my dreams. And when he asked me to marry him, when we exchanged vows, it wouldn't be for the first time. My heart twisted, my chin beginning to quiver.

I was married.

I was about to have an ex-husband. I would be an ex-wife. Shame spread across my skin like a rash.

There was no erasing what had happened in Las Vegas. My

only option at this point was to fix it.

So I squashed the urge to cry, to scream, and collected my clothes from the floor, bundling them against my chest. I carried them down the hallway to my bedroom, where they were dropped in my hamper, then I rushed through a shower, erasing Jasper's cologne and the scent of sex from my body.

With my damp hair twisted in a knot, I dressed in a pair of sweats and grabbed my laptop from my tiny office. I spent the next three hours researching Montana divorce lawyers.

My top choice was a woman in Missoula. She was far enough away from Quincy that hopefully no one local would ever find out. But she was also close enough I could drive there to meet if needed. I put her at the top of my list, noting my second and third choices to call in the morning. Then I steeled my spine and made a call.

To my husband.

"Yeah," Jasper answered.

"I'm sorry. About earlier. About running from you and pretending like I didn't know you. I panicked."

He blew out a long breath. "It's all right. This is…"

"Fucked up?"

He barked a dry laugh. "Yeah."

"I'm going to call a lawyer in the morning."

"'Kay. I left a message with mine."

"We'll let them get this sorted. And I'll tell my family." Somehow.

He hummed his agreement.

The silence stretched for a few heartbeats. This was when I should hang up, but I just sat and listened to the nothing. Jasper's scent might not be on my skin anymore, but I was sitting on the couch and his spicy, woodsy scent still clung to the air in the living room.

If they made that smell into a candle, I'd burn it twenty-four seven.

"We should probably stop having sex." I hated the words the moment they came off my tongue. But it was time to start fixing those mistakes.

"Probably a smart idea," he said.

It was the smart idea. So why did that make my spirits sink?

"Night, Jasper."

"Bye, Eloise."

He ended the call.

As I stared at the screen, something twisted in my stomach. Like that goodbye wasn't only for tonight.

CHAPTER 6

JASPER

You are cordially invited...
The wedding invitation in my hand might as well have been a knife. The sheet of textured ecru paper sliced straight through my heart.

"Fuck." I tossed it on the kitchen counter beside the stack of mail that had been delivered today.

Ironic that the first day I received mail at the A-frame as its official owner was the same day that invitation arrived.

My mail had been forwarded from my place in Vegas to Montana for weeks. Whether I'd bought this cabin or not, that card still would have found its way into my mailbox. Still, it felt like a bad omen.

Why would they send me an invitation? Why couldn't everyone just leave me alone?

I left the kitchen, walking through the house—my house—to the slider that opened to the deck. The babble of the nearby creek played quietly in the background. The breeze rustled the pine and fir trees, making their trunks sway. The air nipped at my arms, cool despite the sun streaming through the sky. Last night's dew had mostly disappeared but there were still a few damp, shady spots that gave the air an earthy, rich aroma.

In the past month, the snow had melted in the mountain valleys, replaced with shoots of green sprouting from the forest floor. Spring was coming, and though I'd been warned that we'd likely have at least one more snowstorm, I could feel the energy of a new season.

Winter had been vicious. But this? This I could live with for a while. For however long it took for Eloise and me to get this annulment.

The wheels of the legal process were grinding at a glacial pace. At this rate, I'd be here through summer.

It had been a month since I'd spoken to Eloise. One month since I'd fucked her against the couch in her living room. One month since that woman had twisted me into a goddamn knot.

One month since I'd seen my *wife*.

Turns out, she didn't need to pretend not to know me. I'd avoided her spectacularly.

Her attorney had contacted mine, and as I remembered from the first round of this bullshit, legally ending a marriage was more time consuming than it should have been. We'd gotten married in less than an hour. Yet a month later, Eloise was still legally my wife.

Had she told her family, like she'd promised? *No.*

If she had, Foster would have confronted me about it. But as far as I could tell, beyond Eloise and me, not a soul in Quincy had a clue.

Still, I'd kept my mouth shut, just like Eloise had asked. I hadn't told Foster even though it was getting harder and harder to face him with every passing day. The putrid, crawling guilt churned my insides.

This secret was eating me alive.

Maybe if it had been any other woman, a stranger, keeping this quiet wouldn't have burned so fiercely. But Foster and Talia were engaged now. Eloise was his soon-to-be sister-in-law. This betrayal extended to his family.

And fuck, he was going to be pissed.

Another irony. Of all the people in this world, having Foster as my brother was a dream. Except when this came out, it would likely ruin our friendship.

Maybe I'd get lucky and he'd understand.

Unlikely, but a man could hope.

My phone vibrated in my pocket. It could have been a hundred different people. But that uneasy feeling came back with a vengeance. The bad omen. And sure enough, when I dug out my phone, a familiar name was on the screen.

Sam must have known I would have received the card by now.

My heart began racing. With it came that familiar disquiet I couldn't seem to overcome no matter how many years passed. "Hello."

"Hi." Once upon a time, I'd lived for that *hi*. "Did you get my wedding invitation?"

"Yes."

"And?"

I pinched the bridge of my nose. "And what?"

"Are you coming?"

"No."

"Why not?"

"Because it's fucked up." Of all the people in the world, I was the last one who should go to that wedding.

"It is fucked up. But isn't that who we are? Isn't that who we've been since we were kids?"

I wanted to argue. "Maybe."

"Good. Then you'll come."

"I'm not coming."

"Why not? Did you develop a dislike for Italy? Or are you afraid to see me again?"

Yes. "No," I lied.

"Prove it."

It had been years since I'd seen Sam. There'd been a time when our relationship had been the only good in my life. From the day we'd bonded over mutual disdain for our asshat parents, we'd filled a void in each other's lives. We'd leaned on one another.

For so long, it had just been us. Together.

Until it had all fallen apart.

Was I scared to face Sam again? Maybe. Mostly, I was afraid of what I'd see in myself. I was afraid I'd find the man I'd been once, lingering beneath the surface. That years of distance, years of trying to be better, hadn't really done a goddamn thing.

That no matter what, when I looked in the mirror, an unworthy man would be staring back.

Yeah, I was afraid to see Sam again.

"I have to go." I ended the call, then I turned away from the view, stalking inside.

Foster and I were meeting at Eden Coffee this afternoon to catch up. Since his fight last month, he'd taken a break from training so I hadn't spent every day with him like usual. When he'd texted this morning to see if I wanted coffee, I'd almost declined.

His lack of training had been my salvation. If I didn't have to face him, then it was easier to keep Eloise a secret. But if I stayed away too long, he'd suspect something. So I walked through the house, swiping my keys from the counter and paused to take one last look at that invitation.

You are cordially invited…

That card had been sent to rub this wedding in my face, hadn't it? Sent so I'd have to say no. Sam had to know that I wouldn't go, not in a million years.

Unless…

What if I did?

What if I went to this wedding? What if I showed up, just to spite the past? What if I had changed?

Would I be able to finally let go? Finally get that freedom I'd been chasing for years?

"What if I went?" I picked up the invitation and ran a finger along the handwritten calligraphy.

Was I seriously entertaining this idea? Yeah. Damn it, maybe I should go. If nothing else, it would at least give me satisfaction to see everyone's faces as I waltzed into the reception. To prove to myself I was over the past.

That I could face my parents and Sam, then walk away again.

And if I came with a date…

A wife, maybe?

"What am I even thinking?" I tossed the invitation on the counter and headed for the door.

I wouldn't—*couldn't*—do that to Eloise, even if one look at her would send Sam into a tailspin. Besides, it wasn't like Eloise would want to go. Why would she? I was her soon-to-be-forgotten ex-husband. Which meant my only option was to check the *With Regrets* box on the RSVP card.

My molars ground together.

You win, Sam.

I wanted to go. But yeah, I was afraid. Especially to go alone.

Hurrying outside, getting far away from that invite before I did something reckless like accept, I climbed into my SUV, then drove into Quincy, doing my best to shake that phone call.

Main Street was busy, like it typically was on Saturdays. A cluster of teens walked toward the theater. A woman pushed a baby stroller toward the local toy store next door to the kitchen goods shop. Two men, each with salt and pepper hair, emerged from The Eloise Inn.

I didn't let myself glance through the front windows as I passed the hotel. Was she working today?

It hadn't been as hard as I'd expected to stay away from my wife. Turns out, I was scared to be in the same room as Eloise Eden. I didn't trust myself around her. She was too tempting. Too irresistible. And I clearly had no control.

If I got addicted to sex with her, the taste of her tongue and the feel of her lips, that amazing perfume, it would only make it harder to walk away.

And though I might have bought a house, that didn't mean much. I'd be leaving Quincy soon enough.

Just not today.

I parked in an empty space on Main. Foster's truck was in front of Eden Coffee.

The name Eden was splashed all over this town. In my time here, I'd learned that the Edens were Quincy's founding family and had lived here for generations. Basically, small-town royalty.

I'd mistakenly married their princess.

My stomach knotted as I headed for Lyla's café. *Eden Coffee* was stenciled in gold letters on the front door. Today's special

was written in white, swirly script on a chalkboard sandwich
sign in the center of the sidewalk. Through the black-paned
windows, I spotted Foster at a table.

The bell above the door tinkled as I walked inside.

He looked up from his phone, jerked his chin and grinned.
"Hey."

"Hi." I drew in a breath, smelling coffee and cinnamon.
"I'm grabbing a coffee. Want a refill?"

"Nah." He picked up his half-full mug. "I'm good."

I walked to the counter where Lyla was waiting with a warm
smile. "Hey, Lyla."

"Hi, Jasper. What can I get for you?"

"Just a coffee. Black."

"You got it." She smiled wider, then moved to a large coffee
pot, plucking a ceramic mug from the nearby shelf. "Haven't
seen you around much lately."

"Been busy." Avoiding my wife.

Lyla filled my cup, then brought it over. "Anything else?"

"No, thanks."

"Sure, um, I was wondering..." Lyla hesitated, like she
wasn't sure what to say. But before she could finish, the door's
bell jingled, stealing her attention.

A couple walked toward the counter, so I slipped away to
let her take their order.

I took the chair opposite Foster's. The gurgle and hiss of
the espresso machine sounded from the counter.

"How's it going?" Maybe if we kept the conversation about
him, he wouldn't ask too many questions about me.

"Good. Damn good."

"How's Talia?"

"Also good." He smiled. It was the happiest I'd ever seen

my friend look. "She took Kadence to the ranch today to ride horses."

"Sounds like fun." I lifted my steaming mug, carefully taking a sip.

Foster leaned in a bit closer, then jerked his chin toward Lyla. "Talia would kick my ass if she knew I was saying this, but I thought you should know. I think Lyla's got a thing for you. Don't be surprised if she asks you out."

My hand shook, so hard that a scorching dollop of coffee sloshed into my mouth. I winced, setting the mug down as my tongue burned. *Well, fuck.*

"Nah, I don't think so." I risked a glance toward Lyla. "She's just friendly. I'm a customer."

"Think it's more than that but...just letting you know." Foster held up a hand. "I've had enough secrets to last my lifetime. I'm all about having everything out in the open these days."

Son of a bitch. The guilt was as bitter as my coffee.

What was Eloise waiting for? Why hadn't she told them? Maybe she'd never planned to share the truth. Maybe she'd promised with no intention of following through.

I took a sip, not caring when it scalded my tongue. Then I glanced to Lyla again.

She was sweet. Pretty. She was Talia's twin and the sisters were close. But when I looked at her, there was no uptick to my pulse. No crippling desire to taste her mouth.

There was only one Eden I couldn't get off my mind.

And her name was on the hotel.

"It wouldn't bother me," Foster said. "You, dating Talia's sister."

And if I'd married one? Would that bother him? I swallowed

down the questions with another searing mouthful of coffee.

This wasn't going to end well, was it? Every time I delayed the truth was another day Foster would have to resent me.

He'd spent years living a lie before he'd moved to Montana to win back Talia. Maybe he'd understand my reasoning for keeping this marriage a secret. Or maybe he'd hate me even more for hiding the truth.

If Lyla did have a crush, it would only make things worse. Damn it. That was an added complication I didn't need.

She'd been at the club in Vegas with Eloise. I'd noticed her staring a few times but hadn't thought anything of it. Mostly because I'd had my eye on Eloise in that sultry black tube top and sexy-as-fuck jeans.

Yes, Lyla was pretty.

But she wasn't Eloise.

The coffee shop door opened again and boots pounded across the floor.

"Daddy!" Kadence raced through the shop, her chestnut braid swinging across her shoulders.

Talia came in behind her, smiling as she followed.

Foster hopped out of his chair in time to catch Kaddie as she flew into his arms. "How was it?"

"So much fun." She giggled as he tickled her side. "Can we go again, Talia?"

"Of course." Talia nodded.

"Tomorrow?" Kaddie asked.

"Um, sure?" Talia laughed. "As long as it's not raining."

The rain, I'd take. Too many years living in the desert. I craved a wet, rainy spring.

"Want a snack?" Foster asked, setting his daughter down, nudging her toward the counter where Lyla was waiting. Then he bent to give Talia a kiss. "Good?"

"Really good. It was fun." She smiled at Foster, the two exchanging a few quiet words before she greeted me. "Hey, Jasper."

I raised my hand. "Hey, Doc."

"Foster told me you're going to stick around for a while."

"Yeah, a little bit."

"He can't live without me," Foster teased.

I gave a quiet, nervous laugh as I shook my head.

They thought I was staying to keep training with Foster. I'd let them believe I'd bought the A-frame because I was growing attached to Montana.

In truth, buying the cabin had been easier than moving. That would come soon enough.

While Eloise and I sorted through the legal bullshit of an annulment, it would be easier if we were in the same town. So three weeks ago, I'd called the owners of the A-frame to extend my vacation rental. Except they'd informed me they were going to sell it this spring. They wanted to capitalize on the peak market time.

I liked the A-frame. I liked its solitude. Its cozy nature.

So I'd bought it myself. In cash.

When this marriage was annulled, I'd be the one to sell it. Maybe even make a slight profit if the timing was right.

Though it all depended on the courts.

Eloise was set on getting an annulment. She wanted a judge to say this marriage had never existed in the first place. But the grounds for an annulment were limited. According to the latest update from my attorney, he was skeptical that we'd be granted one. Meaning we'd have to go through with a divorce.

Either way, when this thing with Eloise was done, I'd leave

Quincy. I'd bid farewell to Montana, hopefully long before another insufferable winter.

My place in Vegas was still an option. Maybe I'd head back toward the East Coast. I wouldn't live in Maryland again, but I had a house in North Carolina. I could spend a few months in the Outer Banks figuring out my next move.

Or maybe I'd leave the country all together. I also had an apartment in Edinburgh, and if I wanted rain, Scotland wouldn't disappoint.

"I'm going to say hi to Lyla and get some water," Talia told Foster, patting his abs before heading to the counter.

Foster took a seat but his eyes stayed locked on his woman.

Talia smiled as Lyla slid a to-go cup to Kadence, the top nearly overflowing with whipped cream. Then as Kaddie returned to our table, Talia leaned in closer to talk to her twin.

Lyla had been about to ask me something earlier. As she spoke to Talia, her eyes flicked my direction, and with that quick glance, the flush of her cheeks, my stomach plummeted.

She did have a crush, didn't she? How had I missed it? Did Eloise know?

"You all right?" Foster asked.

"Yeah." I shifted my attention, watching Kadence as she sipped her hot cocoa. "Great."

Maybe Lyla had mistaken my frequent visits to the coffee shop as interest. Lyla was a fantastic pastry chef. I liked her croissants. They reminded me of the ones our chef had made when I was a kid. But romantically? No.

Besides, I was already married.

The door's bell chimed again, and a familiar face came inside. Vivienne, Kadence's mother, walked to our table. Like me, she was new to Montana.

After her divorce from Foster, she'd been engaged to a guy in Vegas, but they'd recently split, so she'd moved here to be close to Kadence.

For years, Vivienne and Foster had been best friends. Their marriage had been a farce but they'd done their best for Kadence. Except last month, before the championship event, Vivienne and Foster had gotten into a huge fight.

Ever since, he'd been cold and distant, Foster's grudge taking on a life of its own. I hoped like hell he wouldn't hold one against me too.

God, I hated this. I hated the secret. I hated lying.

It wasn't right. The longer this continued, the worse it would get. A month would be hard enough to explain. But two? Three?

One look at Foster and Vivienne, the two of them barely making eye contact, and I knew we couldn't continue on this road. Not if I wanted to keep Foster's friendship.

Fuck me. Eloise was going to be livid.

Vivienne and Foster traded details about Kadence's schedule while Talia grabbed a lid for Kaddie's hot chocolate. Then, after a tense goodbye, Vivi took her daughter's hand and left the coffee shop.

"Are you going to be pissed at her forever?" Would he hate me someday too?

"No." Foster dragged a hand through his hair. "Time to let it go, isn't it?"

Talia took the empty seat beside him, holding out her hand.

Lyla wasn't behind the counter. She must have ducked into the kitchen for something. Which meant if I wanted a captive audience with Foster and Talia, this was my chance.

I'd warned Eloise.

Her time was up.

I couldn't keep this a secret any longer.

"Since you're both here. I, um, need to talk to you about something." Damn it to hell. This was going to be painful. I sat straighter, trying to find the right words. "I, uh, well... I fucked up."

Not the right words. *Shit*.

"What happened?" Foster asked. He tensed. So did Talia.

"I sort of...I, um...fuck." I rubbed my jaw, swallowing hard. Then I closed my eyes and blurted, "I married your sister."

"What?" Talia's jaw dropped. "You married Lyla?"

Lyla. Of course she'd think this was Lyla. Because she had a crush on me. While Eloise pretended I was a goddamn stranger.

"Uh, not exactly," I muttered.

Another jingle sounded from the door, and then there she was. The source of my misery.

"Oh, uh, hi." Eloise came to stand by Talia's side. The color rose in her cheeks. Her eyes darted everywhere but at me.

How could she ignore me? I couldn't tear my damn eyes away.

And that, well...that fucking pissed me off. If she called me sir, I was going to lose my ever-loving mind.

"Hi," Talia said. "Jasper just told us that—"

"Oh my God, you told them?" Eloise shrieked. "How could you tell them? We agreed to keep this a secret until it was annulled!"

No, we'd agreed she was going to tell them.

"Wait." Foster leaned forward, pointing between the two of us. "*You* two got married?"

I was about to explain, but Eloise kept on talking.

"Now everyone is going to find out. Gah! Damn it. I'm never

drinking again." She spun around, jogging for the door.

I shot out of my chair and chased. "Eloise, wait."

She didn't.

She just kept on running.

Again.

So I chased her down the sidewalks of Quincy.

Again.

CHAPTER 7

ELOISE

"Eloise." Jasper's hand wrapped around my elbow, stopping me before I could round the corner and disappear down the block toward my house. "Let me explain."

"No." I whirled, shaking loose his grip. "How could you do that? How could you tell them? We agreed to keep it a secret. Maybe you don't care what people in Quincy think about you. But I do. This is my town. This is my home. This is my *family*. You told Talia. *My* sister. You are a thief, Jasper Vale. You are a *thief*."

He'd robbed me of the chance to explain.

Gone was my opportunity to fix this. Gone was my hope to keep this quiet until I'd worked up the courage to tell my family the truth. I glanced across the street, toward The Eloise.

Did this mean my hotel was gone too?

My chin began to quiver, fury and frustration bubbling to the surface as tears. "This changes everything."

"You said you'd tell them."

"I didn't, okay?" My hands flew out at my sides. "Not yet. I was going to but…"

But I was a coward.

"You should have checked." I poked a finger into his chest. "You should have waited."

"Fuck. I know." He dragged a hand through his dark hair, and that was it. End of explanation.

"'I know'? Just…'I know'?" My hands balled into fists. Never, not once in my life, had I wanted to hit someone. Even as a child when I'd fought with Lyla or Talia over a toy. Even my freshman year of high school when Mateo had snuck into my room and read my diary. Today? I wanted to punch my husband in that handsome face.

"I'm sorry." Jasper sighed. "I'm sorry. I didn't plan on telling them. It's been festering. We were sitting in the coffee shop and it just came out."

"It just came out. Seriously? It just came out?"

We'd kept this a secret for a month. Jasper and I had avoided each other, relying on texts and emails for the few times we'd needed to exchange details. Otherwise, we let our lawyers do the speaking.

But today, it had just come out?

"I can't believe this is happening." My phone vibrated in my coat pocket. I pulled it out and turned it so Jasper could read Talia's name too. "Would you like to answer this?"

Jasper's jaw ticked.

"Didn't think so." I declined the call and returned it to my pocket. Before I spoke to anyone, I needed to think of what to say. "Oh my God. My parents."

Mom and Dad were going to kill me.

My hands dove into my hair, pulling hard at the strands.

"Eloise—"

"We were so close to having this behind us." My voice was practically a shriek. "So freaking close. We just need the annulment and—"

"We're not going to get it."

Now he sounded like my attorney. "We might."

"We won't. Which means we're looking at a divorce."

Divorce. My insides twisted. My lawyer had warned me about this. She'd said it would be easier if we just got divorced, if we didn't even bother asking for an annulment because they were so tricky to obtain.

But I didn't want a divorce. I wanted this marriage gone. Erased.

I wanted it to be like it had never happened.

I wanted it to be my secret.

Forever.

That was the real reason I hadn't told my family. Because I'd let myself hope for the annulment. I'd convinced myself that I could make Jasper agree to keep this secret permanent. Then no one would ever have to know. Not my parents. Not my siblings. No one.

Stupid Eloise.

Another stupid idea.

I should have told them. Now it was too late.

Jasper had done it first.

The lump in my throat began to close, but I managed to croak out a single word. "Why?"

He checked over his shoulder, taking in the sidewalk, making sure no one was close enough to hear. "Lyla has a crush on me."

I blinked, leaning in closer because I couldn't have heard him right. "Say that again."

"Lyla. Your sister."

"Yes, I'm aware that Lyla is my sister," I deadpanned.

"Apparently she's got a thing for me."

"No, she doesn't." Did she?

Lyla hadn't mentioned it. Though we'd both been busy lately and hadn't spent a lot of time alone together. In the past month, I'd only seen her at Mom and Dad's, when we'd all met at the ranch for a family dinner. The house had been noisy and chaotic. Not exactly the best time for sisters to gab about their crushes. But still, she would have hinted, right?

"How do you know? Did she ask you out or something?" My head began to spin. "Do you...do you like her too? Wait. Was that why you told Foster and Talia? Because you want to date Lyla? Does she know we got married too?"

I'd run from the coffee shop so fast that I hadn't even thought about Lyla.

"Oh my God. You want to date my sister. And we're married." I swayed on my feet, about to double over and vomit on his boots.

But Jasper's arms were there, wrapping around me, holding me steady. "Breathe."

My lungs wouldn't work. My stomach was doing cartwheels.

This was happening too fast. Nothing was going according to plan. Jasper was...mine.

He wasn't mine but he was mine. Sort of.

How was I ever going to face him if he fell in love with Lyla? How was I going to forget that he'd given me the best orgasms of my life? How was I going to see them together, knowing what it felt like to have him inside my body?

"Breathe, angel." Jasper's voice, low and smooth, sounded in my ear.

"I can't." My chest heaved. The world tilted sideways. Was this an anxiety attack?

Yep, I was going to puke.

One moment I was swaying on my feet, the next, they were swept out from beneath me.

Jasper cradled my body, holding me against his chest as he walked.

I stiffened, opening my eyes because I wasn't ready to go back to the coffee shop. To face my sisters.

But Jasper walked toward the street, carrying me to his Yukon.

With a pop, the passenger door opened and he set me on the black leather seat. He closed me inside, then rounded the hood, climbing behind the wheel and starting the engine. With a quick glance in his mirrors, he reversed away from the curb and headed down Main.

He hit a button on the console. My seat warmers. Then he turned up the temperature, glancing over with his eyebrows furrowed.

How did he know I was cold?

Oh, right. I was shaking. Was it the cold? Or was it sheer panic?

I didn't ask where we were going. I didn't care. I just closed my eyes, waiting until the warmth seeped into my skin and the trembling in my fingers stopped.

The SUV slowed before Jasper took a corner. Then the whirl of the tires changed to a crunch as we turned off the pavement and onto a gravel road. I cracked my eyes as a street sign flew by.

Alderson Road. He was taking me to the A-frame.

Strange, how I'd only been there once, but the idea of that cabin soothed some of my worries. And this conversation, no matter the outcome, would be best had in private.

"Sorry," I whispered. "For freaking out."

"My fault." Jasper shifted, his wrist draped over the wheel. "Better?"

I nodded. "Getting there."

The drive down the gravel road settled more of my nerves. The rumble of the wheels, the bounce and jostle you didn't have on asphalt. It reminded me of the ranch, of the countless hours I'd spent riding shotgun with Dad as he'd checked pasture fences or counted cattle.

My queasy stomach and clammy palms were gone by the time we reached the A-frame. My knees wobbled, just slightly, as I hopped out of the Yukon and followed Jasper inside, where I was greeted by the scent of a wood fire and Jasper's cologne.

"What happened to your dining room table?" I asked. Instead of the round oak table that had been here the last time I'd visited, there was a black folding card table with four matching chairs.

"I bought this place." He tossed his keys on the small kitchen island. "I called the owners a few weeks ago to ask if I could extend my rental. They were wanting to sell the place. So I bought it. Most of the furnishings too. But they wanted the table."

"You bought this?" Did that mean he was staying in Quincy? Even after the annulment?

My head started to spin again, so I walked to the card table, sinking into one of the folding chairs.

"I'm sorry," Jasper said. "I'm sorry I told them."

"Who knows?"

"Just Foster and Talia. It happened a minute before you came in."

I swallowed hard. "And Lyla?"

He blew out a long breath, leaning against the island. "I'm guessing Talia will tell her."

"But you didn't?"

He shook his head. "I didn't know she felt that way."

My heart began to race. "And do you? Feel that way about her?"

"No."

Relief crashed through my bones, my muscles sagging. Maybe it was silly, feeling this claim on Jasper. Okay, it was definitely silly. We were former lovers and soon-to-be former spouses. But still, the idea of him with Lyla made me want to scream.

"I'll have to tell Lyla," I said. "If Talia didn't already."

My phone vibrated in my coat pocket again. I didn't want to check to see who was calling this time. I was too scared to see *Mom* or *Dad* on the screen.

"I'm mad at you," I murmured.

"I'm mad at you too. You said you'd tell them in a couple weeks. You didn't."

I frowned. "I'm aware."

"Don't you think it will be better this way? If people find out from us instead of gossip?"

"Or not at all," I murmured.

Jasper studied my face, his eyes narrowing. "You weren't going to tell them, were you?"

The blame, the scorn, in his voice made me wince. "No one needed to know."

His jaw clenched. "That's why you want the annulment."

"Do you really want everyone to know?"

Jasper didn't answer. He just cast his gaze toward the island and the stack of mail on its surface.

It turned quiet. Too quiet. He might be okay with these long stretches of silence but they made me squirm. The vinyl beneath my thighs squeaked.

He had a right to be angry. So did I.

But the damage had been done. By both parties.

Hiding this marriage was no longer an option.

"How did you tell them?" I asked Jasper. "Foster and Talia? How did you tell them?" Maybe I could steal his explanation because at the moment, my own eluded me.

He sighed. "Told them I fucked up."

Brutal. But effective. And true. "Then what?"

"Said I married your sister. Talia assumed it was Lyla. Then you walked in the door."

To freak out and announce our marriage.

"Ugh." I dropped my elbows to the table, letting my head fall into my hands. "What a cluster."

My phone vibrated again. The curiosity was too much, so I slipped it out. Talia. She'd called three times. Lyla, only once.

"How do we fix this?" The question was for myself, but Jasper answered.

"What if we called off the lawyers?"

"Huh? What do you mean? We have to get the annulment. Or…a divorce. We need the lawyers."

Jasper stared at that stack of mail on the island, his expression focused on whatever was on the top. "What if we stay married?"

I rubbed my ears. They didn't seem to be working right today. "Say that again."

He stood straighter, his gaze whipping to me. "What if we stayed married?"

"You want to stay married. How does that fix this?"

"Hear me out. What if this marriage wasn't some drunken mistake?"

"Except it was a drunken mistake." Had he forgotten that we'd both been riding the alcohol express as we'd walked into the Clover Chapel and messed up our lives?

"We know that," he said. "No one else does."

"I don't understand." I pressed my fingers to my temples, to the headache that had sent me to Lyla's coffee shop in the first place. It had faded momentarily, during my panic attack. But it was brewing again, raging behind my skull.

"Instead of hiding this, what if we owned it? Tell everyone we got married. Admit it was rushed and reckless. But tell them there's something here and we're going to see if it works."

My hands fell along with my jaw. "Stay married. To me? But I just announced to the coffee shop that we're getting an annulment."

Jasper lifted a shoulder. "We tell them it's not a for-sure thing. Which it isn't. And that we're just exploring our options."

Stay married. That was impossible. Wasn't it?

Jasper's gaze flicked to the stack of mail again. It was subtle. But something on that stack kept drawing his attention.

"What are you not telling me?" I asked.

He faced me, pinning his shoulders back, making them seem even broader. "I need a favor."

"And I'm guessing that favor has something to do with whatever you keep staring at." I pointed to the mail.

Jasper nodded, plucking a square card from the stack. "I need to go to a wedding at the end of June. Go with me."

"As your wife?"

"As my wife." The way his voice dipped, low and gravelly, sent a shiver rolling over my shoulders.

"And after the wedding?"

"We'll get divorced."

Divorced. There'd be no annulment. No erasing this mistake.

"I know you want this to be annulled," he said. "But there was always a good chance we'd have to go through with a divorce instead."

My shoulders slumped. "I know."

"I'll take the blame," he said. "You can tell the world it was my fault. Tell your family I was a horrible husband. Tell them I cheated or something."

"No." My lip curled. I wasn't going to paint Jasper out to be a person he wasn't. "They'd hate you for that. Foster would hate you. We'll just tell them it didn't work out."

Jasper took one step toward me, then stopped. "Does that mean you'll do it?"

Did it? My mind was reeling.

I'd gone to Eden Coffee for some caffeine to chase away a headache. Less than thirty minutes later, Jasper and I were discussing a fake marriage.

"Who?" I asked. "Whose wedding?"

Jasper dropped his gaze, staring at his boots for a long moment. Then he lifted his chin and whatever openness he'd had a moment ago in those dark eyes was gone. They looked shielded. Hard.

"My ex-wife's."

CHAPTER 8

JASPER

There was a gap in the trees surrounding the A-frame. It was no more than twenty feet in diameter, but it was enough to see past the needles and boughs and sweeping limbs to the glowing midnight sky above.

The breeze brought with it the scent of pine. Smoke from the fireplace trickled from the cabin's chimney. An owl hooted in the distance, but otherwise, it was quiet. Peaceful. Empty.

If I stood here long enough, neck craned to the heavens, would the stars offer some advice? I could use some tonight.

Not long after I'd handed that wedding invitation to Eloise, watching closely as she'd read it twice, she'd stood from that cheap folding chair and asked to be driven back to town. She needed time to think about my proposal.

So I'd taken her home, dropped her off at the curb, then watched as she'd dug her key from beneath the mat and slipped inside.

It had gone against every gentlemanly manner my parents, tutors and nannies had instilled in me not to escort Eloise to the door. But damn it, I didn't trust myself.

A hot, mind-blowing fuck wasn't going to change the fact

that my life was a dumpster fire. Eloise and I had enough complications at the moment.

When I'd returned to the A-frame, I'd spent an hour online, searching for a new dining room set. The card table had always been temporary. It hadn't bothered me, not until today. Not until Eloise had sat in that cheap, flimsy chair.

She deserved better.

In furniture.

In husbands.

What was she thinking? What was *I* thinking?

The guilt I'd thought would vanish by spilling our secret had only grown. I'd fucked up. Again.

Eloise had called me a thief.

She hadn't been wrong.

Telling Foster and Talia, taking that chance from her, might just be the worst thing I'd done in years.

Was that why I'd pitched this idea to stay married? Because I just kept screwing everything up?

Not that it was a horrible idea. The more I thought about it, the more it actually made sense.

Could it help Eloise save face with her family? I owed her that.

Foster had called me earlier, but I'd let it go to voicemail. That was a message I was ignoring until tomorrow.

I'd deal with the fallout tomorrow.

Tonight, I just wanted to be alone. To stare at the stars.

A flicker of light burst through the trees. Headlights. Apparently alone wasn't in the cards tonight either. It was probably Foster, here to have the conversation I wasn't ready to have.

I sighed, dropping my gaze and rubbing at the slight kink

in my neck. It was too dark to make out the vehicle that turned off Alderson. So I stood in the clearing, waiting until the car neared. When I made out the shape of a Subaru, my pulse jumped.

Eloise.

She parked in front of the cabin and climbed out. The porch lights caressed her face, chasing away the shadows. She'd changed out of the black slacks and soft, blue turtleneck she'd been wearing earlier. Her long, toned legs were encased in dark leggings. Her torso was covered with a racerback tank top, too thin and strappy for the cold night. Her hair was tied up in a messy knot.

"Hey."

She jumped, startled by my voice and slapped a hand over her heart. "Shit, you scared me."

"Sorry." I lifted a hand as I walked over. "Didn't expect to see you tonight."

Eloise shrugged those bare shoulders. "I was doing laundry and ran out of soap. I was on my way to the grocery store, but my car sort of just drove itself this way instead."

"Come on in." I led her inside, waiting as she kicked off her shoes.

She padded toward the living room, gravitating to the fireplace. "Have you talked to anyone?"

"No. You?"

"Not yet." She shook her head, stepping even closer to the stove, extending her hands to soak in its warmth.

A tendril of hair draped down the line of her neck, like a crooked arrow down her spine. I followed its trail to the sweet curves of her hips in those leggings.

I'd rather see them on the floor than on her body. All of this seemed simpler, easier, when I was inside her.

"Okay," she murmured, more to herself than to me. Her shoulders sagged. Her hands dropped to her sides. Then she turned. "Okay. We'll stay married. We'll go to that wedding. Then we'll get divorced."

For the first time in hours, I breathed. *Thank fuck.* "Okay."

Eloise shuffled to the couch, slumping on its edge. "Maybe if everyone thinks this is real, I'll still get my hotel."

She'd mentioned this before, last month in her ramble of desperation to keep this a secret. I hadn't asked at the time what she meant, but if we were going to do this, then I needed to know what she was after.

"You said your parents didn't want to give you the hotel. They wanted to give it to your brother Knox, right?" I asked, taking the seat beside her.

"Yeah." She blew out a long breath. "I've been managing it for years. Ever since I came home from college. My mom used to run it but she's stepped away, just like my dad did with the ranch. My oldest brother, Griffin, manages the ranch now."

I hadn't met Griffin Eden, but I'd heard the name around town. His wife, Winslow, was the chief of police.

"The hotel is *mine*." The aggressive way she spoke, the growl of that word *mine*. A twinge pinched my side. Almost... jealousy?

Was I really jealous of a hotel? No. That would be ridiculous.

"It's my dream," she said. "But it's been in our family for five generations. I'm not the only Eden who loves that hotel. My parents, my siblings, my extended family. The town. Failure isn't an option."

"And you think you'll fail?" Or was that coming from her parents?

"No." She sighed. "Maybe. I had an issue a few years ago and it rattled my confidence. Mom and Dad's too. Hence why they wanted to give the hotel to Knox."

I shifted, turning sideways in the couch to put an arm across the back. Then I crossed a foot over my ankle, wanting to be able to see her as she spoke. "What happened?"

Eloise traced a pattern on the leather cushion between us, drawing imaginary squares and rectangles. "My tender heart. Or that's what my mother calls it."

Not once in my life had anyone called my heart tender. I liked that about Eloise. That she was affectionate. Genuine. Unguarded. I liked that she could ramble when she was drunk, saying whatever was on her mind, and lose herself in a moment of passion.

"I had an employee," she said. "It's not easy to find reliable, hardworking people all the time, especially those who are willing to clean rooms and scrub toilets. Maybe that's because Quincy is small. Or maybe I'd have the same problem in a large city. I don't know. But it's difficult. I don't have the luxury to always be choosy. If I don't have employees…"

"Then you do the work yourself," I said as she trailed off.

"Exactly." She glanced up but her fingers kept skimming the couch's leather. "I hired a guy to do housekeeping a few years ago. He seemed nice. He was sincere in his interview. He didn't have any previous hospitality experience, but it's rare to find someone who does. And he was only working part-time. I figured we could train him along the way, and if the fit was right, we could bump him to full-time."

This asshole had taken advantage of her, hadn't he? "I'm guessing the fit wasn't right."

Eloise gave me a sad smile. "I thought it was. At first. He

showed up on time. He was nice to me and polite to guests. He didn't go above and beyond but he did what I asked him to do. Until one day, he skipped a shift. I'd been doing some schedule changes and thought maybe he just missed the calendar update. So I covered for him. The next day when he came in, he apologized over and over. Said he had a lot happening and had gotten confused about the schedule."

He'd probably seen an opportunity to exploit Eloise's *tender heart*.

"It happened again. And again. And again." She tensed, her shoulders curling inward as that fingertip kept drawing patterns. Circles now, instead of squares. "My mom found out. Which means my dad found out. He came into the hotel one day, called the guy into the office and gave him a warning. Another skipped shift and he was gone. Guess what happened?"

"He skipped another shift."

"Yep." Eloise sighed. "Dad fired him. I would have done it, but Dad said he'd take care of it. Mostly, I think Dad was worried I'd cave and give the guy another chance."

"Would you have?"

"I wish I could say no," she said quietly. "But I'm honestly not sure."

"So your parents got mad because they had to fire someone for you?" That didn't seem like a big deal.

"Oh, no. It gets worse." She scrunched up her nose. "Back then, most of us would go out to Willie's for a drink once a month. I invited him to come along. I didn't want anyone to feel left out. He came once, that first month after he'd started. There was a whole group of us at the bar. We had a few drinks. Played pool. Laughed. And at the end of the night, I hugged him goodbye. I hugged everyone. No big deal."

There was shame in her voice, like someone had made her feel bad for who she was. For that heart. It pissed me off instantly. Especially if that someone had been in her family.

"I was trying too hard to be a friend instead of a boss. Professional boundaries weren't exactly my forte."

"Who told you that?" I asked.

"Well, my parents. But mostly, experience." Her lip curled. "The week after Dad fired the guy, we were sued for wrongful termination and sexual harassment."

"Damn."

"He said I propositioned him." Eloise's arms wrapped around her waist. "I've never felt so dirty. And you know the worst part? I started to doubt myself. I replayed that night at Willie's a thousand times. Every smile. Every laugh. Every word. I wondered if I'd gone too far. If anything I'd done could have made him feel uncomfortable. When all I wanted was to be nice. Include him."

I leaned forward, dropping my elbows to my knees, shifting just a bit closer toward that hand drawing on the couch. "I doubt you did anything wrong."

"We still got sued. If I had fired him after the first shift he'd skipped, it would have been done."

"He probably would have sued you anyway."

She gave me a sad smile. "That's what my dad says. That no matter what, the guy was always going to be trouble. He got a smarmy lawyer and thought he could get rich suing my family."

"What happened with the lawsuit?"

"We won." There wasn't an ounce of joy in her voice. No victory. "It was stressful and horrible, but at least we won. Mom and Dad dealt with most of it. They knew it was hard on me so they took care of it."

But in doing so, her parents had decided she couldn't handle the hotel.

"I've worked hard these last few years," she said. "Really hard. No more friendships with the employees. No more nights at Willie's. Whenever my parents need a favor, I drop everything to say yes. And I've apologized to them more times than I can count. My life is that hotel, and it's paying off. We're having one of the best years ever."

"Then isn't that enough?"

"It should be." She blew out a long breath. "My parents came to me last month. They think I'm ready. And in my heart of hearts, I know I can do it. I know I'm the right person to do it."

"So what's the problem?"

"It's taken three years. Three years of being perfect. No mistakes. No reckless decisions. Until—"

"Me."

Her finger stopped moving. "Please don't take that the wrong way."

All that, and she was worried her confession would hurt my feelings. That I didn't see our marriage as a mistake.

That tender heart was as beautiful as the starry night sky outside.

"I don't."

She brought her hand to her lap to fidget with her fingers. "My parents think I'm soft. Too trusting. Too naive. Maybe I am."

"You're worried they'll think I'm taking advantage of you."

"Yes."

"Do you worry about that?" I held my breath, waiting for her answer. Waiting to hear what kind of man she thought I was.

"No. I think you need a date to a wedding. And as your wife, I'm the obvious choice. You're helping me. I'll help you."

My frame relaxed. How she trusted me, I wasn't sure. But she could. I didn't need any of the Eden fortune. I wasn't interested in getting involved with their businesses or meddling with the family dynamic. I just...was too much of a coward to face Sam alone.

"Why are you going to your ex-wife's wedding?" Eloise asked.

"It's complicated."

She gave me a sideways glance. "She's not marrying your brother or father or something strange like that, is she? I saw that in a movie once."

I chuckled. "No, nothing like that. I'm pretty sure she invited me as a dare."

"A dare? What do you mean?"

"To see if I'd show. She told me once that I'd never be happy without her. This wedding is her way of testing me."

Except the joke was on her. This wedding was going to be my way of testing myself. Of facing those old demons.

It was probably a horrible decision—wouldn't be my first or last where Sam was concerned. The smart thing to do was say no. To do my best to forget. Except I'd been trying that for ten fucking years.

And I still couldn't shake her.

"I get it." Eloise nodded. "If you don't go, then she wins. She'll think you're miserable or still in love with her."

"Something like that," I muttered. "Like I said, we have a complicated relationship."

"Sounds like it." Eloise relaxed into the couch, her head against the back. "Thank you for doing this."

My finger reached out, acting on its own, to touch a wisp of hair at her temple. "I'm the one who should say thanks. It was my idea."

"Think it will work?"

I shrugged. "No idea. But at this point, I figure...it can't hurt."

She leaned into my caress, those brilliant, blue eyes looking up at me from beneath long, sooty lashes.

My heart thumped. A spark zinged beneath the finger still toying with her hair.

"We'll have to convince my family this is real."

I nodded, my gaze shifting to her soft lips, watching how they formed every word.

Eloise talked fast. At times, the words ran together, and if I wasn't listening closely, I'd miss something. But if I watched those lips, I caught every word.

Or maybe I was just totally fixated on her mouth.

"Not to jump straight into the fire here, but we should talk logistics," she said. "First, we probably need to start by living under the same roof."

The A-frame. I hadn't seen more than the entryway and living room of her place, but I wanted to stay here.

"Actually..." I shifted, inching closer. My hand in her hair threaded deeper, sliding into the thick tresses at her temple. "That's not the first step."

"It's not?" Her breath hitched as I leaned in closer.

"No." I bent to run my nose along the long column of her throat. "First, we do this."

I wanted Eloise on my tongue.

Her pulse fluttered beneath my lips as I kissed my way down her neck to her collarbone. Her head lolled to the side as her hand drifted to my hair. "Jasper."

The way she said my name…

I turned hard as a rock.

My hands trailed down her thighs, stopping at her knees. I stood from the couch, and with a fast yank, I pulled her until she was flat on her back.

Eloise reached for me, but I swatted her hand away, reaching for her leggings instead. With the waistband balled in my fists, I peeled them off her legs, whipping them away so fast she yelped and slid even deeper down the couch.

She wore a black thong, the lace delicate with a scalloped edge.

With one swift tug, I shredded the seams, sending the scrap sailing over my shoulder to the floor.

"Hey." She scowled. "I liked those."

"When you move in here, panties are optional."

"Who said I was going to move in here?"

"Me." I grabbed her ankle and tossed a leg over the back of the couch. Then I dove for her, dragging my tongue through her wet slit.

"Oh my God." Her hands threaded into my hair. She hummed, relaxing and letting her other leg fall toward the floor. Opening herself up for me entirely, her body so fucking responsive it made my cock weep.

"You taste so good, El." I lapped at her, flattening my tongue against her center before dropping to my knees to lick and kiss the inside of her thighs.

Eloise trembled, her hips lifting to meet my mouth.

"You like my tongue, angel?"

"Yes." Her hands wandered over my shoulders, then up my nape. Like she'd done with the couch, for every lick, for every suck, she drew a circle in the back of my hair.

I feasted on her, lost in her sweetness and the sexy moans escaping her throat. When I latched on to her clit, she gasped, her back arching off the couch as her legs began to tremble.

But before she could come, I eased away.

"Make me come." She lifted, seeking more. "Please. Don't stop."

I slid a finger through her tight heat.

Her whimper filled the room. "More. Babe, I need more."

Babe. I'd do this every fucking day to have her call me babe. Eloise wasn't the first woman to use that endearment. But I liked it in her voice the best.

It was just more paint. More color, more beauty, covering up my ugly past.

My arousal was painful, straining against my jeans, but I kept my pants on. "Come on my tongue. Then you'll get my cock."

Eloise moaned, writhing against my mouth as I devoured her, fluttering my tongue while I plunged two fingers inside, curling them to the spot that made her limbs shake. Her fists gripped my hair, holding me in place as her inner walls began to pulse. "Jasper, I'm—"

Her warning was cut off by a scream, her body nearly rocketing off the couch as she exploded. Every muscle in her body quaked. Her grip on my hair was unforgiving. But no matter how hard she pulled or pulsed, I kept at her, drawing out her orgasm until every last tendril of her pleasure was mine.

She collapsed, boneless and panting, her legs spread wide and her drenched center glistening.

I'd have her in bed next. I'd have that lithe body spread across my sheets, that hair undone and tangled with my pillows.

"Okay." She let out a dreamy sigh, her mouth turning up at the corners. Her cheeks had a beautiful flush.

"Okay, what?"

"I'll move in with you. But only because you asked me so nicely."

CHAPTER 9

ELOISE

"Do you think it's a bad idea for us to keep having sex?"

"Now?" Jasper's cock, still buried inside me, twitched. "You want to talk about this now? When my come is leaking down your legs?"

I giggled. "Okay, let's talk about it later."

"Yeah." He held me tight for a moment. His arms were wrapped around my shoulders, his chest pressed to my back.

But like always, he let me go too soon and slid out. Then he tucked himself into his jeans before bending to pull up my panties and joggers.

"Back to work." He swatted my ass. "What room do you want to pack next?"

"Bedroom?" We'd been in the middle of sorting through the kitchen when Jasper and I had brushed against each other.

He'd been closing a box. I'd been filling another. Our elbows had touched. That was all it had taken for the spark to ignite.

We'd flown at each other, kissing wildly. Then he'd ripped down my pants, freed himself and fucked me against the counter.

Since last night at the A-frame, we'd had sex three times.

Once last night in his bed. Once this morning in the shower. And now in my kitchen—former kitchen. This desire for him was overwhelming. Startling. Every time we were together, I wanted more and more.

That was normal, right? This was just chemistry. It would fade eventually. Most newlyweds probably couldn't keep their hands off each other too.

Granted, most newlyweds had probably intended to get married. And to stay married.

While I was lost in this sexual haze with Jasper, I'd asked my attorney to get a jumpstart on preparing our divorce papers. That way they'd be ready once we returned from this wedding at the end of June.

"So." I put a set of measuring cups in the open box. "Do you think it's a bad idea for us to keep having sex?"

"No." Jasper hefted a box in his arms, the muscles of his biceps flexing as he strode from the room.

I waited, thinking he'd just set it with the other boxes in the living room and come back to expand on that answer. But then the front door opened and closed.

"Good talk." With an eye roll, I went back to packing.

My husband, I was learning, had a proclivity for tiny sentences. The shorter the better.

I'd just finished packing the last of the kitchen boxes when he strode into the room.

"Do you want to stop having sex?" he asked.

"No." Before Jasper, I'd had no idea sex could be like this. Addictive. Freeing. Thrilling. There were no inhibitions. We came together with fireworks. The moment he touched me, the world beyond us disappeared.

He snared my focus with that gorgeous face. With the way

every muscle in his body flexed and bunched with raw, primal power as he drove inside me. Jasper delivered twice as much pleasure as he took.

Sure, maybe sex would muddle feelings. Maybe it would make it harder in the end when we parted ways. Or maybe we could just take it for what it was.

Sex. Crazy, phenomenal sex.

"I like fucking you, Eloise."

A flush crept into my cheeks. That rugged voice, his rasp, always made my breath catch. He might not be a man of many words, but when he used them, I listened.

Jasper crossed the kitchen with that slow swagger, like a man on the prowl. Even his walk was hot. As intoxicating as his voice. He stopped, towering in front of me. It forced me to tilt my chin to keep his gaze. "I'm going to keep fucking you."

"Right now?" I was okay with right now.

The crinkles at the sides of his eyes were the only sign of his amusement. It was like Jasper's secret smile.

And it was all mine. For now.

"Let's wrap up here." He lifted his hand to my face, his fingertips skimming my cheekbone. "Head back to the cabin. Spend the rest of the day in bed."

"Yes, please," I breathed.

"You like that, don't you? I talk about fucking you, and your face turns this pretty pink. Almost as pretty of a pink as your pussy."

"Jas," I whimpered. If my face had been pink before, now it was a flaming red.

He bent, his mouth a whisper against the shell of my ear. "You call me Jas later, okay? When I'm so deep inside you that you'll feel me in your throat. You call me Jas. And I'll make you come so hard you'll scream."

God, I loved his dirty mouth.

His fingers came to my throat. His hand was so large that he could wrap his palm all the way around my nape and his thumb could still trace the line of my windpipe. His teeth nipped at my earlobe before his lips skimmed my cheek.

Then he was gone, chuckling as he strode from the kitchen.

The air rushed from my lungs, and I gripped the counter behind me, holding tight until my head stopped spinning. *Wow*.

Foreplay with Jasper was an experience like no other. It had been an education.

With him, foreplay didn't start the minute we hit the bedroom. It started first thing in the morning. A casual touch as we crossed paths. A sensual stare. A chaste kiss. Dirty words and promises of what was to come.

It had been mere minutes since he'd given me an orgasm, but I ached for another already. Waiting until the packing was finished might kill me.

I shook my head, clearing the fog. Then I swallowed hard and followed him down the hallway to the bedroom.

Jasper had already taken the suitcases out of my closet and had them strewn open on the mattress. "You start on clothes. I'll get another box for shoes."

"Okay." I moved for the dresser just as he passed by.

His arm touched mine, intentionally. Tingles cascaded across my skin.

"You're an evil man."

He chuckled from the hallway.

I smiled, collecting my panties and bras from the top drawer, tossing them in a suitcase before moving to the second drawer.

We'd be taking most of my things to the A-frame today.

The plan was to haul over everything that could fit in boxes. The furniture, we'd deal with later. This was our second trip so far, and we'd need at least one more.

Though if Jasper wanted to delay packing and spend the rest of the day in bed, he'd get no arguments here. I could grab the rest after work this week. And if we were in the bedroom, I could continue to avoid reality.

For just another few hours.

Then I had to face my family.

My stomach twisted. Other than my sisters, no one had called me since the coffee shop yesterday. Maybe they hadn't told anyone. Or maybe they'd told everyone.

The fact that I hadn't heard from anyone was both relieving and stressful. But before I made the announcement, I wanted to be able to tell everyone that Jasper and I were living together.

I was going to confess that Jasper and I had gotten married on a whim. That the past month, we'd been spending time together. Getting to know each other. And the reason we'd kept it a secret was because I'd been unsure. Hence my outburst about the annulment at the coffee shop yesterday.

Then I'd tell them the truth. We were staying married. I'd moved into the A-frame. We were giving it a shot.

No one needed to know that that "shot" had a deadline.

The idea of lying to my parents and siblings made me queasy, so I focused on packing. Packing, I could control.

We'd already finished the bathroom and office. The kitchen hadn't had much to begin with because, unlike Knox and Lyla, I didn't hoard gadgets and cookbooks.

Once everything was at the cabin, I'd start the process of sorting. What we wouldn't use for the next few months I'd put in storage. There was an empty shed tucked into the trees behind the A-frame that was about to get stuffed with boxes and my furniture.

I'd lived in this house for nearly two years, but my lease was up in June. I hated letting this place go, mostly because it was so close to work. But if I kept this house, my parents would ask questions. They'd have doubts. So in an attempt to convince my family and the community this marriage to Jasper was real, I'd let it go. Even if that meant a major headache this summer finding a new house. Rentals in Quincy, decent rentals, didn't pop up often.

I spun in a slow circle, taking in the bedroom's tan walls and thick crown molding. I'd miss this little home.

This house was cute. Old, but cute. Yes, the winters were too cold and the summers excruciatingly hot because this place had been built long before decent insulation was a standard. Still, it had been mine.

When Jasper and I parted ways, where would I go next? With any luck, maybe I could just come back here. There might be something else within walking distance to downtown. Worst case scenario, I could move to the ranch.

There was a loft apartment above the barn at home. My uncle Briggs had been living there for a while, but his dementia had progressed to the point where he needed more care, so Mom and Dad had moved him into a local home with nursing staff to help.

Mateo had lived in the barn loft for a while before he'd moved to Alaska. It wouldn't be horrible. Mom would cook for me. That was a major bonus since I was still working on refining my cooking skills. But the drive to town alone would be time consuming, especially in the winter when the roads were icy.

And my poor pride might never recover if I had to move home after the divorce. I could already hear the snickers at my ten-year class reunion.

"Last resort," I told myself, then finished unloading the dresser, zipping both suitcases closed.

My closet was next. Maybe we could just leave everything on the hangers. Was there enough room in the A-frame's closet for all this?

Wait. Did the A-frame even have a closet? I hadn't noticed one in the bedroom this morning. Maybe it was downstairs by the laundry room or bathroom.

"Jasper, how much room is in the closet at the A-frame?"

No answer. Where was he? Where was that box for my shoes?

"Eloise," Jasper called.

"Yeah?" I hollered back.

"Come out here."

I hefted a suitcase off the bed and popped the handle, dragging it behind me down the hall. "How much room do you have in the closet at the cabin?"

Jasper still didn't answer.

"Can you not hear me?"

Silence.

"Apparently not," I muttered, trudging to the living room. When I reached the mouth of the hallway, I came to an abrupt halt.

Oh shit.

Jasper stood, legs planted wide, arms crossed over his broad chest, staring at two angry men.

They also stood with their legs planted wide and arms

crossed over their chests.

Griffin and Knox didn't so much as glance my direction. Their glares were locked on Jasper.

Okay, so I guess Talia hadn't kept this quiet.

My heart climbed into my throat as I risked a step into the room. The testosterone was stifling. It was like walking through a dense fog.

"Hey!" I smiled too brightly, hoping it would cover up my nerves.

Nope. My voice was shaky. *Damn it.* Someday I'd master cool and collected when faced with my angry, scowling brothers.

One hesitant step at a time, I walked straight through the wall of alpha-male energy to stand between them and Jasper.

Still, they ignored me completely. They looked straight over my head to scowl at Jasper.

This was the problem with marrying a man just as big as your brothers. I was ignorable.

"Did you bring one truck or two?" I asked.

No response. Could anyone hear me today?

"Griffin." I reached out and poked him in the gut. His scowl deepened but he dropped his gaze, finally shifting his focus to me.

I realized my mistake too late. Because his gaze might as well have been a flamethrower.

"Is it hot in here?" I gulped. "Maybe we should all go outside where there's more air. You can carry this suitcase for me."

Nothing. Not even a blink.

"Okay, I'll just wheel this one out myself."

"You got married." Knox's voice was as lethal as Griffin's glare.

"Right. Um…about that."

Griffin's nostrils flared.

"I see that Talia called you yesterday," I muttered, my gaze flicking to Knox.

"It was Lyla," he said. "Would have been nice to hear from you."

I winced. "In my defense, I called both Winn and Memphis earlier. Neither of them answered."

My strategy for breaking this news was to tell the easy people first. Hopefully earn a couple of allies. So I'd called their wives, breathing a huge sigh of relief this morning when neither had answered.

"You called at five o'clock this morning," Knox said. "Memphis was asleep since she spent most of the night up with the baby."

"And you called Winn's personal phone," Griffin clipped.

I knew that Memphis didn't sleep with her phone in their bedroom, and Knox had been taking the early morning shift with the boys. And Winn always had her work phone close by in case the police station needed to get ahold of her. But I'd counted on her personal phone being out of battery or lost, like normal.

"I'm sorry." I clasped my hands in front of me, a silent prayer for forgiveness. "I'm really, really sorry. But given you're standing in my living room, it's not like you've been in the dark for long. And I was going to tell you today. I swear."

A muscle in Griffin's jaw flexed. The scary muscle.

"I'm sorry."

My apologies weren't helping. Because we all knew I shouldn't have waited. I should have talked to everyone yesterday. But the dread had been crippling. So instead of dealing with it last night, I'd escaped reality by sleeping in

Jasper's bed.

No more escaping.

It was time to face the consequences of my actions. And so far, this was playing out exactly as expected. They were mad, rightly so. And worse, they were disappointed.

"Do Mom and Dad know?" My breath lodged in my chest as I waited for Griff's answer.

Griffin gave me a single nod.

My arms wrapped around my stomach. The regret swallowed me whole. I sucked as a daughter. "How mad are they?"

Knox scoffed. "Guess."

Mad. Super mad.

"What the actual fuck were you thinking?" Griffin uncrossed his arms, planting his fists on his hips. "You got married. When? Where? Why the hell didn't you tell your fucking family, Eloise?"

"See? This was why I wanted to talk to Winn first." I shied away from that furious glare. "Because I knew you were going to yell at me."

"You married a stranger. In secret. And you hid it from us. I'm going to fucking yell."

"Griff—"

A strong arm wrapped around my shoulders, stopping another lame apology.

Jasper hauled me backward, flush against his chest. "That's enough."

Griffin's gaze leveled on Jasper. "This is a private conversation."

"You're yelling at my wife."

My jaw dropped.

It took a brave man to stand up to my brothers. That calm

and collected I dreamed of? Jasper had it. Maybe he'd teach me.

Knox blinked. Then he dropped his chin, lifting a hand to rub over his mouth. Almost like he was surprised.

I stared up at Griffin, expecting to see that murderous glare he'd inherited from Dad. Except his scowl was gone. He looked...shocked. Intrigued? What the hell was happening?

"Sorry," Griff muttered.

Jasper just kept staring at Griffin, his gaze as hard as I'd ever seen. Goose bumps broke out on my forearms as I stood between them, my head whipping back and forth, waiting for someone to speak or make a move.

But they were locked in this strange staring contest. Was this a good thing? A bad? Why were men so complicated?

We needed to go back to the yelling because then at least I knew what was going on.

Griffin was the first to break. His arms fell relaxed to his sides. He dropped his attention, his blue eyes finding mine. "You need to call Mom." His voice was so gentle it hurt.

"I will."

"Now. Not later today. Now. I know you're avoiding this because it's going to be hard. But she's hurt."

Ouch. "Okay."

"Better add Talia and Lyla to your list." Knox gave me a sad smile.

Griffin sighed, shaking his head. "Do you need help hauling stuff out of here? I can go home and bring in a horse trailer."

My chin began to quiver. Tears welled. They might be mad, disappointed, but they were still my big brothers. And they'd help me move.

"Rain check?" I asked.

Griffin nodded, touched the tip of my nose, then without another word, turned and walked out of the house.

Knox jerked up his chin to Jasper, then followed.

It wasn't until the rumble of Griffin's truck vanished down the block that I relaxed, sagging into Jasper's hold. "Sorry."

"It's not your fault." He let me go, then stepped around me, taking the suitcase I'd hauled out, carrying it to the Yukon.

I walked toward the door, watching as he loaded it inside.

Well, that had gone...it had gone.

"Stupid Eloise," I muttered.

Not only had I hurt my family but Jasper hadn't deserved that ambush from my brothers. The person at fault here was me.

And I had more apologies to make.

So I squared my shoulders and headed for the kitchen, to where I'd left my phone earlier.

By the time I was done making phone calls, Jasper had taken the SUV to the A-frame and unloaded the boxes. When he came back to pick me up, I'd already cried three times.

Once, while talking to Mom. Again, while talking to Dad. The third time, after I'd left a message for Lyla.

I'd called Talia after my parents, and she'd warned me that Lyla might not want to talk.

It was heavy. Carrying around the weight of this kind of mistake was heavy. Maybe Jasper felt it too because when we got back to the cabin, he changed clothes and left for a run.

I spent the rest of the day unpacking, claiming the small closet in the tiny office for myself. Dinner was quiet. Afterward, Jasper built a fire and read a book while I continued to unpack. And after darkness fell, he retreated to the loft.

"You coming up?" he asked from the top of the stairs.

"In a bit."

He gave me a sad smile, then turned off the light.

This was going to end in a disaster, wasn't it? We were doomed.

Instead of climbing the stairs, I found a blanket and pillow. And fell asleep on the couch.

CHAPTER 10

JASPER

The moment I opened the front door and stepped inside the A-frame, the acrid scent of burnt food slapped me in the face. Smoke hazed the kitchen, clouding the air as the early evening light shined through the windows.

"What the fuck?" I set my backpack on the island and hurried to the stove, yanking the door open. It was empty. And off. But something had clearly died in there today.

"Eloise?" I called.

No answer.

No surprise.

She'd been avoiding me all week, ever since that encounter with her brothers at her rental.

Over the past six days, the reality of our situation had crept in, bitter and harsh, just like the scent in the cabin. We were strangers. And we were acting like it.

Not even sex was a commonality at this point, not with Eloise choosing to sleep on the couch.

A week ago, I'd thought this agreement of ours would be a damn breeze. The two of us would pretend for a while. We'd enjoy some hot, uncomplicated sex. Then after the wedding, we'd call it quits. Get a simple divorce. Part ways.

I was a fucking idiot for thinking this would be easy. Eloise and I were as fucked as whatever had been in my oven.

The smell stung my nostrils, so I strode for the closest window, only to find it already open. Then I glanced toward the back of the house to the sliding door, also open.

My wife sat on the deck.

I ducked into the laundry room, taking out the small fan stashed on the top shelf of the storage closet. With it in the kitchen window, running full blast, I propped open the front door to get some air flowing, then I headed outside.

The deck only rose about a foot off the ground. Eloise was sitting on the edge, her legs crossed, her gaze aimed to the trees. There was something black in her hand that looked a lot like a hockey puck. "I made cookies."

The hockey puck. The source of the smoke and smell.

"Want one?" She held it up in the air, turning enough that I could see her face.

The look in those blue eyes made my chest pinch. There were tear tracks on her cheeks. Smudges of black from watery mascara that she'd tried to rub away. Or maybe that was from the cookie.

"Chocolate chip?" I asked, taking the burnt cookie.

"Yeah."

"I don't like chocolate chip cookies." Winding it up like it was a Frisbee, I threw the cookie as far as possible, sending it sailing through the air and crashing into a tree trunk. Then I wiped my hands together, brushing away the charcoal dust, before I took a seat beside Eloise.

"You don't like chocolate chip cookies?" she asked.

"No."

"What's your favorite cookie?"

"I don't really like cookies. But if I had to choose, oatmeal raisin."

"Oatmeal raisin? Oh my God, I married a monster."

The corner of my mouth turned up. It was the first time I'd smiled in, well…a week.

"Sorry I stank up the house," she said.

"It'll fade."

"Stupid Eloise," she muttered.

"Call yourself stupid again, and I'll take you over my knee."

She gasped, her eyes widening.

"You're not stupid." I knew it was one of those off-handed, self-deprecating remarks, but I still didn't like it. If I heard it again, I'd spank her beautiful ass until it was red. "So don't say it."

"Okay," she whispered, her gaze running over my T-shirt and shorts. "Were you at the gym?"

"This morning. Then I went for a hike. Did you work today?"

"No, I took it off."

Eloise had spent every day this week at the hotel. Either to avoid me or because she was busy. Probably both. Normally when I woke up each morning around six, she was already gone, leaving behind her scent, that earthy, floral vanilla, in the bathroom.

Except this morning, there'd been no perfume. When I'd come down from the loft, she'd been asleep on the couch, her eyelids fluttering as she'd dreamed.

So it had been my turn to sneak out early.

Foster had asked me to come to his gym this morning to work out.

Today was the first time we'd seen each other since the coffee shop last weekend. We'd talked on the phone a couple times, short, clipped conversations. Not that our face-to-face today had been much different. We hadn't spoken much before we'd climbed into the ring to spar.

Inside the ropes, there hadn't been the need for words. Foster had let his fists do all the talking.

Eloise's eyes locked on the fresh cut on my lower lip. She reached out to touch it but stopped before she actually made contact. Then that sad look in her eyes doubled.

So did the pinch in my chest.

"How was Foster?" she asked.

Pissed. Seriously fucking pissed. "Fine."

He was angry that I hadn't told him about Eloise. He was mad that I'd spent a month concealing the truth. But mostly, I think he was hurt because he knew I was still hiding something.

Maybe I should have fessed up. Maybe I should have laid it all out there, explaining that this marriage was a sham. That Eloise and I were gutting this out so she could have a shot at her hotel and I wouldn't have to show up to Sam's wedding alone.

But I'd kept my mouth shut. My reward? An ass kicking.

Foster had landed a kick to my gut that had knocked the wind out of me. Then he'd popped me in the mouth, the skin splitting instantly.

It had bled on and off during my afternoon hike. Whatever blood was on the sleeve of my black shirt was invisible.

"You didn't, um...tell him about our arrangement. Did you?" she asked.

I shook my head. "No."

"Thank you." She sighed.

More secrets. But for some reason, keeping our motives

from Foster didn't bother me as much as hiding this marriage to Eloise.

Why? No fucking clue. I'd tried to figure it out on my hike. I'd spent a couple hours trying to sort through these feelings. Clear my head. It hadn't worked. I still felt...off.

Maybe I was just tired. Sleep had been shit all week.

"Where did you go hiking?" she asked.

"The Sable Peak Trailhead."

Even after a punishing workout with Foster, I'd had this restless energy coursing through my veins. So I'd searched for local trailheads and headed for the mountains.

The loop had been six miles. My legs were dead, and tomorrow I'd pay for overexerting myself. And only a sliver of that energy had faded.

"That's always been Mateo's favorite trail." Eloise pulled her knees up, hugging them to her chest. "Maybe I should have gone hiking with you instead of yet another kitchen fail."

Those beautiful eyes flooded with tears.

This wasn't about the cookies. But if she needed to cry over them, I'd sit beside her.

Even though I needed a shower, even though I was starving, I didn't move. We stared at the trees until Eloise filled the silence.

"My mom is an amazing cook. She jokes that Knox and Lyla inherited her talents, and by the time Mateo and I were born, there was nothing left for us. But I still try. I bake cookies for family dinners and pretend not to notice when they all disappear to the garbage can in the garage. I make sangria that no one drinks."

"Do you like to cook?"

"No."

"Then why not quit?"

She lifted a shoulder. "I don't know. I guess it would be nice to do it right. Just once."

Eloise was still trying to cover up those ugly horses with pretty pictures.

"After today, I think…I give up." Her voice was so small. Gone was the strong, vibrant woman who'd caught me in her spell in Vegas. And at the moment, I'd give anything to make those tears disappear.

"I like to cook," I said. "Hate doing laundry."

She sniffled, wiping beneath her eyes. "I don't mind laundry."

"Then you do my laundry. I'll cook. No more peanut butter and jelly sandwiches for dinner. Deal?"

"Deal." She gave me a tiny smile. "Our first assignment of duties. Look at us, crushing this marriage thing already. Other newlyweds would be jealous. If they only knew it was all fake."

Fake. My shoulders tensed. She was right. This marriage was as fake as my father's handshakes and my mother's interest in her son's life.

I hated fake as much as I hated chocolate chip cookies.

"What?" Eloise nudged my elbow with hers.

"Nothing." I stood from the step and walked inside.

The smell was better already, that fan blowing in the fresh, forest air. Or maybe my nose had just adjusted after the shock of the stench.

I made my way to the kitchen, my muscles already heavy and tired. My body needed fuel, so I opened the fridge and took out leftovers from dinner last night. Grilled chicken breasts, roasted vegetables and wild rice.

Eloise followed me inside, coming to stand beside the

island. There was a pitcher on the countertop, one I hadn't noticed when I'd come inside. Orange slices and apple rings floated in a ruby red liquid.

"Want some sangria?" She walked to a cabinet, taking out a cup. Then she poured herself a glass, taking a sip and grimacing. "Yum."

"Hungry?" I asked, taking out a plate.

"Not really. I ate a lot of cookie dough."

I frowned and took out another plate. Nutrition was important. Cookie dough and sangria weren't going to be her dinner. So I dished us both food, my plate twice as full as hers, and carried them to the card table with forks and napkins.

Eloise took the chair beside mine, slouching in the cheap seat.

We needed to get the rest of the furniture from her rental, including the dining table. Most of her larger pieces wouldn't fit in my Yukon, so I was going to ask Foster to borrow his truck and give me a hand lifting the heavy pieces.

But before I asked for a favor, I was letting him chill. We'd agreed to meet on Monday morning at the gym. Hopefully by then, some of his anger would have passed. Knowing Foster, he was probably at home, stewing over my lip. He'd already texted me an apology. And, unlike any of the Edens, a congratulations.

Foster and I would get past this. Probably. We'd get back to normal. Hopefully. Then in a week or two, I'd finish at Eloise's house and we'd be done with moving.

Without any help from her fucking brothers.

The way they'd treated me had been fair. If I had a sister and she'd married a stranger in Vegas, I probably would have confronted the bastard too. But to yell at Eloise? To scold her like a child?

No. Fuck no.

Had anyone been happy for her? Or were they all just pouting because she hadn't included them? That she'd done something without their approval first?

Foster had told me about the Edens. He had a lot of respect for Talia's family. But they had a lot of work to do to earn mine.

Not that it mattered. Sooner rather than later, I'd just be that man who'd married Eloise. A mistake. The guy who'd disappeared after a quick divorce.

Eventually, I'd become a no one. A distant memory.

My fork stabbed a piece of chicken too hard, scraping against the plate.

While I inhaled my food, Eloise picked at hers. Every sip of her sangria looked pained but she seemed determined to drink the glass.

"Have you, um...gone to the coffee shop?" she asked, poking at a cube of squash.

"No."

"I've gone every day." Another piece of squash got added to her fork but she didn't lift it to her mouth. "Lyla made my favorite pumpkin scones yesterday. She hasn't made me pay for coffee all week."

"And that's a bad thing?"

"Lyla always makes us pay. Not that any of us mind. We want to support her business. But she's refused when I offered. And she only bakes with pumpkin in the fall."

So Lyla was pissed too. Or hurt. Or both.

Eloise set down her fork. "Fake marriage is hard."

I stabbed another bite of cold chicken, again harder than necessary. Did she need to keep reminding me this was fake? I was well aware.

"My parents asked me to come to the ranch for a family dinner tomorrow night. That's why I made cookies. And sangria." She took a drink, swallowing hard. "I think I'll just stop by the grocery store tomorrow and buy a bottle of wine."

I chewed, my jaw tensing as I waited for her to invite me along.

But Eloise sipped that sangria, not uttering a word. By the time her glass was empty, the cringing had stopped and my plate was empty, unlike hers.

"Done?" I asked, standing.

She nodded.

I took care of the dishes, then dug my phone from my pocket, pulling up a recipe. Then I rifled through the cupboards for a bowl and mixer.

"What are you doing?" Eloise asked, coming to the kitchen to refill her glass.

I didn't answer. I just worked with quiet efficiency, knowing she'd figure it out.

When I hit the button on the oven to start it preheating, I knew the burnt smell would return, but hopefully the sugar and cinnamon would beat it out.

And while I made oatmeal raisin cookies, something I hadn't done in years, Eloise stood beside the island, watching and drinking.

Thirteen minutes after I put the first batch in the oven, they were on a cooling rack and the last dozen was baking.

Now she wouldn't show up at the ranch empty-handed. Even if she didn't like oatmeal raisin.

"You're incredibly sexy in the kitchen," she said. "And when you smile. Except you don't smile enough. Why is that?"

I lifted a shoulder, leaning against the counter. Maybe there just wasn't much to smile about.

She shifted away from the island, taking the space beside mine. "I'm tipsy."

So whatever popped into that gorgeous head of hers was coming out of her pretty mouth.

"Will you smile for me?"

I smiled.

Her nose scrunched up. "That's not your real smile. Your eyes aren't doing the crinkle thing."

"Crinkle thing?"

She waved it off, lifting her glass. But before she could take another drink, I stole it from her hand, bringing the sangria to my mouth.

Fuck, it was awful.

She'd used too much orange juice or too much rum or too much wine. Maybe too much of everything. It was like drinking diluted sweet and sour sauce.

"Bad, right?" She pouted.

I answered by finishing her glass in a single gulp.

"Jas," she whispered. Damn, but I liked it when she called me Jas. Her gaze dropped to my mouth. "I don't want to sleep on the couch anymore."

Thank fuck. I set the empty glass in the sink. The pitcher would get poured down the drain later. The cookies had a minute left, but I took them out anyway, shutting off the oven and leaving them on the stovetop.

Then I took Eloise's hand, leading her to the bathroom. With a quick flick on the knob, I turned on the shower.

"Turn around," I ordered.

She obeyed without hesitation, facing the mirror.

I reached behind my head, yanking off my T-shirt. Then I shoved my shorts and boxers from my legs, kicking them off with my shoes. My cock jutted out, hard and throbbing, aching for the beautiful woman who stood silently staring at our reflection.

When I came up behind her, Eloise's entire body shivered. I pressed my nose into her hair, breathing in that intoxicating scent. It held a bit of the burnt cookie smell too.

With one hand, I took her face in my grip, turning her chin up so she had to look up at me. She tried to turn around, but I shook my head, keeping her body aimed toward the mirror.

"Have you ever watched yourself come before?"

Her breath hitched. "No."

"Watch." Releasing her chin, I nodded to the mirror, already fogging at the edges from the shower's steam.

Then I reached for the hem of her tee, pulling it up and over her chest. Her sports bra came next, landing with a thump on the floor. When her joggers and panties joined the heap, my hand snaked around her waist, skating across her hip before dropping down her thigh.

"Are you wet for me, angel?" I asked.

She nodded, her breaths coming in pants. Her eyelids fluttered closed the moment I dragged a finger through her slit.

"Fucking soaked," I murmured against the skin of her shoulder. "Don't close your eyes."

Her blue eyes popped open, locking with mine through the glass.

"Watch how exquisite you are when you come." I stroked her flesh, drawing that wetness from her core to her clit with slow, lazy circles. My cock was rock hard, weeping to sink inside her wet heat. I wedged it in between her ass cheeks.

Eloise whimpered, rocking her hips against my arousal.

I wrapped my other arm around her waist, holding her to me as I worked her clit, faster and faster. Her body began to tremble. Her mouth opened, her breaths heavy. And just like I'd ordered, she kept her eyes locked on our reflection.

"Fuck, but you're gorgeous." I slipped my middle finger inside. Then I shifted to her clit again, stroking and flicking. "Look at you. Look at how fucking sexy you are. Who gives a damn if you can bake cookies or make sangria. You're perfect, El."

"Jas." She turned her chin, reaching back to cup my head, drawing my mouth toward hers.

I slammed my lips on hers, our tongues tangling the moment her orgasm broke. I swallowed her cry, refusing to let up as her body trembled and shattered. Pulse after pulse, she came apart in my arms until her body sagged against mine.

We shuffled into the shower, our mouths colliding again as soon as we were under the spray. Then I hoisted her up, her mouth fused to mine, her hands coming to my cheeks as she took control of the kiss, letting me press her against the slippery tiled wall.

When I slid inside, burying myself to the root, she wrapped her arms around my neck, holding tight while I fucked her hard, not letting up until we came together in a frenzy of cries and groans.

"No more couch," I said, my cock still deep inside her.

She pushed her fingers through my wet hair. "Okay."

I eased out and set her on her feet. While I washed my hair, she dragged a soapy puff across my shoulders and back. Then the two of us moved to the loft, ignoring the mess in the kitchen.

We fucked again, slow and lazy, until we were both spent.

The restless energy was gone. Finally. And even though she fell asleep cuddled into my side, making me too hot and uncomfortable, I crashed, waking only when dawn crept through the windows.

And found Eloise still sleeping against my side.

CHAPTER 11

ELOISE

The rows and columns on my spreadsheet were blurring together. The color coding had taken on a life of its own today, and now it looked like a rainbow had puked on the hotel's shift schedule.

But it was done. Hopefully.

Summer was hard. It had taken me the entire day of shuffling and juggling to iron out the tentative schedule for the summer. Fingers crossed I'd managed to accommodate everyone's vacation plans. It *should* work.

Until someone called in sick. Or quit.

"Nobody can quit," I told my computer screen. At least not until I hired another part-time housekeeper. *If* I could hire another housekeeper. I'd had an ad in the local newspaper for a week without a single bite.

Worst case, I'd have to clean rooms myself. It certainly wouldn't be the first time, but I was already working six days a week.

For the first time in my career at The Eloise, I wanted just one day off. One day to spend in bed with Jasper. If we only had two more months together, then I wanted to make the most of it.

Though maybe I was going about this all wrong. Maybe I needed to live and breathe this hotel for the next sixty-ish days. Maybe that would make it easier in the end.

Despite my best intentions to confine our relationship to sex, I was growing attached to Jasper. Everything about him was appealing. From that handsome face to his ripped body. From the way he forced me to eat more vegetables to the way he buried his nose in my hair to inhale its scent.

The nightly orgasms were just a bonus.

Ever since the burnt cookie incident, Jasper and I had settled into a routine. I woke up early each morning and left for work. When I got home in the evening, he'd make us dinner. Then we'd do...nothing.

I loved the nothing.

He'd listen to me talk about whatever was happening at the hotel. He'd sit beside me on the couch reading while I flipped on the TV for an hour. Then we'd retreat to the loft where we'd exhaust each other's bodies to sleep.

The past two weeks had been good. Borderline great.

Except the pressure from my family was starting to crush me. They'd planned that family dinner two weeks ago to meet Jasper, but the moment I'd mentioned it, I could tell he hadn't wanted to go. So I hadn't even invited him.

When they'd asked us to last week's family dinner, I'd lied. I'd told Mom and Dad that Jasper and I were having a date night. Was it a lie if the date just happened to be at the A-frame?

Yes. With every lie and half-truth, the icky feeling in my stomach came crawling back.

Something had to give. I couldn't keep this up for another two months, not with every Eden within a fifty-mile radius trying to poke their noses into my marriage.

Two of my aunts had stopped by the hotel this week, asking when they were going to get to meet my mysterious husband. I'd bumped into one of my cousins yesterday at the gas station and he'd wanted to hire Jasper as his personal trainer.

Did Jasper even do personal training for anyone but Foster? A wife should know the answer to that question.

I pressed my fingers to my temples, rubbing at the headache caused by the rainbow spreadsheet and lack of caffeine.

I'd spent the past two weeks avoiding Eden Coffee because Lyla was still acting too...nice. The coffee at the hotel was okay, but it was nothing like Lyla's. I missed good coffee. I missed my sister.

The lobby door opened so I tore my eyes away from my screen, smiling and ready to greet my guests. But it was my parents who walked inside, their hands locked.

I loved that my parents held hands. For as long as I could remember, they were always linked when they walked.

Did Jasper hold hands in public? Then again, we didn't walk together in public.

"Hi." I braced, steeling my spine and holding my breath.

Mom tried to mask it, but she still looked sad. Disappointed. Dad didn't even bother to hide the hurt from his blue eyes.

Mom stopped at the counter and frowned. "Don't look so scared to see us."

But I was. "That's not it." Another lie that made me feel gross, but I forced my frame to relax. "I've just got a miserable headache. What's up?"

"We were hoping to have dinner with you and Jasper tonight at Knuckles," she said.

"Oh." My stomach dropped. "Um..." *Shit.* "I'd love to but can we have a rain check?"

"Why?" Dad's eyes narrowed.

"This headache is killing me. I sort of just want to go home and take a bath. It's been a long day."

Mom and Dad shared a look, one I hadn't seen since high school—since the night I'd come home slightly tipsy and five minutes past curfew. They'd both been waiting up. I'd tried to convince them I was entirely sober.

They hadn't bought it then, and I'd scored a two-week grounding.

They weren't buying it now either, were they?

"How about dinner tomorrow night?" I blurted. "I'm not working, and I'm sure I'll feel better. We could come to the house. Or meet you here in town."

"The house." Mom nodded. "We'll see if everyone else can make it too."

"Great." My voice was too bright.

What was worse? Mom and Dad alone at Knuckles, where Dad would no doubt interrogate Jasper? Or at the house with my parents, siblings, nieces and nephews?

The house. Definitely the house. But it was too late. Mom was already rattling off potential dinner options.

"Burgers? Does Jasper like burgers?" she asked.

"Yes, he likes burgers." Probably. Did he eat red meat? He normally cooked chicken.

Whatever. I'd eat two burgers if necessary.

"We'll see you then," Dad said. "Hope your headache goes away."

"Me too." I gave them a small smile.

"Oh, before I forget." Mom held up a finger. "Did you talk to Brittany about swapping Sundays and Tuesdays?"

"Um, no." What?

"I bumped into her the other day at the grocery store. She mentioned she was trying to make a little extra money before their summer vacation to Disney. So I offered to have her come out and do some cleaning at the house. I was thinking Tuesdays if you can switch her schedule so she's working here Sundays instead. Then I could go to Griff and Winn's and watch the kids there Tuesdays and stay out of her way."

Tuesdays. I needed Brittany here Tuesdays. She was the only housekeeper on the schedule that day.

If she wanted extra money, why hadn't she asked me first? I would have given her more shifts. Why hadn't Mom told her to talk to me first instead of offering her a side gig?

But instead of getting mad, I smothered my frustration. At this point, I'd do anything to get back to normal with my parents. Even if that meant changing the schedule. Again.

"No problem. I'm sure I can adjust the schedule."

"Thanks." Mom smiled. "Let me know if it becomes a hassle and we'll forget the whole thing."

"I'm sure it will be fine," I lied. It was going to be a cluster. "I'll call Brittany."

"See you tomorrow night."

"Bye." I waited until they were outside and past the hotel's gleaming windows before I dropped my head to the desk.

If my head had hurt before Mom and Dad's visit, it was unbearable as I left the hotel.

My skull throbbed, and when I hit the gravel on Alderson Road, my teeth rattled, making the pain worse.

Jasper's Yukon was parked outside the A-frame when I got home. I found him in the kitchen, wearing a simple gray T-shirt and a pair of faded jeans. His feet were bare, his hair damp, like he'd showered recently.

That stubble on his jaw was begging to be touched, and his lips needed to be kissed.

This man, this gorgeous man, was mine. Temporarily mine, but mine nonetheless. It took me by surprise each and every night. I'd walk through the door, and my heart would skip.

Would my real husband be as handsome as Jasper? Would he make me cookies so I wouldn't show up at a family dinner empty-handed? Would he have a dirty mouth and wickedly talented tongue? Would he kiss me like he was a man drowning and I was his air?

Jasper spotted me standing inside the door. He was beside the counter, seasoning two small steaks on a cutting board. "Hey."

"You eat red meat." I sighed. Thank God.

"What?"

"Nothing." I shook my head, about to set my purse down when I noticed the dining room table. *My* dining room table. "You went to my house?"

He nodded, washing his hands at the sink. "Foster and I took a few trips today. Hauled out the rest of the furniture."

"Oh. Thank you." I pulled out a familiar chair, sinking into the smooth, walnut seat. "I would have helped."

He shrugged. "We had it covered."

That meant all that was left was to clean. Then the owners could find another tenant.

"Most of the stuff I put in the shop," he said.

"All right." There wasn't much need for my furniture inside the A-frame.

If I had kept sleeping on the couch, I would have insisted we bring in mine because it was more comfortable. But Jasper's bed was a dream, soft and plush and warm. Not once had I woken in the middle of the night with cold feet, and the crook of his neck was better than any pillow.

"How was your day?" he asked.

"Long. My parents stopped by. We need to go to the ranch for dinner tomorrow." I braced, just like I had at the hotel. Shoulders pinned. Breath held.

That muscle—the angry muscle—feathered Jasper's jaw. "I'm not one for family functions."

"And I'm not one for anal play but I still let you shove your finger up my ass last night."

"This is not the same." His look flattened. "And you liked it last night."

Yes, I had liked it.

Jasper was pushing my sexual boundaries, and each time we were together, he seemed to unlock a new level of pleasure. Last night had been nerve-racking and exhilarating. The combination had led to the most intense orgasm of my life.

"You might enjoy dinner with my family. If you tried."

He walked to the fridge, taking out a sweet potato. Ignoring me.

"My family thinks I have horrible taste in men."

"Okay," he drawled, rifling through a drawer for the potato peeler. "I'll try not to take offense to that."

"You could prove them wrong."

He turned on the faucet and started peeling a potato.

"The last guy I brought home was for Foster's first dinner at the ranch. Did he tell you about it?"

"No."

"He was a guy I met at Willie's. He was sort of lanky with a hippie vibe. Cute though."

The peeler scraped harder against the potato as Jasper's

frame tensed. Was that jealousy? If so, I liked it. Though he had nothing to envy. That guy had been a solid two compared to Jasper's eleven.

"We'd gone on a couple of dates," I said. "Nothing serious. But since Foster was coming to the ranch, I thought, why not bring a date too? We'd get all of the introductions over with. So we get to the house and it turns out my date wasn't entirely a stranger to everyone in the house."

Jasper's focus was still on the potato and peeler in his hand, but he'd slowed, listening.

"Winn knew my date. She'd gotten a call at the station from the general manager at the grocery store because he'd caught this guy stuffing a cucumber down his jeans."

"What the fuck?"

"Exactly." I huffed a dry laugh. "Come with me. Show everyone my taste isn't as bad as they think."

Jasper set the peeled potato aside and picked up a towel to dry his hands.

"Don't make me beg," I whispered.

Jasper crossed the room, towering in front of me. His hand came to my cheek, tilting my face up so I could stare at him while his thumb stroked my jaw. "It's better this way. Keep some separation."

Begging it was. "Please."

"Go without me, angel." His voice was soft, smoother than I'd ever heard before. Either because he talked more when I was home. Or because he was trying to lessen the blow of his refusal.

"This is important to me."

"Why?"

I blinked. Why was it important that he meet my family?

What the hell kind of question was that? "Um, because it's my family. And you're supposed to be my husband."

Not supposed. He *was* my husband. Temporarily.

Was this about his family? We hadn't spoken about them. I had no idea where he was from. Where his parents lived. If he had siblings. Curiosity bubbled but I tamped it down, saving those questions for another day. There was begging to do.

"Jas."

His hand fell away from my face. "I'll be gone in a couple of months."

My heart squeezed. Why was that so painful? It wasn't a surprise, not really. We hadn't exactly talked about what would happen after the divorce but I'd known the chances were high that he'd leave Quincy. Still...it stung.

"Please go with me."

"El—"

"This is ridiculous." I shot out of my chair, slipping around him to pace in front of the island. "I shouldn't have to beg for you to go with me. Why is this even a debate? You're going. You promised me that you'd help me prove to everyone that this was real, so you're going."

Jasper looked up, crossing his arms over his broad chest.

I mirrored his posture, mostly so I wouldn't squirm beneath the intensity of his stare. It took all my willpower to breathe evenly and keep my chin held high. "You're coming with me."

His eyes narrowed. "You're awfully bossy today."

"I've been taking lessons from my husband."

His jaw flexed. But then I saw it, a crack in that steel armor. He dropped his arms. "You're right. I just...I struggle with family. But I'll go."

The air rushed from my lungs. "Thank you."

Jasper crooked a finger, luring me closer. Then, when I'd stopped in front of him, my arms still crossed, he shook his head. "They don't need to like me."

Yes, they did. I wanted them to be proud that I'd married a good man. Just for a little while, I wanted them to like Jasper. Because when he walked away, no matter how hard I tried to convince them otherwise, he would become the enemy.

So for now, for two more months, sixty-ish days, I wanted them to like him. To be happy for us.

Starting Sunday with dinner at the ranch.

CHAPTER 12

ELOISE

This dinner was either going to be incredible or an incredible disaster. I was betting on the latter. Regardless, even if this was an epic failure, I wasn't sorry for pushing Jasper to come.

"Turn off up there," I told him, pointing to the gravel road that teed into the highway ahead.

Jasper slowed and took the left without so much as a nod. He was as silent now as he had been all day. Hell, other than a few groans, he'd barely made a sound when we'd had sex this morning.

Still, no regrets.

My family was a huge part of my life. He was my husband. At some point, the two had to learn how to play nice. Besides, it was only for a couple months.

The ranch's open gates greeted us as we rolled down the gravel drive. My stomach, already in knots, twisted tighter as we passed the log archway emblazoned with the Eden ranch brand—an *E* with a curve in the shape of a rocking chair's runner beneath.

"That's our brand," I told Jasper.

Not even a hum of acknowledgment.

Why was he so against this? I still didn't understand his resistance. It was just dinner.

Last night during our argument—if that counted as an argument—I should have pressed for more of an explanation. But the moment he'd agreed to come to dinner, I'd dropped the subject entirely.

While he'd made dinner, I'd changed into sweats. Then the two of us had shared a quiet meal before we'd retreated to bed, doing what we did best.

Each other.

"Thank you for coming."

He nodded. Progress. Though his eyes stayed locked on the road ahead.

I studied his profile, letting my gaze wander down his forehead to the bump on the bridge of his nose. To the soft lips and stubbled jaw that had woken me this morning as he'd kissed my neck and slid inside my body.

Was it such a crime for me to ask for this meal?

I wanted my family to know Jasper. To remember him. I wanted them to see the man who'd shared this wild, reckless adventure with me. The man who'd only be in my life for a short time but whose memory would undoubtedly last for years.

Forcing this issue was probably silly, considering this was all just a charade. But with every passing day, this felt less and less like a mistake. And if they knew him, then maybe they'd realize why I'd married him that night. Maybe they wouldn't hold it against me.

And I wanted Jasper to know my family. To see the best of them.

Here on the ranch, we were all our best.

This was home.

Spring weather in Montana, especially in May, was always unpredictable. It could snow one day and be sunny and seventy degrees the next. But for Jasper's first visit to the ranch, the scene through the windshield couldn't have been more picturesque.

Barbwire fences bordered the road. Beyond them, the meadows were a lush, vibrant green as they stretched beneath tall evergreens toward the foothills. Mountains, capped with snow, towered in the distance. Their jagged peaks kissed the brilliant blue sky.

It was magnificent. I'd lived my whole life in Montana, yet it never failed to steal my breath.

"Griffin and Winn live on the ranch," I told Jasper, pointing out my window in the general direction of my brother's house. "You can't see their place from here but it's that way."

Not that Jasper had asked for that information, but this silence was only making the nerves fluttering in my belly worse. If he wouldn't talk, then I would.

"Griff runs the ranch now. It's one of the largest in the state." That wasn't a brag. It was simply pride in my family. For generations, the Edens had owned this land, expanding it when possible, adding more acreage and more cattle. "It runs along the mountains for miles."

Normally, I offered to take visitors on a tour, maybe even spend a Sunday riding horses along the path that tied one end of the ranch to the other. That was, if they showed any interest in this place.

But Jasper just kept driving, not even bothering to look my way. And by the time the trails dried out enough so we wouldn't be riding in the mud, he'd be gone anyway.

I swallowed down the lump in my throat. "Griff and Winn have two kids. Hudson and Emma. Knox and his wife, Memphis, have two boys, Drake and Harrison."

Did Jasper want kids? I couldn't picture him with a baby in his arms. Though until my brothers had become fathers, I hadn't been able to imagine them as dads either.

It was hard to remember what these family dinners had been like before the babies had been born. When I thought of Griffin, I saw him wearing his scuffed cowboy boots and faded Wranglers, Hudson perched on one arm and Emma on the other. And Knox wasn't Knox without Drake toddling behind him, an adorable shadow with blond hair and a smile that would thaw even Jasper's icy indifference.

I was counting on those kids. I was counting on my brothers and sisters, Mom's cooking and Dad's bellowing laugh to win Jasper over tonight.

My hands began to tremble so I slid them beneath my legs.

Ahead, in a clearing of the trees, my parents' log house came into view. "That's Mom and Dad's. My room was that first window on the second floor."

Jasper shifted his grip on the wheel, but otherwise, he gave nothing away. He was as unreadable as a piece of blank paper.

"Penny for your thoughts?" I asked.

He blinked.

"Apparently I'll have to pay more," I muttered. "Are you going to be like this all night? Brooding and, well...grumpy?"

Jasper glanced over, his jaw ticking, as he arched an eyebrow. Finally, a reaction. "I'm here, aren't I?"

"Are you?"

This wasn't the Jasper I'd been living with for the past month. Or maybe it was. Maybe I'd gotten used to filling the silence. Maybe I'd forgotten how rare it was to earn a smile because I'd been winning them more often.

"Never mind." I shook my head, dismissing the subject before it caused a fight. Then I sat a little taller, once more talking to battle my nerves. "My grandfather built the barn behind the house. Dad was the one who put in the shop and stables."

The enormous buildings, together with Mom and Dad's house, formed ranch headquarters. There were three Eden Ranch trucks parked in the open lot, employee vehicles left for the weekend. Four more vehicles were lined up in front of Mom and Dad's place.

Which meant we were the last to arrive.

Jasper eased into the space beside Foster's truck. It had been quiet on the drive, but the moment he shut off the engine, I could hear my heart pounding against my sternum.

My hand trembled as I reached for the door, but before I could touch the handle, Jasper's hand settled on my thigh.

"Here." He popped open the console, taking out a square, velvet box.

A ring box.

"What's that?" Dumb question, Eloise.

"We're married," he said.

"So you got me a ring?"

Was that where he'd gone this morning? I'd assumed he'd left after breakfast for a workout. But he must have stopped downtown and bought me this ring.

The jewelry store owners and their clerks were horrible gossips. But if they thought it was strange for Jasper to buy me a ring now, after we'd been married for a month, I didn't care.

I flipped open the box's lid and my jaw dropped.

A round diamond, at least two carats and utterly flawless, sat atop a platinum, jewel-studded band. Beneath it was a wedding ring made entirely of diamonds. It was dainty. Elegant. Exactly what I would have picked out for myself.

"Jas. This is…" Too beautiful. Too expensive.

Too real for a fake wife.

I couldn't find the right words, so I just stared at the diamonds through blurry eyes, wishing I could parse the emotions swelling inside my chest.

Jasper plucked the box from my hand, taking out the set. Then he took my hand, pulling it across the console to slide the jewelry onto my finger. A perfect fit.

"I didn't buy you a ring." My gaze whipped to his as panic rushed through my veins. "I should have bought you a ring."

"I don't wear rings."

"Oh." Why not? Was it because he trained with Foster? I guess if it came down to wearing a ring or losing a finger, I'd rather he not wear a ring either.

"Okay. Well, thank you." My gaze dropped to the ring again, mesmerized by the gleaming jewel. I soaked in the glitter and sparkle, then leaned across the console.

The moment I pressed my mouth to Jasper's, his hand cupped the back of my head, pulling me closer. His tongue licked at the seam of my lips, sliding inside when I opened.

I sank into the kiss, the languid strokes of his tongue and the soft press of his lips. It was slow and unhurried. Different than the way he kissed me in bed.

What was this? Affection? Intimacy? An apology? Or just another form of foreplay?

Before I could figure it out, the sound of a door slamming filled the air.

Jasper and I broke apart as Griffin came striding across Mom and Dad's wraparound porch with Emma on his hip.

"Thank you for the ring," I told Jasper.

He nodded, then opened his door.

I did the same, climbing out and walking to Griffin.

"Hey." Griffin gave me a hug, then held out Emma so I could kiss her cheek. But she didn't want me to carry her. She was content with her daddy. When he let me go, he extended a hand to Jasper. "How's it going?"

"Good." Jasper nodded, shaking Griff's hand.

That was a good thing, right? No angry glares or scowls.

"Everyone is in the stables," Griff said, jerking his chin that direction. "One of the horses had her foal this morning."

"Aww. Cute." I fell in step beside my brother, reaching back for Jasper's hand.

He took it but he didn't hold it. Not the way Dad would hold Mom's hand. Not even the way Jasper would hold my hand at night while we were having sex, with our palms pressed together like he wanted to fuse them together.

Jasper's grip was too loose as we walked. His fingers barely clasped mine. All it would take was a quick flick, and he'd be free.

Fine. If he wouldn't hold tight, then I'd do it. I laced my fingers through his. If he wanted to escape, he'd have to work for it.

The earthy scent of hay and horses greeted us as we walked into the stables. When my eyes adjusted to the dimmer light, I saw my entire family clustered around a stall, heads peering past the door. At the sound of our footsteps, everyone turned.

"Hi." No one paid me any attention. All eyes were on Jasper. So I held up our clasped hands. "Everyone, meet Jasper. Jasper, this is my family."

I hadn't expected him to smile but he didn't even wave.

Didn't nod. Didn't say hello. Seriously? Why was he acting like this? Even Foster gave him a sideways glance.

Jasper said that he struggled with family. *Um... understatement.*

Dad walked over, standing in front of us.

When he extended his hand, I had no choice but to let Jasper's go.

"Harrison Eden."

"Jasper Vale." He shook Dad's hand.

Thank God. Otherwise he would have been known for eternity as the only man I'd brought home to snub my father.

Mom joined us, standing at Dad's side. "And I'm Anne."

"Nice to meet you both." Jasper dipped his chin. "Thanks for having me for dinner."

He sounded like this visit was a one-time trip. Maybe it was.

"Hey." Lyla came over with that too bright, too friendly smile on her face. "How are you guys?"

"Good. You?"

"Great." Her gaze flicked to Jasper for a split second before it dropped to the ground. Except on its downward path, it landed on my left hand. She tensed when she saw my ring.

We hadn't talked about her crush. But I should have forced it. I should have gotten the awkward over with before a family gathering. How could I have not realized she'd been into Jasper? I was such an asshole. Worst sister ever.

"Heard we have a new addition," I said, desperately wanting the attention to go anywhere else.

"A colt," Dad said, leading the way to the stall.

Inside was a black foal with a white star on his forehead.

"Isn't he handsome?" I smiled. It was as fake as my marriage. I knew without turning around that Jasper hadn't followed us over. That he was standing apart.

Dad's arm came around my shoulder, pulling me into a side hug.

I looked up, meeting his blue eyes. They were full of concern, probably because Dad always saw what his children were trying to hide. Not all of it, but enough.

"Well, now that you're here, we can name him," he said.

"No planets," Knox said from where he stood beside Memphis. She was holding baby Harrison while he had Drake in his arms.

"We're out of planets anyway," I told him.

Years ago, Dad had bought eight horses. At the time, I'd been doing a school project about the solar system, so I'd asked to name the horses after planets. My horse was Venus. Her stall, three down, was empty, probably because she was out grazing in a meadow with the others.

Jupiter, Griffin's horse, was at his house. But otherwise, the other seven lived here. Mars belonged to Knox. Saturn was Mateo's. Neptune and Mercury were Lyla's and Talia's. Mom and Dad had volunteered for the least desirable planet names.

Ever since those horses, I'd been naming our animals. The dogs. The milk cow. The kittens. Whenever a creature needed a name, they came to me.

But it was time to pass the torch.

"Let's let Kadence name him," I said.

Foster's seven-year-old daughter stood on her tiptoes beside Mom, her eyes locked on the foal. At my suggestion, her gaze whipped to me, then Dad.

"Really?" she asked. "Can I?"

Dad nodded. "He needs a name."

"What should I pick?" she asked.

A deep voice filled the air. "Anything other than Earth or Uranus."

Mom gasped.

We all turned as a man strode into the stables.

Mateo.

"W-what are you doing here?" Mom rushed toward him, pulling him into her arms.

She blamed her recent gray hairs on the fact that her baby was flying planes in Alaska. That, and Mateo hadn't been great about visiting.

"Hey, Mom." He swept her into his arms, looking bigger than when he'd left. Grown up, like Griffin and Knox.

When Mom stepped aside, Dad claimed him next for a back-slapping hug. "Welcome home, son. This is a surprise."

"Good to be here, Dad."

Something settled. Something clicked. With all of us on the ranch, it was like being hugged by home. I glanced at Jasper, wondering if he felt the love too.

His arms were crossed. He stared blankly at an empty stall.

My good feeling dimmed.

Matty got mobbed with hugs and handshakes. He became the center of attention, and I breathed a sigh of relief, moving to stand beside Jasper. Maybe we'd survive tonight after all.

"Hi." Mateo walked over, pulling me in for the last hug, keeping me tucked against his side as he held out a hand for Jasper. "You must be the husband. Jason? James?"

"Matty." I elbowed him in the ribs.

He chuckled. "Kidding. Nice to meet you, Jasper."

"You too," Jasper said, shaking Mateo's hand. It was the first genuine sentiment I'd seen from him since we'd arrived.

"Congratulations." Mateo glanced down, pinching my

cheek like he used to when we were kids.

"Don't." I swatted his hand away. "What are you doing here?"

"Can't I come home?" he teased.

"How long do we have you?" Mom's voice was cautious, like she already despised his answer. "What's your plan?"

He shrugged, letting me go to drag a hand through his hair. It was longer now than I'd ever seen it, like he hadn't cut it in months. "Well, first I was hoping for dinner. Then I'm going to find an empty bed and sleep for two days. After that, whatever. See who needs help around here."

"Me." My hand shot in the air. Griffin had his mouth open, like he was about to offer Mateo work too, but I pointed my finger at his nose. "Don't even think about it. I called dibs first."

Griff chuckled. "Fine."

Matty, like the rest of us, had spent his teenage years working here on the ranch and at the hotel.

"Even if it's just for a few days, I'd love some help," I told him. "Thank you."

"How about if it was for more than a few days?"

"Wait." I blinked. "What do you mean? What about Alaska?"

"Alaska's great. But it's not Montana."

"Does that mean you're home?" The hope in Talia's voice was written on every Eden face. "For good?"

He nodded. "For now."

Mom coughed, clearing her throat. She had tears in her eyes. "I need to get started on dinner."

Without another word, she turned and walked out of the stables. She'd retreat to her kitchen and shed a few tears of joy. Then she'd fuss over Mateo the moment he crossed the threshold.

Everyone trickled out behind her, one by one, heading for the house.

Except Jasper.

He walked toward the stall, peering inside to look at the foal.

I took the space beside him, but I didn't look at the baby. I stared at his profile, waiting for him to look my way. "Are you okay?"

"Yeah."

Liar.

He'd told me last night he wasn't one for family functions. Why? What was I missing? What was his family like? Maybe I shouldn't have pushed so hard for this. Part of me wanted to beg, to plead with him to just...try. Instead, I told him what was in my heart.

"I don't want them to hate you when this is over," I whispered.

"Don't you think it's easier that way?"

"What do you mean, easier?"

He lifted a shoulder. "They don't need to know me to hate me."

"But I don't want them to hate you." My heart twisted. Why would they hate him?

"I don't care if they do."

"Jasper." My voice cracked. "I do."

Was that how he saw us ending? With hate in our hearts? Part of me wanted to hug him. The other part wanted to throw a handful of horse shit in his face for being such an idiot.

"I don't want them to curse your name," I said. "To talk about you for years as the bad guy who broke my heart. I don't want them to think of you that way, because it's not how *I* want to think of you."

He sighed, snagging my hand and pulling me into his arms. He kissed my hair. Then together, we walked to the house.

But nothing changed.

Through dinner, he hardly spoke. He only answered questions that were directed at him.

Yes, he was quiet normally. But this was different. Tense. Even when Foster engaged with him, he gave the shortest answers possible. Until people stopped trying. Everyone gave their attention to Mateo instead, while I fought the urge to cry.

Jasper seemed determined to be the villain.

Maybe he was right. Maybe that would make it easier. Maybe it didn't matter what anyone thought of my husband.

This was just a lie anyway.

CHAPTER 13

JASPER

Foster and I sat across from each other on the mats at his gym, stretching our hamstrings after a three-mile run.

"So did you see the announcement?" he asked.

"I did."

This was the subject I'd been waiting for him to bring up all morning. I'd thought he might want to talk about it during the run. Instead, he'd stayed quiet, letting me push him faster and faster. Until now, when he was ready.

"Great statement," I said.

"Talia helped me write it."

Foster had announced his retirement today. In the news article I'd read this morning, he'd thanked the UFC and his fans for supporting him throughout his career. He'd even thanked me.

His retirement wasn't news, not to those of us who knew him personally. He'd told me about it weeks ago but had chosen to hold off on the announcement to ride the wave of his final victory for just a little bit longer.

Until now, when it was time to say goodbye.

"It feels strange." He dragged a hand over his beard. "Not

bad, just… I don't know the right word."

"Official."

"Something like that."

"You all right? No second thoughts?"

He shook his head. "No regrets. I'm where I need to be."

And he had a whole future ahead of him, a life to build with Talia and their growing family.

"Even though I'm retired, you're still my trainer," he said.

"I know."

He'd told me the same thing when he'd shared his decision to step away from fighting. There wasn't a doubt in my mind that Foster would pay me for the rest of his life just to run alongside him around Quincy. To spar with him at his private gym. To stretch in this very spot.

But training had never been about the money. I didn't need money.

I'd started training because I'd needed…something.

More than ten years I'd been doing this and I still couldn't exactly articulate that *something*.

The physical release was part of it. So was the thrill of watching a student or athlete win. And when I'd started down this path, it had been the first time in my life when I hadn't felt like a second thought. When I'd walked into my first dojo all those years ago, I hadn't been a burden.

Finally, I'd been in the right place at the right time.

Montana had been the right place, initially. With Foster's retirement, well…I wasn't sure what was next.

For years, Foster had forged the path. He'd led. I'd followed. That had suited me just fine. But he'd finished his journey. He'd found that pot of gold at the end of the rainbow.

So where was I headed?

The last time I'd been in this position, staring at a blank future, I'd managed to find a career. A best friend.

But that friendship was about to change. When Eloise and I got divorced, Foster would choose a side, and I wasn't foolish enough to think it would be mine.

Damn, but I'd miss him. The worry of what was to come was like an endless cloud hanging over my head.

Foster jumped up to his bare feet, rolling his arms in big circles, loosening his muscles. "Is Eloise working today?"

"No, she's at home. The weekend desk clerk needs Saturday off so she's going to cover and take today off instead."

When I'd left the cabin this morning, she'd been folding laundry. She'd mentioned running errands later and swinging out to the ranch. There'd been no invitation to tag along, probably because she knew I would have said no.

It had been a month since that awkward and tense dinner with her family. Other than occasionally crossing paths with Talia here at the gym or my infrequent stops at the coffee shop where I'd bump into Lyla, I hadn't seen much of the Edens.

I preferred it that way.

Eloise didn't bring them up. Even Foster rarely mentioned them anymore.

I'd only gone to that dinner because Eloise had insisted, but it had taken all my willpower not to call out her parents on their bullshit.

How could they not see how hard she was trying? I had no doubt that they loved her. But there was a reason she was faking this marriage.

Her family, her parents, had put so much pressure on Eloise to change that she'd convinced herself she wasn't good enough. That to get that hotel, she couldn't say no. That she had to be perfect.

She already was.

They wanted her to harden that beautiful heart, to put up walls and shut people out. To guard herself so no one, including me, could take advantage of her trusting nature. If they kept pushing, they'd snuff out all of the wonderful that made her Eloise.

But this wasn't my fight. Considering the unhealthy relationship I had with my own parents, I had no place to speak up. So I'd stayed quiet at dinner.

Did I have to like the Edens? No. And despite Eloise's wishes, they didn't need to like me either. I'd be gone soon. The wedding was at the end of the month.

It would be Eloise's turn to deal with family—mine.

And Sam's.

After that, she'd realize just how messed up this entire situation was, how shitty it was of me to ask her to go with me to Italy. She'd probably put a rush on drafting our divorce papers.

"What else do you feel like doing?" Foster asked. "Want to spar?"

"Do you?" We'd spent so many years together, I knew what answer was coming.

He shrugged. "Not really."

"Let's call it quits." I stood, walking over to the bench where I'd left my sweatshirt and phone.

"How about we go to lunch?" he asked.

"Sure." I pulled on my hoodie, covering my sweaty T-shirt. If I only had weeks left in Quincy with Foster, I'd do just about anything he wanted.

Except another painful dinner at the ranch.

"You good with Eden Coffee?"

"Sounds good."

Although going there felt like a slight betrayal. According to Eloise, Lyla was still acting strange, so she'd been avoiding the coffee shop. But if that was where Foster wanted to eat, I'd let him choose. He had to live in Quincy for the rest of his life. He had to deal with the Edens.

Eloise and Lyla would patch things up after I was gone.

"Mind if I take a quick shower?" Foster jerked his chin to the gym's small apartment. It was where he'd lived when he'd first moved to Quincy.

"Not at all." I swept up my phone, taking a seat on the bench while he disappeared into the apartment. A moment later, the water turned on.

I was just about to scroll through the news when my phone rang. My insides knotted at the name on the screen.

Samantha.

The call shouldn't have surprised me. Ever since I'd mailed the reply to that wedding invitation with my name and a plus-one, I'd known another call was coming. Still, my pulse quickened as my heart crept toward my throat.

"What, Samantha?" I answered, gripping the phone too tight as I pressed it to my ear.

"Oh, my full name. You're in a bad mood."

When was I going to stop answering her calls? I regretted it each and every time. Yet here I was, listening to her voice on the other end of the line for the thousandth time. "Did you need something? I'm working."

"Are you though? I read an article today about Foster Madden's retirement."

I gritted my teeth, holding back a snide comment that would just drag this out.

So she'd called to rub it in my face. Sam had always criticized my job as a trainer. To her, it was a hobby. Not something any self-respecting man would do, because it would never make me rich.

I was already rich, something she very well knew, but no amount of money would ever be enough for my ex-wife.

"What's new? Fuck anyone interesting lately?" she asked.

"Do we really need to do this?"

"Oh, that's a yes. Tell me all about her. Does she tug your hair just the way you like it?"

As a matter of fact, yes. Eloise was always pulling on my hair when we were having sex. But I kept my mouth shut.

"Tell me."

"No," I clipped.

"Jasper."

I stayed quiet, having learned a long time ago that whether I talked or not, it wouldn't matter, not to Sam. She didn't give a damn what I had to say.

She'd fill the lull in conversation.

Eloise did that too.

Though Eloise never spoke with the intention to hurt. Her tongue wasn't her greatest weapon. No, when Eloise talked, that heart of hers shined even brighter.

"How many times have you fucked her?" Sam asked. "More than once? Is she the first since me?"

Yes. At thirty-three years old, I could count on two fingers the women I'd slept with more than once. Samantha.

And Eloise.

"Your silence is telling, Jasper."

I always regretted these calls, but none so much as today's.

When had we started this sick game? I wished I could go back in time, to that first phone call after our divorce, and block Sam's number.

There'd been a woman in my bed when she'd called. I'd just moved to Vegas. I'd met a pretty woman at a bar and had forgotten her name as soon as she'd spoken it. But I hadn't needed a name to take her to bed.

The morning after, Sam's call had woken me up early. It had woken the woman too. Sam had heard her in the background, and instead of hanging up, she'd asked if I'd liked fucking another woman.

I'd lied and said yes, mostly to make Sam jealous.

But Samantha had called me on the lie. We'd known each other too damn long to pull off convincing lies.

Two weeks later, Sam had called again. Asked if I'd been with another woman. So I'd told her all of the vivid details, rubbing my sex life in her face, thinking maybe it would hurt her the way she'd hurt me.

It hadn't.

Ten years had passed since our divorce.

When would this stop?

"I had sex last night," she said. "I thought about you. I thought about our first time. Remember that? We were so young."

And stupid. We hadn't used any protection. Thank fuck she hadn't gotten pregnant.

"It was so…bad." She laughed. "It was sweet. You were so gentle. But we were so bad in the beginning. Then we got better, didn't we?"

"Yeah, I guess so." I dragged a hand through my hair. We'd

learned with each other. Taught each other. I'd never forget the two of us sitting on my bed, shoulder to shoulder, reading a book on tantric sex.

Any other woman and I probably would have been embarrassed. Not Sam.

"Who is this mystery woman? Is she any good?"

"Goodbye, Samantha."

"Wait."

Hell. "What?"

"Tell me. Does she make you lose your mind? Does she rake her nails down your back and leave marks?"

"Yes. It's the best sex I've ever had."

It was the truth.

And I'd never felt so fucking slimy in my life.

"Are you bringing this woman to my wedding?" Sam asked.

"Yes, I am."

"Who is she?"

If I couldn't hang up the phone, then what I was about to tell Sam would do the trick. "My wife."

The line went quiet.

No one in my family knew I'd gotten married. There was no way Sam could have known before now.

Sam cleared her throat. "I'm excited to meet her." A lie.

"She's a treasure." A truth.

Without a goodbye, Sam ended the call. Probably to make another. To scatter her minions in search of gossip and information on Eloise. But whatever drama Sam conjured wouldn't touch us, not in Montana.

And anyone who might have cared that I'd gotten married in secret, well…they'd stopped talking to me a long time ago. My parents included.

I stood from the bench suppressing the urge to puke.

Foster walked out, dressed in clean clothes, his hair wet. He held up his phone. "Okay, change of plan. Tally's not feeling well. She's, um…"

"Pregnant." It was a guess, something I'd suspected for a while. But my hunch was confirmed by Foster's wide smile.

"We haven't told many, but I wanted you to know."

"Congratulations." I pulled him into a hug. "I'm happy for you. Truly."

With all that he'd endured, losing Talia, the fight to win her back, Foster deserved this happiness.

He clapped me on the back, letting me go. "Thank you."

"Go home. Check on Talia. You up for a workout tomorrow?"

"Definitely. Nine?"

"I'll be here." With a wave, I headed for the door, climbing in the Yukon. Then I breathed a sigh of relief. I wouldn't have been able to sit through lunch today. Not after talking to Sam. So I took the familiar road toward town, grateful to have a few minutes to shove it aside.

Main Street was crowded with people. Tourist season had arrived in full force and happy strangers crowded the sidewalks. Kids, free from school on summer break, skipped along the blocks, their parents trailing behind.

There was an energy in the air, one that hadn't been here this winter. Quincy was no longer in hibernation but flourishing along with the rugged countryside. The snow had melted, making way for blooming flowers.

If someone had asked me in January if I'd miss it here, I would have said fuck no. But maybe I'd miss it after all. Of all the places I'd traveled in my life, there weren't many as captivating as Montana.

Eloise's car was still parked outside the A-frame when I got home.

I headed inside, dropping my keys and phone on the kitchen island just as she walked out of the laundry room, carrying a full basket. "Hey."

"Hi." She was wearing a simple green dress that hit her midthigh. Her feet were bare, showing off her polished toenails. White. This morning they'd been pink.

Her hair was down, the silky strands draping over her shoulders. When she smiled, her blue eyes sparkled like jewels. It was that smile that stopped me in my tracks. She looked at me like watching me come through the door was the highlight of her whole day.

And not that long ago, I'd told Sam how much I liked fucking my wife.

I wasn't supposed to like that label. My heart wasn't supposed to stop whenever Eloise walked into the room.

"What's wrong?" She set the basket down on the couch, coming closer. Her gaze raked over me from head to toe. "Did Foster punch you again?"

"No. It's nothing." I shook my head, turning away and walking to the fridge. "Thought you were going to the ranch."

"I changed my mind. I didn't feel like driving out there today."

I took out a Gatorade, twisting off the cap and drinking half in a few gulps. Then I set it down on the counter, staring blankly at the bottle. "Foster announced his retirement today."

"Oh." She rounded the island and hopped up on the counter, sitting right beside my drink. "You okay?"

"I knew it was coming."

Her hand lifted, her fingertips going to my hair. Exactly the way I liked. "That doesn't answer my question."

I sighed, leaning into her touch. "The biggest commitment I've made in the last decade has been to Foster's career."

"What now?" she whispered, voicing the question in my head.

"I don't know." I leaned in closer, dropping my forehead to hers.

My entire childhood, I'd been handed a plan. It had been drawn out for me before birth, sculpted from generations of Vale men who had unyielding expectations that their footsteps would be followed.

It hadn't been as hard as I'd thought to shun those expectations. The criticism, or lack thereof, had been mild. Tolerable.

My parents would have to care to be disappointed.

Those days, I'd embraced the lack of plan. I'd done whatever I'd wanted, whenever I'd wanted. Spontaneity had been an adventure.

It didn't feel as exciting this time around.

Eloise's fingers drifted over my face, tracing my cheekbone to my lips. Touching. She was always touching. Just like she was always curled against my side when we slept because apparently she was allergic to her own side of the bed.

I'd miss the touching when this was over. Not so much the cuddling.

"Hey." She pulled away, giving me a sad smile. "You'll figure it out."

"Yeah." I'd decide when the wedding was over.

"Hungry?" she asked. "I could cook us lunch."

"Peanut butter and jelly doesn't count as cooking." I nipped at her lower lip. And if she was here today, I didn't want to spend it in the kitchen.

With a quick sweep, I lifted her from the counter.

She gasped, her long legs wrapping around my hips.

"Kiss."

She dropped her mouth to mine, one arm sliding around my shoulders while the other tucked a lock of hair behind her ear. Her eyes drifted closed but I kept mine open, watching as her tongue fluttered against my lower lip.

I'd taught her that flutter.

Two weeks ago, when I'd done the exact move with my tongue against her clit, she'd come apart. Then before she'd drifted off to sleep, she'd said she wished she could do it. So for the past two weeks, we'd practiced.

She had it down now. That flutter was fucking perfect.

I tore my lips away, waiting until she opened her eyes.

"What?" she asked, breathless.

My arms tightened around her, hauling her so close she could feel my arousal. "That flutter is mine. Only mine."

"Huh?"

I waited, giving her a minute to understand.

No other man got that flutter.

The sparkle in her gaze dimmed, like a sheer curtain had been draped across a window. "Don't talk like that."

"Like what?"

"Jas." She unwrapped her legs, wiggling to be set down, but my hold on her only tightened.

"Promise me, Eloise. Don't give it to anyone else."

This was it. In all the vows we'd made, this one was the only one I wanted her to keep.

Her eyes searched mine for a long moment, sorrow creeping into those pretty blue irises, until she nodded. "Promise."

I slammed my mouth on hers, our tongues twisting. I kissed her with everything I had, marking, claiming, needing to memorize her sweet taste. Then I changed my hold, cradling her with an arm beneath her knees, the other banded around her back as I walked through the cabin, carrying her to the bed we'd share for another month.

The sun streamed through the balcony's sliding glass door, illuminating the loft. I set Eloise on her feet, and she reached for the hem of her dress, dragging it from her body before I had a chance to strip it free myself.

Her body was a fucking dream, firm but soft in all the right places.

My own clothes puddled on the floor beside hers as she unclasped her bra and shimmied out of her panties.

Then we collided. Mouths. Hands. Skin. When we fell into bed, her legs spread wide. My hips settled into the cradle of hers, and then I slid home.

"Jas." Her fingernails, also white, dug into the flesh of my shoulders. It wouldn't take more than a few strokes and she'd come apart. The flutter of her inner walls was as addictive as her tongue.

There was only so much I could demand for myself. Her orgasms were mine, for now. Then she'd give them to another man. Just the thought sent red through my vision, a jealous rage as powerful as any feeling I'd had in months.

I thrust into her body hard, wanting her to remember what it felt like when I fucked her.

"Look at me," I ordered, my breath hot against her ear.

When I leaned back, her eyes were waiting. I slammed

inside of her, all the way to the hilt.

"Remember." *Remember me.*

Her hand came to my cheek. "Will you?"

For the rest of my life.

CHAPTER 14

ELOISE

Mateo leaned against the reception counter at the hotel, looking like he was about to broach the subject I'd managed to dodge for over a month.

My marriage.

"So…" he said.

"We still have three guests coming in tonight." I clicked the mouse, waking up the computer. "Hopefully they'll get here soon. I'd love to check them in before I go home tonight. There's been a lot of changes to the reservation software since the last time you worked the desk."

As promised, Mateo had spent the past month helping me at the hotel. He'd mostly been covering shifts in housekeeping. There'd been a few maintenance projects I'd asked him to tackle too, but this was the first time I'd needed him as a desk clerk.

My regular night desk clerk had called in sick this morning, and I'd planned to cover myself. But I'd been here since seven, and when Mateo had come in this afternoon, he'd volunteered to work tonight.

"I can figure out the software," he said.

"Okay." I looked to the doors, praying a guest would walk

inside so the two of us weren't alone. So we didn't have to talk about Jasper.

"What's Jasper going to do now that Foster is retiring?" Mateo asked.

I shrugged. "He's not sure yet." Or maybe he had a plan. Mateo's guess was as good as mine.

It had been a week since Foster's retirement had been announced, and if Jasper was sure of his next steps, he hadn't shared them with me. Why would he? We only had a couple more weeks to go until the wedding, then I'd no longer be his fake wife.

I was trying my very best not to let that chafe.

Just like I was trying my very best to not think about what July would bring.

Divorce.

Dread had become a constant companion these past couple of weeks. It was as unwelcome as it was troubling. Wasn't I supposed to be looking forward to this divorce? To having my normal life back? To righting the wrong I'd made in Las Vegas?

This marriage had to end. Jasper and I weren't in love. This wasn't some fairy tale. Yet the idea of watching him leave made my heart sink.

"How's it going with Jasper?" Mateo asked. "Be honest."

"Good." Not great, but good.

Good enough.

When Jasper and I were at the A-frame, when the rest of the world was a blur beyond the bedroom, it was easy. But the other twenty hours of every day were a bit more difficult.

Prying anything but orgasms out of that man was impossible.

I still didn't know anything about his family. He never asked about mine. I had no clue what had happened with his ex-wife and why this wedding was so important.

Was I just a tool to spite her? Or did he still love her? When the officiant asked if anyone objected to the marriage, would Jasper raise his hand?

Either way, I doubted I'd like any of the answers to those questions. My curiosity was crippling, but I refused to ask.

Mateo glanced around the lobby, making sure we were alone.

Unfortunately, we were. Why was it that whenever I wanted a quiet minute alone at the hotel, I'd be swamped, but when I needed someone, anyone, to provide a distraction, the lobby was as silent as a grave?

"You should know... Mom and Dad are worried."

My stomach pitched. It shouldn't have surprised me, but it did. "Why? I'm fine."

"They don't like Jasper."

I winced. "Ouch. That's pretty severe, don't you think?"

"Is it? Come on, Eloise. Put yourself in their shoes. Their youngest daughter goes to Las Vegas for a weekend and comes home married, which she then hides for a month. The truth finally comes out, and when they attempt to get to know their new son-in-law, he blows them off."

"Jasper came to dinner."

Mateo arched an eyebrow. "And wanted to be anywhere else. That was the most awkward dinner that table has seen in years."

"Give him a break, Mateo. We're a lot as a group. Not everyone adjusts to the Eden chaos immediately." It was a flimsy deflection. That dinner had been awful.

No surprise, Mom and Dad hadn't bothered with another invitation this past month. We certainly hadn't made any attempts to visit them either.

"I don't want them to be worried." I sighed. Soon, this would all go away.

"Well, they are. They're worried Jasper is taking advantage of you."

"He's not."

"Are you sure? Where's he from? What's his family like? How is he going to support you now that Foster is retiring?"

"I can support myself, thank you very much."

I had no idea what Jasper's monetary situation was but it wasn't my business. But I doubted he was broke. He'd bought the A-frame. He'd bought the diamond ring on my finger. Nothing about him struck me as a man seeking his wife's paycheck.

"So he's counting on you to support you both?"

"What the hell is with this interrogation?" I snapped.

"You're my sister, Eloise." Mateo's voice gentled. The concern in his face nearly broke me.

For a split second, I wanted to confess it all. To tell him the truth about Jasper. But I kept my mouth shut.

Admitting the lie felt impossible. This hole I'd dug for myself just kept getting deeper. If I told them the whole story, they'd resent me.

But if I stayed quiet, then I was letting them resent Jasper instead.

Ironic, that I'd told him I didn't want my family to hate him when this was over. But I'd made that impossible, hadn't I? By keeping this secret, it was never going to end peacefully.

Stupid Eloise.

Shame, disgust crept beneath my skin, making me shiver.

"He's a good man." I believed it to my very soul.

"Okay." Mateo held up his hands, dropping this topic. "I'm

going to run to Lyla's for coffee. Want anything?"

I shook my head. "No, thanks."

"See you in a minute." As Mateo strode across the lobby, I sat frozen, my heart racing as I replayed that conversation.

Mom and Dad were worried. How worried?

Jasper and I had stayed together in an effort to prove I was responsible enough to take over this hotel. But if they didn't like Jasper, if they thought he was taking advantage, or that maybe he wanted a slice of the Eden fortune, would that change everything?

What if I'd ruined this after all? What if they wouldn't let me have the hotel *because* I was still married?

"What a mess." A headache bloomed behind my temples. Why did we have to get married? If I had a time machine, I'd go back to that night and change everything. Wouldn't I?

"Just a couple more weeks." A couple more weeks until I could make this right. A couple more weeks with Jasper.

The countdown should have eased my headache.

It only seemed to make the pain worse.

The lobby doors opened but it wasn't a guest who came inside. It was Mom.

I sat straighter, forcing a bright smile. "Hey, Mom."

"Hi, sweetheart." She rounded the counter, kissing my cheek. "How are you today?"

"Oh, fine. Busy. You know how it gets in the summer." There wasn't a single vacancy until September, and we'd been running at full capacity since Memorial Day.

I loved tourist season, when fresh faces flooded the sidewalks of my hometown, when people got to experience the enchantment of Quincy. Normally, I'd spend as much time as possible at The Eloise, not only to care for guests but to soak in their energy. But this year, more often than not, I found myself itching to leave each evening. To return to the cabin and get lost in Jasper for the night.

As soon as Mateo returned from Eden Coffee, I'd be out the door.

"I'm glad Mateo is here to help," I told Mom.

"I'm glad he's here too." Her eyes softened. Mom was in heaven now that all six of her children were at home. Add to that her grandkids and it was rare I saw her without a smile these days.

"How's, um… Jasper?" Her smile dimmed. I doubted she even knew it was happening, but it hurt.

Not that I blamed her. This was all my fault.

"He's great," I said, turning the rings on my left hand. "He promised me fish tacos for dinner tonight."

"Yum." Mom looked like she was going to say something else, maybe to ask for a recipe. But instead, she glanced around the lobby. "Everyone checked in for today?"

"Not quite."

Mom might share a bond with Knox and Lyla in the kitchen, but she shared something important with me too.

This hotel.

The ranch had kept Dad busy for years, and Mom could have worked there too, like many couples did on Montana farms and ranches. But Mom had taken an interest in the hotel, and rather than hire a manager for the inn, she'd taken it on herself. Somehow, she'd balanced six children and a career.

I'd always admired just how capable she was.

As a little girl, I'd spent countless hours with her here, sitting on the floor at her feet behind this same mahogany counter while she'd chatted with guests. I'd reenacted her conversations with my dolls. I'd pretended they were my hotel guests, visiting Quincy from faraway places.

When I'd gotten to kindergarten, my teacher had been amazed at how well I knew geography for a five-year-old. It was because Mom would show me on a map where every guest was from.

Maybe other girls would have wanted to travel the world, to see those different places. But I was content to stay here.

My dreams weren't beyond the walls of this hotel.

They *were* the walls.

Mom and Dad had made some renovations and updates, though I had some ideas of my own to play up the boutique feel for The Eloise. Except those ideas would need to wait until it was officially mine.

If it was ever going to be officially mine.

"I wanted to talk to you about something," Mom said.

I tensed, not sure I had the energy for another discussion about Jasper. "Of course. What's up?"

"Do you remember Lydia Mitchum?"

"Um, do I?" But maybe this wasn't about Jasper. *Thank God*.

"She was my college roommate. You met but it's been ages. You were probably only eight or nine."

"Sorry, I don't remember. Why?"

"Well, she moved to Quincy. I haven't talked to her in probably ten years, but out of the blue, she called and told me she'd just bought a house on Evergreen Drive."

"Oh, that's nice."

"We just met for coffee and to catch up. That's why I'm in town."

"Mateo was headed that way."

Mom nodded. "I passed him on my way here. Anyway, Lydia has a son. Blaze."

"Blaze. Interesting name."

"He's seventeen. She didn't get into the whole story, but I got the impression Lydia's had a rough decade. I met the man she married once and didn't like him much. She divorced him this year. Good for her. But Blaze is struggling. They were living in Missoula, but I guess he had some major problems in his high school there. She thought maybe a move would be a good reset."

"Ah. Well…this is a good place to reset."

"She's still not sure if she's going to send him to high school or just home school him for his senior year. But if she does keep him home, she's worried he won't get enough social interaction. Apparently he's very introverted and would be happy playing video games twelve hours a day."

"Okay," I drawled, feeling the real question coming.

"Lydia wants him to get a job."

I swallowed a groan. "I'd be happy to interview him."

"Or you could just hire him for that open part-time position."

The position I still hadn't been able to fill. Three people had applied. Two had come in to interview—the other had ghosted me—but the fit had been off. So I'd passed them up, not wanting to get into a situation where I had to fire someone.

"Mom, you know I'm trying to be regimented in hiring decisions." It was an employee who'd gotten me into trouble in the first place. Mom, of all people, should want to make sure we avoided that situation again.

"I know you are," she said, holding up her hands. "I respect that. But just…do me a favor? Give him a part-time job. If it doesn't work out, let him go."

She made it sound so easy. But I hated firing people. It was the worst of the worst part of my job. Hell, I'd happily scrub toilets and scour bathrooms for the rest of my life if it meant I didn't have to fire anyone.

Hence the reason we'd gotten involved in that lawsuit. Hence why I'd been more careful about hiring.

"Mom, I don't know."

"Please?"

The lobby door opened, covering the sound of my groan.

Jasper strode inside, wearing a simple black T-shirt and his favorite pair of faded jeans. They had buttons on the fly instead of a zipper, which made them my favorite jeans too because they came off so easily.

"Hi," I said.

"Hey." He stopped beside Mom, giving her a nod. "Hi, Anne."

"Hello, Jasper." She smiled but it didn't reach her eyes. Instead, there was a wariness in her gaze. She watched his every breath like she was waiting for him to turn around and walk away.

"Am I interrupting?" he asked, hooking a thumb over his shoulder. "I can go."

"No, you're fine," Mom said. "I actually need to get going. Think about Blaze?"

I nodded. "I will."

She turned, casting Jasper one last suspicious glance before heading to the doors.

Was this really where we were? My own mother was avoiding the man in my life? It was wrong. Every cell in my being screamed *fix it*.

"Mom," I called before she could leave.

"Yeah?" She stopped beside the door, looking back.

"I'll hire him. Have Lydia send him in tomorrow." It was a mistake to shortcut my process and skip the interview. But apparently mistakes were becoming my specialty.

"Thanks," Mom said on a sigh, the relief on her face only making the knot in my stomach tighter. Had she already promised Blaze a job? She lifted a hand to wave, then pushed outside.

It would probably be fine. If it wasn't, then I'd deal. If Blaze did a bad job or had a problem cleaning rooms, well...at least Mom could tell Lydia that we'd given him a chance.

"You okay?" Jasper asked.

"Long day." I forced a smile. "What are you doing?"

"I need to go on a trip."

I blinked. "A trip? When?"

"Tonight."

"Tonight?" What about fish tacos? Or a little advance notice? Had something bad happened with his family? Did he need me to go with him? "Is everything okay?"

"Yeah, I've got an interview in Vegas with an up-and-coming fighter. It's last minute."

"Oh." Someone might as well have kicked the chair out from underneath my ass. "That's...great."

That was great, right? This could be a new challenge for Jasper. He'd need that now that Foster was retired.

"What time is your flight?" It was supposed to come across as supportive but it sounded like a whine.

"I'm driving. I don't need to be there until Friday, but I don't want to bother with the airport in Missoula."

Driving? To Las Vegas? "I could take you to the airport

tomorrow." It was only two hours away. Not that I had two hours to spare, but I'd find the time.

"Nah. I'll hit the road. Find a hotel along the way. Get there tomorrow before my interview Friday."

"Oh. Um, all right. When are you coming back?"

If Jasper heard the desperation and disappointment in my voice, he didn't let it show. "Next week sometime. I'm not sure. I might stick around Vegas for a while. Check in on my house. Hit the old gym."

In my imagination, I heard a piece of paper tear in two. *Rrrrrip.* There went our marriage certificate.

This was Jasper stepping back, wasn't it? Planning his life. Leaving Montana.

I was supposed to have a couple more weeks.

Guess not.

"Drive safe." My voice wobbled.

Jasper rounded the corner, forcing me to turn and face him. Then he framed my face with his hands, dropping a chaste kiss to my mouth. "The fridge is full of food. I even made you cookies. Which means there's no reason for you to turn on the oven."

I gave him a small smile. "No oven. Got it."

Jasper's brown eyes searched mine. So I searched his right back, wishing I could hear whatever thoughts were in that gorgeous head. Would he miss me?

I'd miss him.

Now. Later.

I was afraid that I'd miss him for the rest of my life.

"Will you text me updates as you drive?" I asked. "So I won't worry?"

He nodded, kissing my forehead. Then he was gone, walking

out the door.

To start the next phase of his life.

It was time to plan mine.

The Eloise Inn. That was the goal. I couldn't let a couple months of incredible sex with Jasper steer me off that path. So I waited until Mateo returned with his coffee, then spent an hour wandering the hallways, up and down each floor, smiling to guests passing by. Taking mental notes of what I'd change when—if—the hotel was mine.

By the time I made it home, I was starving. Jasper hadn't lied about the food in the fridge. It was teeming with storage containers, each labeled. I snagged the one marked fish tacos. The tortillas were on the counter. So were the cookies.

Everything was set.

For me to eat alone.

For me to stay alone.

How long had he known about this interview? How long had he planned this trip?

"Last minute, my ass," I muttered.

Instead of taking the food to the table and eating my dinner alone, I balanced it in one hand while I snagged my purse with the other and marched outside, climbing in my car and driving back to town.

Lyla was dressed in sweats when she answered the door to her house. Gray joggers and a matching hoodie. She was also wearing that freaking fake smile. "Hey. What are you doing here? Everything okay?"

"No, it's not okay. Stop being so nice. And happy. It's weird."

"Me being happy is weird?"

"You know what I mean, Lyla. You've been acting strange since you found out about Jasper. I'm sorry. I'm so sorry. I had no idea that you liked him."

The façade slipped as she crossed her arms over her chest. "It's fine."

"No, it's not. You're upset."

"I'm embarrassed," she corrected. "It was just... embarrassing."

My heart pinched. "I'm sorry."

Lyla straightened, waving it off. "You didn't know."

"Why didn't you tell me?" It wasn't like Lyla to keep her crushes a secret, especially from Talia and me. Usually half of Quincy knew she liked a guy before they even had a date.

"I don't know." She lifted a shoulder. "But if you're happy with Jasper, then I'm glad I didn't."

Because had I known she liked him, our night beside the fountain in Vegas would have been entirely different.

That made both of us glad. Otherwise I never would have known Jasper.

"What's that?" Lyla pointed to the container and tortillas in my hand.

"Dinner. Jasper had to leave, and I don't want to eat alone. How do you feel about fish tacos?"

"Um, well, that depends. Did you make them?"

I giggled, feeling some of the tension in my frame melt away. "No, Jasper did."

"He made sure you had food while he was gone? Aww." Lyla pressed a hand to her heart. "That's sweet."

It was sweet. And annoying. Because he hadn't told me he was leaving.

"This dinner comes at a price," I told her.

"Wine?"

"And your guest bedroom. Can I have a sleepover?"

CHAPTER 15

ELOISE

Blaze, you are killing me. I spun in a slow circle, taking in the hotel room he'd just cleaned.

Or attempted to clean? At what point did people stop giving an A for effort?

The bed was rumpled, the pillows askew against the headboard. The towels in the bathroom weren't folded into neat piles, but rather tossed together haphazardly. The trash can beside the television hadn't been emptied and he'd forgotten to vacuum.

"Okay, Blaze." I turned, ready to rattle off the list of everything he needed to fix. Except Blaze wasn't standing beside the cleaning cart where he'd been a minute ago. "Blaze?"

Nothing.

I groaned, walking to the door and checking the hallway. Empty.

"Seriously?" I muttered. If I wasn't correcting this kid, I was chasing him around the damn hotel.

At least this time I had a hunch where he was hiding.

I tucked the cleaning cart closer to the wall so it would be out of the way for people walking by, then headed for the stairwell, jogging from the second floor to the first. As expected, Blaze was at the reception counter, talking to Taylor.

From the strained expression on her pretty face, she was sick of Blaze too.

"Blaze," I snapped, drawing his attention.

Behind his thick, black-framed glasses, he rolled his eyes. This kid didn't even try to hide his annoyance. I needed both hands to count the number of eye rolls and muttered insults I'd earned since Friday.

"Go upstairs and fix that room," I said. "Make the bed nice. Fold the towels in a stack. Empty the garbage can. And vacuum."

"I did vacuum," he argued.

"Then vacuum again." Maybe if I sent him up there to vacuum three times, he'd manage to get the whole floor.

"Fine," he grumbled, his footsteps heavy as he passed by. Blaze walked with his eyes on the floor, shoulders rounded in. His black hair, severely parted down the middle, flopped into his face, probably hiding another eye roll.

We didn't have a dress code for the housekeepers. It was more important to me that they were comfortable as they cleaned than to have them in a uniform. Most cleaned in jeans, tees and tennis shoes. Not once had I needed to ask an employee to wear something different. Not once, in all my years as manager.

When Blaze had come in on Friday to complete his new-hire paperwork, he'd arrived in a pair of jeans that he'd decorated with black marker. He'd written line after line of *Fuck You Mom* on those jeans, down his thighs all the way to his ankles.

Poor Lydia. I hoped she didn't do his laundry.

He'd paired those pants with a red hoodie that had a middle finger drawn onto the front.

I'd told him that he was required to wear a plain, gray or white shirt with clean jeans. No profanity.

Clearly, he wasn't happy that his mother had arranged for him to have this job. Maybe he was doing a shitty job because he hoped I'd fire him.

Oh, it was tempting.

But I'd promised myself I'd give him an honest two weekends.

He was working Saturdays and Sundays to start. Which meant I was working Saturdays and Sundays.

Instead of spending my weekend at the cabin alone, I'd been here, training Blaze. Yesterday, we'd worked together as I'd shown him how to clean a room and what was expected. Today, I'd let him do the work, but for every room he finished, I did an inspection.

So far, not a single room had been done correctly. Though they were getting better. Slightly. Maybe he'd do a decent job if that meant impressing Taylor.

Except I wouldn't put that on her.

Taylor would be a senior at Quincy High in the fall. She was as reliable as she was friendly. With her blond hair and sparkling brown eyes, she was a ray of sunshine. She'd worked at the hotel since last summer. During the school year, she only worked weekends because she played volleyball and basketball. But during the summer, she was always willing to do whatever was necessary, from manning the desk to housekeeping, anything to add to her college savings.

"Sorry, Eloise," she said once the stairwell door slammed closed behind Blaze. "I told him I was working and couldn't talk but he just wouldn't leave."

"I know." I sighed. "It's not you."

"He's, um…different."

If different meant creepy and rude. "Does he make you uncomfortable?"

"He hasn't really done anything. He just talks about his video games a lot. They sound violent and that's not really my thing."

"If he does make you uncomfortable, text me immediately."

She nodded. "I will."

"Okay. I'll go monitor his progress. Again." With heavy shoulders, I turned and marched upstairs.

It took Blaze the three times I'd expected for the vacuuming to be sufficient. His shift was the longest I'd endured in years, and by the time the rooms were finished, I wanted to scream.

This wasn't going to work, was it?

Not only was his work shoddy, his attitude was grating on my nerves. If he wasn't grumbling under his breath or rolling his eyes, he was making bold, insulting statements about Quincy.

He fucking hated this shithole of a town.

Blaze's words, not mine.

Part of me felt bad for the kid. New town. New house. His mom had shoved a job down his throat. That sympathy was the only reason I hadn't fired him yet.

"That's all for today," I told Blaze, walking with him to the staff room.

While he went to the locker I'd assigned him, I filled a coffee mug. It was bitter after sitting all day, but I sipped it anyway, needing the caffeine. Sleep this week had been lacking, mostly because I'd spent every night since Wednesday at Lyla's place.

It was too quiet at the A-frame. The bed looked too lonely without Jasper. So I'd packed a bag and raided the fridge, extending my sleepover at my sister's house.

Lyla's guest room was cute and the bed was comfortable, but I just hadn't been able to sleep. I woke up cold and no matter how many blankets I put on the bed, it wasn't the same as snuggling against Jasper.

I yawned as Blaze slammed his locker door closed. "See you next Saturday."

"I guess," he muttered, walking to the time clock to punch his card with a *thunk*.

"Have a good—"

Blaze walked out of the room in the middle of my sentence.

"Week." It was my turn for an eye roll. Then I stood in the quiet, sipping my coffee, staring at the time clock.

It was old fashioned. Charming. At least, charming up until the first and fifteenth of every month when I had to tally each employee's hours manually before sending the details to our accountant. Replacing it was on my list of future updates. Someday.

When my cup was empty, I washed it in the sink and put it away, then headed to the front desk. "I'm heading out, Taylor."

She only had about an hour left before she'd take off too. "Bye, Eloise. Have a good evening."

I waved, using my hand to cover another yawn, then headed for the alley.

Knox's truck was parked beside my Subaru. Part of me craved a bowl of his homemade mac 'n' cheese and a big glass of wine, but instead of heading to Knuckles to visit my brother, I aimed my car toward home.

The sky was covered in gray clouds, and the scent of rain marked the air, so I rolled my windows down, breathing in the crisp smell as I drove.

My overnight bag and a pile of empty food containers were in the passenger seat. As much as I didn't want to be alone in the A-frame, I'd told Lyla not to expect me tonight. I needed to do laundry and clean. And maybe tonight, I'd work up the courage to actually call Jasper to find out about his interview. Or not.

Phone calls, or communication in general, wasn't really our forte. If our in-person conversations were one-sided, I couldn't imagine what a phone call would be like.

To his credit, he'd done as I'd asked, texting me along the way for his trip. But the last text I'd gotten had been Thursday when he'd made it to Vegas.

Checking my phone for missed notifications had become as regular as yawning.

My eyelids drooped by the time I reached Alderson Road. Cleaning and laundry might have to wait another day. A hot shower and an early bedtime were calling.

But my exhaustion vanished the moment I turned onto the lane for the A-frame.

Jasper's Yukon was outside the house.

My heart leapt.

He was home? When had he gotten back? Why hadn't he texted me?

I parked and scrambled to gather my stuff. The sudden need to see him made my fingers fumble with a couple of the lids. But after some juggling, I had them all tucked close and managed to open the car's door, kicking it closed while I hurried inside.

"Jasper?" I called when I didn't see him anywhere. The containers were all dropped in the sink with a chorus of clattering. My backpack landed on the island with a thud. "Jas?"

The house was quiet.

So I moved through the living room, making my way toward the deck. I found him, sitting on the boards, his legs stretched in front of him as he bent to touch his toes. His hair was wet, like he'd just showered.

"Hi." My eyes swept over his body, from his wet hair to his clean T-shirt to the shorts and his tennis shoes. Something in my chest unlocked. The breath I'd been holding since Wednesday. "You're home."

"Yeah." He glanced up at me, then went back to stretching.

"Are you stiff from the drive?" I asked.

He shook his head, eyes locked on the toes of his shoes. "I showered but didn't stretch at the gym after Foster and I finished up."

The gym? "Foster's gym?"

"Yep."

I blinked, my sluggish brain trying to sort this out. He'd had time to go meet Foster? Wait. "When did you get back?"

"Last night."

"Last night?" My jaw dropped. "Why didn't you call me?"

"Figured you were busy." Jasper shifted, drawing one foot to the inside of the opposite thigh. Then he bent forward again, stretching those long, strong muscles while avoiding anything that resembled eye contact.

I huffed. Was this really happening? Did I mean so little to him that he couldn't even call to tell me he was back in Quincy? Just a minute ago, I'd been so excited to see him. To hear his voice. To bury my nose in his chest and draw in his spicy scent.

But he'd been here. All day long. Probably glad to have the house to himself for a change.

My hands balled into fists. "I wasn't busy."

"Well, you weren't here." Accusation, anger, filled his rugged voice.

Was he mad at me? What the hell?

"I was at Lyla's house because I didn't want to be here alone. I've been at Lyla's since you left me on Wednesday. She loved the fish tacos, by the way. But she said your cookies need some work."

Jasper sat up straight.

Before he could say anything, I spun around and stormed inside, moving straight for the bathroom. I made sure to slam the door as hard as possible, then flipped the lock because he was not coming in here.

"Last night." My entire body vibrated with fury as I stripped off my jeans and The Eloise Inn T-shirt. I balled up the latter, throwing it with all the force I could muster against the tiled floor. Then I turned on the shower, not waiting for the water to warm up before I stepped under the spray.

The moment the icy water hit my shoulders, tears flooded my eyes.

He'd come back last night.

No call. No text. And then to be upset because I hadn't been waiting with bated breath for his return?

"How dare you, Jasper Vale," I whispered as the first sob broke through.

God, I had missed him. I had missed him so much it ached. We could have been together last night. We were running out of time, and he'd wasted a whole night being mad.

I would have come running. All it would have taken was a phone call.

He didn't even care enough about me for a text.

The tears fell hot down my cheeks as the cold water stung the skin on my back. When it warmed, I tilted my head back, letting the water soak my hair and face.

This is fake. This is fake. This is fake.

Over and over again, I replayed those three words. And when the tears had stopped, when my hair and body were clean, I shut off the water and plucked a white towel from the shelf.

Numbness spread through my veins as I brushed out my hair, unable to see my face because the mirror was fogged.

This is fake.

This was a lie. And I'd made the horrible mistake of believing it was real.

The irony was stifling. The one person in Quincy who knew the truth was the one who'd fallen for the lie.

Another wave of tears pricked my eyes but I blinked them away, swallowing the lump in my throat. With my shoulders pinned, my chin held high, and a towel wrapped around my body, I opened the bathroom door.

Jasper stood in the middle of the living room, his arms crossed over his broad chest, his legs planted wide. His gaze was locked on the bathroom door, almost like he'd been standing in that exact spot the entire time I'd showered.

The ten feet between us might as well have been a chasm to the earth's very core.

"Did you get the job?" My voice didn't even wobble. *Go me.*

"He made me an offer."

"You didn't accept it?"

"Not yet. But I probably will."

Then he'd be gone.

Shit. My nose started to sting. More tears were coming, and damn it, I didn't want Jasper to see me cry. I looked around, searching for a place to hide. Except this fucking cabin didn't have enough walls or doors.

I'd have to walk past Jasper for the office or the deck. Since I doubted he'd let me lock him out of the bathroom again, I marched toward the kitchen, bypassing the island, and this time, I slammed the front door.

While I'd been in the shower, the clouds had burst. It was still light outside and the overcast sky made the colors around the A-frame pop. The evergreen limbs and the grasses sweeping their brown trunks practically glowed green. Rain drizzled in a steady stream, soaking the trees. Dirt and gravel and pine needles poked the soles of my bare feet as I stepped off the porch stairs and onto the forest floor.

There was a little clearing in the trees outside the A-frame. It wasn't very big but it was enough that if you craned your neck, you could see the stars.

The stars weren't out yet. There were no tiny sparkles in the sky to give me hope. But I tilted my head to the gray clouds regardless, letting the water drops coat my face.

This is fake, Eloise.

Why was it so hard to align a head and a heart?

"What the hell are you doing?" Jasper's voice was a dull murmur against the thunder rumbling in the background.

Still, I heard him. I ignored him.

Until one moment, my face was catching droplets, the next, the rain had stopped. I cracked my eyes open, my lashes heavy with water. And I stared up into Jasper's eyes.

My heart pounded. Our breaths mingled. I drowned in his dark gaze as his hands cupped my jaw. Then his mouth crushed mine, his tongue sweeping inside with a greedy stroke. The groan that rumbled in his chest echoed in my bones.

Our lips moved frantically as we clung to each other, tongues dueling. He licked and sucked, devouring me whole. And for everything he poured into that searing kiss, I sent it right back. The thunder to his lightning.

We were a storm.

Two souls lost in the pouring rain.

Jasper kissed me until I was breathless, my heart racing. Then he broke away, his eyes searching mine again.

"Eloise."

Just my name. Something inside me cracked. I was so sick of pretending. I was so tired of caring for this man and not knowing fuck all about him.

"I want to be your friend." His best friend. Not Foster. Me. "I want you to talk to me. Or *try*."

The torment in Jasper's gaze twisted my heart. He looked like I was asking for the world.

Maybe I was.

"I want to know you, better than anyone else knows you."

His hands came to my face, his palms pushing away the rain and stroking through my wet hair. "What else do you want?"

I want this to be real.

But it wasn't.

"I want you to kiss me."

He didn't hesitate. He slammed his mouth down on mine again, his tongue sliding along my lower lip.

I moaned, fluttering my tongue against his, just like he'd

taught me. The moan that came from his throat, my reward.

Jasper lifted me off the ground, waiting until my arms encircled his shoulders, before he swept me inside.

Then he ripped away my towel.

And used it to clean the dirt from my feet.

CHAPTER 16

JASPER

Eloise's towel lay puddled on the kitchen floor as she padded for the stairs, every inch of her naked, glorious body on display.

That woman carried an invisible leash.

Where she went, I willingly followed.

Fucking hell, I'd missed her.

So much I stopped moving, needing a moment to soak her in. The smooth skin. Those slender curves. Her chocolate hair and her soft lips. The mouth I loved to kiss.

She noticed I wasn't following and glanced over her shoulder. Those dazzling blue eyes were as stormy as the weather. Frustration. Lust. Defeat.

Our reality was inevitable. It hung over our heads like the current thunderstorm.

Eloise stretched out a hand.

I took it.

We'd ignore that reality for another night.

The moment we reached the loft, she lay on the bed, her wet hair splaying across the pillows. Her gaze stayed locked on me as I undressed, tossing my clothes into a pile beside my discarded shoes.

Then I climbed into the bed, settling on top of her, and without any fooling around, I slid inside her wet heat. And for the first time in days, I could breathe.

She hummed, that sound of ecstasy music to my ears. Her legs wrapped around me, holding tight as I encircled her with my arms, burying my face in the crook of her neck to draw in the vanilla and spice and earth.

Eloise.

She'd ruined me. Somewhere along the way, she'd ruined me for any other woman.

Maybe that should have bothered me.

We moved in tandem, like practiced lovers who'd had years, not months, to learn each other's weaknesses. Our eyes stayed locked, our limbs entwined.

This wasn't fucking, not tonight. It was too intimate to be considered fucking. But I wouldn't put the other label on it, not even for myself. Instead I drowned in Eloise, and when she shattered, I followed her into the oblivion.

Neither of us shifted until our hearts had stopped pounding, our breaths no longer ragged. Then I rolled to my back, taking her with me, positioning her on my chest, knowing she'd want to stay close.

Beyond the balcony door, the thunder boomed, followed seconds later by the flash of lightning. Rain prattled on the tin roof.

Eloise's finger traced lazy circles on my skin, first on my shoulder, then drifting to my pec before she flicked my nipple and her touch trailed up my throat.

It wasn't foreplay. This was just her. She touched, constantly. Aimlessly.

I'd missed this touch, so much so that I'd changed my plans in Vegas, cramming what I'd planned to do in days into hours. After my interview, I'd stopped by my old gym to see a few friends. Then I'd gone to my house, packing the few things I'd brought along so that yesterday morning, when I woke at dawn to hit the road, my stuff would be ready.

Pulling into the A-frame last night, finding Eloise's car missing and a dark house, had been a punch to the face.

Fifteen hours on the road, and I'd been so desperate to see her. To climb in bed beside her and finally get some sleep. Apparently, I'd gotten used to the cuddling. Without her, I hadn't been able to sleep.

Last night had been restless too. I'd stayed awake most of the night, waiting for her to get home, wondering if she was working at the hotel. Worrying that something had happened to her.

I'd finally had enough of the worry that I'd gotten up, put on some sweats and driven into town. But she hadn't been at the hotel's front desk. Through the gleaming windows, I'd spotted the night clerk reading a book.

Rationally, I'd known she was probably with her family. Maybe at the ranch with her parents. But that hadn't stopped me from driving by the two bars on Main, searching out her car. I'd swung by Willie's too before finally returning home.

Then I'd waited. And waited. And fucking waited.

All goddamn day to see my wife.

Yeah, I should have texted her. Or called. Except that would have been too real. Too revealing.

So I'd gotten pissed. Not even a few hours with Foster at the gym had helped me relax.

Then she'd come home and well…I'd missed her.

I wasn't supposed to miss her.

Fuck, but I was tired. Tired of holding up my hand, keeping her at a distance. Tired of pretending that sex between us was our only connection.

"El."

"Jas." She propped her chin on the hand over my chest while the other kept drawing those circles. Across my jaw, then over my cheekbone to my eyes. She skimmed my lashes, then flitted over the line of my nose before tracing my lips.

The defeat and frustration were gone from her gaze. Another flash of lightning brightened the room, making those blue irises flare.

She'd asked me to talk to her. To *try*.

I loved that she knew it wasn't easy for me. And for that, I'd try.

"My ex-wife. Her name is Samantha." This was either the best or worst place to start explaining the disaster that was my family and first marriage. "My parents are close friends with hers, so I've known her since we were kids. And I loved her for most of that time too."

Eloise stiffened. The tracing stopped.

So I clasped her hand, drawing the circles for her until she took over again.

"I grew up in Potomac, Maryland. My mother is in politics. She's an advisor to some powerful officials. And she works on campaigns. During election years, Mom was practically a ghost. The one year when the senator she was advising lost, well... let's just say she stayed in her wing of the house, and I stayed in mine."

"Your *wing*?" Eloise's eyes widened.

"My father is in political fundraising, but he comes from

money." Extreme money. That money had paid for their lives, though both had well-paying jobs. "Because money was never the issue, they work because they love to work." And the notoriety. They craved the spotlight.

"That doesn't sound like such a bad thing."

"Unless you're their son. And you were born out of obligation, not love."

The tracing stopped again, but this time, I didn't make her start again. "What do you mean, obligation?"

I shrugged. "Rich, powerful families have heirs. Heaven forbid all their money go to someone who might actually need it."

Instead, their fortunes were spent on properties across the globe. On homes like my childhood mansion, which was thirty times the size of what three people might need. I hadn't been back to Potomac in years. If that red-brick monstrosity with its sprawling green lawns and sweeping gardens ever became mine, I'd gladly sell it and donate the proceeds to charity.

"It's not that my parents were cruel," I told Eloise. "I can't remember a time when I was reprimanded by my mother or father. They didn't abuse me. They didn't resent me. They were just...disinterested." Wholly and utterly disinterested.

"How could they be disinterested? You're their child."

"They just were." I understood the confusion on her face. For a woman like Eloise, who had a family like hers, it was hard for her to comprehend. "You know how at that dinner at the ranch, there was barely a second of space in the conversation?"

"Yeah."

"Imagine the exact opposite. That was my childhood."

She frowned. "Oh."

"Mom and Dad are both eloquent people. Put them at a

gala or in front of a journalist, you'll see two well-spoken people who will charm anyone in minutes. You wouldn't think that if you put them at a table with their only son, that would be different. But it's like they have on and off switches."

"And for you, it's off."

"Yeah." The pain in her face, the sympathy, made my heart ache. "Don't be sad, angel. I had every luxury in the world as a kid." Nannies to dote on me. Tutors to ensure I was at the top of my class. Chefs to make me whatever food I desired.

"Luxury is not a replacement for love, Jasper."

"No, it isn't." Money wasn't affection. "But until Samantha moved to Maryland, I didn't know any better."

Eloise shifted, like hearing Samantha's name made her uncomfortable. I held her to me, needing to feel her skin against my own after too many days away.

"Samantha's father is also in politics," I said. "They moved from New York City to Potomac when I was ten. Dad and John met through work and became friends. Mom and Ashley hit it off too, and from then on out, if there was an activity or function, our families did it together. I preferred it that way. When John and Ashley were around, my parents were flipped on. And I had Samantha. She was my first everything. Crush. Kiss. We lost our virginity to each other at fourteen."

Eloise dropped her gaze, staring blankly over my shoulder to the pillow.

"What?" I asked.

"Just...jealous."

Fuck, but I loved that she could lay it out there. That she didn't hide it from me.

If our positions were reversed, I wasn't sure I could hear about her past lovers. Hell, the day at the ranch when she'd told me about the guys she'd brought home had been hard enough.

"Are her parents like yours?" she asked. "Disinterested?"

"Yes and no," I said. "Ashley is a surgeon and constantly at the hospital. John works even more than my dad. I don't doubt that they love Sam. But she was always second priority. We had that in common. We gave the attention we each craved to one another."

We'd filled that void. The moment our families would get together, Sam and I would disappear, not a parent concerned with what we were doing. Even as teens, either our parents hadn't known or they hadn't cared when we'd vanish to a closed bedroom and fuck for hours.

Sam was the first person I'd ever loved. The first and only person who ever heard me say *I love you.* I'd given that woman all I'd had. And it still hadn't been enough.

"We went to the same private high school in Maryland," I said.

Sam and I had spent our teenage years as bored, rich kids. With bored, rich kids. Three of my classmates had graduated with substance abuse problems. There weren't many drugs Sam and I hadn't sampled. Drinking had been a casual pastime up until my senior year, when I'd had someone pull my head out of my ass.

"Sam wanted to go to Cornell because that's where her parents met. I wanted Georgetown. Mostly because I wanted to stay in DC."

"Why?" Eloise asked. "You didn't want to get away from your parents?"

"I did. But my senior year in high school, I started taking karate at a local dojo. It was like I'd found a passion, you know? It was the right place for me. I got attached to my sensei and wanted to earn my black belt. Moving to New York meant a different teacher, and I wasn't about to change, start over. So Sam left, and I stayed."

"Did you get your black belt?"

"Yeah. My sophomore year at Georgetown. I got my second degree about two years after that. Right before my sensei passed away. Cancer."

"I'm sorry." Eloise pressed a kiss to my heart.

"Me too." I threaded my fingers through her hair, most of the strands nearly dry now. "His name was Dan. He changed my life."

He'd taken me—an arrogant, spoiled brat—under his wing. He'd taught me humility. Discipline. Grace. Respect. He'd been the father I'd never had.

"He was a widower. No kids. So when he was going through chemo, I went with him a lot. Sat with him at the hospital while they pumped him full of drugs." Toward the end, the doctors had been honest with us both. It had been terminal. But he'd gone to treatment anyway, never giving up hope for a miracle.

I missed Dan every single day. Would he be proud of the man I'd become? I wished he were here so I could ask him myself. I wished he could meet Eloise because he'd adore her. And he'd kick my ass for getting myself tangled in a fake marriage. He'd call me a turd.

I missed being called a turd.

"One day at the hospital, toward the end, I asked him why he picked me," I said. "Why he gave me so much time and energy. What was so special about me. Why he treated me differently than his other students."

"What did he say?"

"He didn't answer." The lump in my throat began to choke

me. "He said that if I couldn't look in the mirror and know the answer to that question, he hadn't done a good enough job. Broke my fucking heart. So I went home that night and stared at the mirror for an hour. Still not sure what he saw."

"Jasper." Eloise's chin began to quiver.

"Don't cry, angel."

She sniffled, her eyes flooding. "I can cry if I want."

"Don't cry for me. Please." It only made this harder.

"Okay," she whispered, blinking away the tears.

This was the most I'd spoken of my past in, well…ever. Not even Foster knew this much about my family. But Eloise had said she wanted to know me better than anyone. There wasn't much I could give her, but I could give her this. And before we went to Sam's wedding, she deserved the truth.

"Dan died a week after I graduated from Georgetown," I said. "I was a wreck."

My exams had been finished, thankfully. I wouldn't have been able to concentrate on a test. But I'd been totally lost without him. He'd become this anchor. This voice of reason. And suddenly, I was adrift, left alone with only the voices in my head.

And Sam's.

"Sam and I stayed together through college. Did the long-distance thing. Saw each other when we could, but we were both busy. If I wasn't at school, I was at the dojo. When Dan pulled back, after he got sick, I stepped up to help teach. And I'd wanted to broaden my martial arts skills, so I'd started doing some Muay Thai too."

There'd been too many emotions stirring at the time. With school. With Dan. The only way I'd known how to deal with them was by shoving them aside. And it had always been easier to shut down emotionally if I was channeled wholly into something physical.

In high school, when my parents had overlooked me, I'd ignored that pain and, instead, gotten lost in sex with Sam. Then I'd started at the dojo, and martial arts training had become my joy in those days.

"Sam was in a sorority," I said. "They always had functions, plus she had school demands. We'd talk every day, but it was shallow. We were both changing. Moving in different directions. Not that I realized it at the time."

Hindsight was a bitch.

The red flags had been endless, but I'd overlooked each and every one.

"Did she know Dan?" Eloise asked.

"A little." And though he'd never admitted it, he hadn't liked her. Looking back, I could see that now too. Maybe if he'd told me, I wouldn't have married her.

"She was there when I got the call that he'd died. She'd graduated too and had moved back to live with me. We got through the funeral, and she knew I was falling apart. She didn't leave my side, just stayed close because I needed her close. I think it scared her, seeing me fall apart. So she planned a trip to get my mind off it."

"To where?" Eloise asked.

I swallowed hard, knowing what was coming would hurt her. But it was truth time. "Vegas."

She sat up, her body still draped across mine but her chin lifted, her shoulders stiffening.

Yep. This was going to fucking suck.

"It was just supposed to be for fun. A chance for me to clear my head. We went out that first night. Partied at a club. An hour later, we were at a chapel to get married."

It had been Sam's idea. If Dan hadn't died, would I have taken her up on it? I'd asked myself that countless times. But that night, I'd just wanted to feel...loved.

"You got married in Vegas," Eloise said.

I nodded.

"Which chapel?"

Fuck. "The Clover Chapel."

"*Our* chapel." Eloise sat up, clutching the sheet to her chest. Horror, betrayal, was written across her expression. "That's how you knew where it was."

"It was an asshole move, taking you there. I'm sorry. But when you were talking about that ugly horse drawing, how you covered it up with something beautiful, I wanted that. I wanted a new picture. I wanted to erase Sam's ugly. And you were the most beautiful woman I'd ever seen."

Her jaw flexed, her nostrils flaring like they normally did when she was pissed. Like she'd done downstairs before marching out into the storm. "You'd seen me before that night."

"Yeah." I shifted, sitting up so I could lock my gaze with hers. "Don't take this the wrong way."

"Which guarantees I won't like what you're about to say." She rolled her eyes. "This ought to be great."

Damn, but I loved that eye roll. That sass.

"I didn't *see* you before that night." I leaned in, dropping my forehead to hers. "I was focused on Foster. On his fight. On shifting my life to Montana, even temporarily. I wasn't in a frame of mind to see anyone."

Eloise sighed, and with that exhale, some of her irritation seemed to fade.

"I should have told you sooner."

"Yup. Like when we were standing at. The. Altar." She poked my chest, accentuating every word. "That would have been a great time to mention you'd been there before."

"I'm sorry." I captured her hand, squeezing so she couldn't fold in that poking finger. Then I brought it to my lips for a kiss. "I'm sorry, Eloise."

Another sigh. And from the softness in her pretty blue eyes, I was forgiven. "What happened then?"

I leaned back, dropping my gaze to the bed, still keeping her hand in mine. "Sam and I went home. Our parents were pissed, to say the least. Not that they hadn't expected us to get married, they'd just missed the opportunity to host a party for their friends. To show off their perfect match."

"What do you mean, their perfect match?"

"They took credit for us being together. Like it was something they'd planned from the beginning." I'd always thought that was ridiculous. How my parents could give so little of a shit about me but, when it came to my marriage to Sam, be so angry to be excluded.

"Things with Samantha were...okay." The changes I'd ignored had started to come to light. But I'd just kept on ignoring them. "I did my thing. She did hers. She'd gotten a job, but I still wasn't sure what I wanted to do, so I kept working at the dojo and started training on the side. That's how I got into it. Spent four years at Georgetown and haven't once used my degree."

"What did you get your degree in?"

"Communications."

"Communications? You're kidding." Eloise snorted. "This is the most I've ever heard you speak. Ever. I think you need to call Georgetown and ask for a refund. Or maybe Georgetown is where you learned how to communicate with grunts and nods? Because if that's the case, then don't worry, babe. You use your degree every single day."

I laughed. Loud. I tipped my head to the ceiling and let it roar. I let it free. I laughed like I hadn't done in years, until all that was left was a smile.

Eloise had a smug grin on her face when I faced her. She knew she'd earned that laugh. She knew, without needing to ask, that it was rare.

"Anyway…" I pinched her rib, making her squeal and swat at my hand. "About six months later, I came home from the gym to find Sam had invited a couple over. They were people she'd met through a mutual friend."

A friend I'd despised. Another red flag ignored.

"I thought she'd planned a double date. So I took a quick shower. Joined them to eat. They were nice. It was just a normal dinner. Until Sam pulled me aside later and asked if I liked the woman."

"Wait. What?" Eloise sat ramrod straight. "Why would she ask you that?"

"Because she wanted to fuck the man and hoped I'd fuck the wife in the guest bedroom. That's the night she informed me we were going to have an open marriage."

CHAPTER 17

ELOISE

"You're kidding."

Jasper shook his head. "Nope."

"You have to be kidding."

He shook his head again.

My jaw hit the sheets.

Oh, how I hated his ex-wife. I hated her for the tension that crept into Jasper's body when he mentioned her name. For the way his voice changed when he spoke about her. It was rougher, harder, like she was this infected wound oozing puss, and just the thought of her caused him pain. But mostly, my hate was driven from envy.

I hated that he'd loved her for so long. I hated that she'd gotten his firsts, marriage included. I hated that she'd been with him at the Clover Chapel.

The night we'd gotten married wasn't exactly special. I couldn't remember the words the officiant had spoken. I hadn't worn a stunning gown. We hadn't exchanged vows surrounded by friends and family.

Still, since Vegas, I'd considered that mine. Ours. Even though this marriage was fake, I'd never forget that beautiful chapel.

Now there was a nasty stain splashed across the doors. The stain's name was Samantha.

She was an ugly horse.

Maybe I should have been more offended that he'd taken me there. But the moment he'd explained why, that he needed a good memory to outshine the bad, well… I was honored that Jasper considered me that good. That I was the beauty he'd needed.

But I still hated his ex.

I'd heard of open marriages through celebrity gossip rags and random social media videos. But the concept wasn't for me. The idea of my husband fucking another woman? No. Hard no. I was too selfish and too territorial to share.

"So was Sam cheating?" I asked.

"She didn't consider it cheating because it was simply physical. She loved me. She was committed to me."

I scoffed. "Then her definition of commitment is different than mine."

Jasper dropped his gaze to the sheet between us and something about the stiffness in his frame made my pulse rocket. Like he was dreading what he was about to tell me.

Oh, hell. Had he gone along with it? Was he okay with an open marriage?

"What did you do?" I asked, not sure I wanted to know the answer.

Jasper looked up and the agony in his gaze cracked my heart. "I took the woman to the guest bedroom. I don't know why. Shock, maybe. Revenge. I was furious and thought maybe if I fucked another woman, Sam would get jealous."

No. My stomach dropped.

"The woman started touching me," he said. "She took off

her clothes. Climbed on the bed. And I just stood by the door, staring at her, wondering when the hell my life had turned to such shit. So I left her naked in the guest bedroom and went to mine. Found Sam and that guy in the throes. Sam was on top, riding him like it was her job."

I cringed, a fresh wave of loathing for his ex-wife coursing through my veins.

"She didn't even stop when I walked into the room." He huffed, shaking his head. I wasn't the only one disgusted. "She just watched me, like it was a turn-on to have her husband see her fuck another man on our bed. So I walked to the closet, packed a bag."

"You left?"

"Yeah. I drove to a bar. Got sloppy drunk. Slept it off in my car."

Oh, Jasper. I wasn't even sure what to say.

"I won't share, Eloise." Jasper locked his eyes with mine. "I won't."

I lifted my hand to cup his stubbled cheek. "I don't share either. If another woman touches you, I'll cut off her fingers and feed them to my dad's dogs."

That declaration came out so suddenly, I froze. There was no way he'd miss how much that had sounded like a claim. A commitment longer than two to three more weeks.

But Jasper only chuckled, that low, gravelly rumble. It was second place to that free, boisterous laugh I'd coaxed out of him earlier. Maybe if I was lucky, I'd hear that laugh again before he walked out of my life.

"What happened after the bar?" I asked.

"Went home the next morning. Found the house was clean. Smelled like laundry soap. Sam had washed the bedding. And she just pretended like nothing had happened."

I blinked. "Seriously?"

Jasper nodded.

"What did you do?"

"Told her to get the fuck out of my house. And that she'd be hearing from my attorney."

Pride swelled in my chest. *Good riddance.*

"It got messy after that," he said. "Sam didn't want a divorce. She kept trying to convince me this open marriage would be good for us. A chance to explore our base desires but stay together."

"Of course she did." I rolled my eyes. *Bitch.*

"That other woman? She lied. She told Sam and her husband that I fucked her."

"No," I gasped.

"Sam believed her. Still thinks it happened. She likes to hold that over my head."

Because Sam was a spoiled, manipulative twat. No wonder Jasper rarely spoke about his past. Between his parents and his ex, I wouldn't talk about them either. *Assholes.*

"Sam wouldn't actually leave the house," he said. "Even though it was mine. So I ended up being the one to move. I packed up what was important, it was less than I'd expected it to be, and left the rest behind. I put the house on the market without telling her. She came home from work one day to find a *For Sale* sign in front."

"You have a vindictive side." I giggled. "I like it."

"So do I." His eyes crinkled, that ghost of a smile. It dimmed too soon. "Sam is rather spiteful herself."

"Uh-oh. What did she do?"

"Threw a tantrum. Told her parents and my parents that we

were going through a rough patch, and that I refused to work on our marriage."

"Did they know she was cheating?" It *was* cheating. If Jasper hadn't wanted an open marriage, then everything she'd done was cheating.

He blew out a long breath. "I could have told them, I just... didn't."

"Why?" This woman had used him, betrayed him, but he hadn't put the blame on her. Why? The answer came to me before he could say it. "Because you loved her."

"Something like that."

Goddamn that stung, knowing a woman who hadn't deserved him was the one who'd earned his love.

Did he still love her? My heart couldn't take that answer, so I didn't ask the question. "Obviously, you got the divorce."

"It took six months," he said. "I didn't want to be anywhere near her, and with Dan gone, it was easier to walk away. A friend of a friend had just moved to Vegas. Had met some UFC fighters. He knew of some gyms looking for trainers and instructors. It seemed like a hell of a good idea to move across the country. So I did and let my lawyer deal with Sam."

"What about your parents?" I asked.

He shrugged. "They reacted as expected. Meaning they didn't really give a flying fuck that their son was going through hell."

My nostrils flared. "Tell me why we're going to this wedding."

At this point, I'd rather shove bamboo shoots up my fingernails than meet Samantha or his parents.

Jasper's gaze dropped to the sheet and he plucked at the cotton. "For a long, long time, I was Samantha's. She's a very possessive person."

"Yet she was okay with you screwing other women? How does that make sense?"

"Her game. Her rules."

"That still doesn't make any sense but whatever." I'd already expended more energy toward that woman than she deserved for breaking his heart. I wasn't going to attempt to understand her motivations.

"Sam has rarely had people tell her no. Not her parents. Not even me. She's…stubborn. She'll push and push and push until she gets her way. I learned a long time ago, it was just easier to let her have it than fight."

Was that part of why he'd taken that woman into their guest bedroom? Probably. I shuddered, using every ounce of mental strength to shove the images of Jasper with any other woman out of my head. Sam included.

"When I walked away from her, she lost. The battle is over. But she's still fighting."

"What do you mean?"

"Sam and I still talk." He swallowed hard. "She calls me."

"And you answer? Even though she's getting remarried. Even though you're divorced. Why?"

"It's, um, toxic."

No shit. "What exactly do you mean, toxic?"

It was probably foolish for me to ask. This was probably opening the door for him to tell me he would always be in love with her. But if they spoke, if I was going to this wedding, I had to know.

"Sam would call and ask about the women I was fucking. And I'd tell her. I'd tell her every detail, my own revenge. She'd ask me if I pictured her face while I was inside another woman."

I gasped. "That's—"

"Fucked up. It's fucked up."

"Wait. Did you tell her about us?" Oh God. If he'd told her, I'd never recover from the humiliation.

Jasper met my gaze, and my chest cracked.

"You did," I whispered.

He nodded.

"How dare you, Jasper Vale." I swept up the only weapon within reach. A pillow. And slammed it into his head.

"I'm sorry."

I hit him with the pillow again. He didn't even try to block it. "What did you tell her?"

"That you were the best I've ever had."

My teeth clenched. My hands gripped the sheets. "What else?"

"That's it."

I hit him with the pillow again. "You had no right. That's private, Jasper."

"I know, angel. I know." He leaned in, his hands coming to frame my face as his eyes searched mine. "I'm sorry."

"Did you mean it?" That seemed like such a silly question in the face of a betrayal. But I needed to know.

"Without question."

Well, at least that was something. "And do you see her? When you're with me?" *Please say no.*

"No, El. I see you. I've only ever seen you."

So why didn't that make me feel better?

"Why do you answer her calls?"

He gave me a sad smile. "For a long, long time, she was all I had."

Understanding dawned. While I had my parents, sisters,

and brothers to lean on, Jasper had only had Samantha. She'd been his person. And he answered her calls because he wasn't ready to let that go.

"Sam tries to keep me connected to our old life," he said, letting me go. "She'll bring up old memories, stories. Mostly of us together. The trips we took. The movies we watched or inside jokes we shared. But she'll remind me of the stupid shit I did in school too. The days before I found Dan's dojo."

"Like what?"

"Drinking. Some drugs."

"Oh."

"I'm not proud. But it happened."

"I get it." There were plenty of kids in Quincy who drank. Some who experimented with drugs. Small-town parties were a rite of passage. "What else does she do?"

"She'll have lunch with my mother, then call and give me some bullshit story about how Mom wishes I'd call. That I'd go home to visit. She tries to make me feel guilty for disconnecting with them."

"You don't talk to your parents?"

"I used to. I stopped."

"Why?"

"Phone goes both ways, angel."

Yes, it did. And if they didn't care enough to reach out, it was their loss.

"Sam knows me well," he said. "Despite how much I struggle with my parents, I'm still their kid. Still never stopped hoping I'd get the on switch."

My heart squeezed. Okay, I hated his parents more than Sam. Maybe. It was a toss-up.

Jasper deserved the on switch. Was that why he was so

hesitant with my family? Because he didn't even know what loving parents looked like? Fuck Sam for playing on his vulnerability.

"So she calls to, what? Guilt you into coming back?"

"Basically. I haven't seen her or my parents since the divorce."

Whoa. That was a long time.

"For years, I think she thought if she could just get me to come home, I'd take her back. Sam, her parents, mine…they all think I went through some sort of mental break and that's why I moved to Vegas. But what none of them have tried to understand is that I have a better life. That I'm content as a trainer. That I don't need or want a spotlight. That their money could sink to the bottom of the ocean, and I wouldn't give a damn."

They didn't see the good in him. They didn't see what made him special.

But I did.

"I'm still mad at you for telling her about our sex life."

"I'm mad at me too." He took my hand, lifting it to his mouth to kiss my fingertips. "Forgive me. Please."

"If you ever tell another soul about us, I'll feed *you* to my dad's dogs."

"Fair enough."

"Fine. Then I forgive you."

Maybe I should have been angrier. Held on to my anger with a steely grip. But as much as it annoyed me, embarrassed me, that a stranger knew we had incredible sex, that stranger was also his ex.

And part of me liked that he'd thrown something in her face.

So I shifted, the sheets rustling as I moved. We were close, but not close enough. So I crawled into his lap, curling against his chest.

It took him a moment—it usually did, especially when he was asleep—but his arms looped around me. Just like they did when he was asleep.

I cuddled.

And Jasper held me.

"I still don't understand why we're going to the wedding." If he'd walked away, if he'd found a better life, why wade into the cesspool again?

"Like I told you, that invitation she sent me was a dare."

"A dare." My hand went to his chest, tracing swirls on his skin. "To see if you had the guts to face her."

"More or less. And I'm sure she wants to rub her new husband in my face."

"Who is he?"

Jasper shifted us, scooting back to lean against the pillows, but he kept me in his lap. "A guy who went to our high school. He was a prick back then. I doubt that has changed."

"What if you just told them to fuck off?"

"Then she'd win."

So Jasper was still fighting too. Still holding on. He was still trying to prove he'd made the right decision. That he wasn't a failure by walking away.

"I'm going because I need to see her. To face her."

Because he still loved her? "Does she know you're bringing me?"

He nodded.

"Does she know that we're married?"

He nodded again. "She called me a while ago. I told her."

Probably the same call when he'd told her I was the best sex of his life. *Take that, Sam.* "Do your parents know about me?"

"I got an email from Dad a few days after that. It said he heard congratulations were in order. That he was looking forward to meeting you at the wedding."

"Oh. That's it?"

"That's it."

A polite, shallow email. Meanwhile, my brothers had stormed into my house to confront Jasper. My parents were likely writing letters for an intervention.

Jasper had said that his parents weren't cruel, but I wholeheartedly disagreed. His parents were the definition of cruel. Ignoring a child was cruel. Having a child so your wealth would have a landing spot...cruel.

It was heartbreaking. No wonder he'd clung to Dan.

I only wished that when he'd asked Dan why he'd been special, Dan had made it crystal clear. I wished that Dan had told Jasper he was incredible. That he was kind. And though it was guarded behind a plethora of locked doors, that Jasper had a good heart.

Dan should have told him he was important.

Well, I wouldn't make the same mistake. Before this was over, Jasper would have at least one person in his life tell him he was worthy of love.

"I'm using you, El." Jasper's arms banded tighter. "By taking you to this wedding, I'm using you because I want to throw your beautiful face in theirs."

Did he expect that to surprise me? Or piss me off? It didn't. "Hell, yeah. We're going together, and I'm going to look hot."

Jasper stared down at me, eyes wide and unblinking.

"What?"

"Nothing." He dropped his forehead to mine. "Thank you."

"Welcome."

"Not sure I deserve you."

"Oh, you probably don't," I teased, earning a chuckle. Not quite the laugh, but I'd take what I could get from this man.

"It won't be a fun trip," he muttered.

The wedding was in Italy, something I'd learned about six weeks ago when Jasper had asked me if I had my passport. It was in the gun safe at Mom and Dad's house. I'd gotten it simply to have, in case of a spontaneous trip. It still had Eden as my last name. So did my driver's license.

There was no point in changing them to Vale, only to change them back.

"This will be the first time I've been to Europe," I told him. "I'm having fun, no matter what."

"All right." He tucked a lock of hair behind my ear. "Then we'll have fun."

"I, um, actually got you something." I'd been waiting weeks for the right time to do this. A rush of nerves spiked as I shifted off Jasper's lap, stretching for the nightstand on my side of the bed.

Pulling the drawer back, I felt around until my finger grazed the small, metal circle. I tucked it into my palm, then returned to my spot on Jasper's lap, letting him draw the sheet around my shoulders.

"Since we're going to this wedding for some revenge, and you got me a ring before my family's function. Here." With it pinched between my fingers, I held up the ring I'd ordered online.

It was titanium. Simple but bold, like Jasper. The inside and outer edges were polished to a shine, but the center had a matte sheen.

Jasper stared at the ring but made no move to take it from my hand.

My nerves doubled. "You said you didn't wear rings."

He kept staring at it, like if he touched it, the metal would burn his hand.

Okay, bad idea. I was about to throw it back in the drawer, to pretend like it never existed, when he moved, twisting us both so fast I barely realized what he was doing until I was flat on my back.

"Thank you. For the ring." Jasper hovered above me, his eyes searching mine.

"Welcome. You don't have to wear it. It was just a thought."

"Okay," he whispered. Then his mouth claimed my own, his tongue sweeping inside. He kissed me until I was breathless, until I pleaded for more.

We clung to each other until long after the thunderstorm outside had passed. Until I was boneless and fell into a deep sleep.

At some point during the night, the ring slipped out of my fingers and disappeared. Lost in the tangle of sheets.

The next morning, when I left Jasper sleeping to go to work, all I knew was that the ring wasn't on his finger.

CHAPTER 18

JASPER

There were three couples inside the lobby at The Eloise Inn. Two were chatting with each other while the third stood at the reception counter, talking to Eloise.

She smiled as she talked, radiating that gorgeous light, and handed them their key cards. Her hair was up today, not a tendril out of place. The white, button-down shirt she wore was pressed and crisp across her slender shoulders. When she pointed to the elevators, my ring on her finger glinted beneath the lobby's lights.

I slipped inside, walking toward the fireplace.

Eloise's gaze flicked my way. She smiled a little wider but otherwise didn't miss a beat with her guests.

She'd snuck out this morning. Or maybe she'd said goodbye and I'd missed it. Last night was the hardest I'd slept in years.

It was strange to have my past out in the open. Part of me was relieved. Eloise should know what she was getting into before this wedding. But an unease, a vulnerability, had stirred this morning, mixing with the relief. The combination had left me raw.

No one knew the whole truth about my parents or Samantha.

And though Sam had been there, I'd told Eloise things about Dan Sensei that even Sam didn't know.

Eloise wanted to know me better than anyone. Now she did.

How long until she realized she could do a hell of a lot better?

Maybe she already had. Maybe she was counting down the days until this wedding was over and she'd be free.

Meanwhile, I was beginning to fear each and every day that passed. Time was going too damn fast.

Eloise finished with one guest, motioning the next in line forward. So I took a seat on one of the lobby's leather couches, glancing around as I waited.

The morning sunlight streamed through the crystal clear windows. I hadn't visited the inn often, but this was my first visit when a fire wasn't burning in the hearth. Instead of a woodsy, smoky scent, it smelled like spring. Fresh. Clean. Fragrant. There was a small bouquet of flowers on the coffee table beside three artfully arranged magazines.

Every detail was designed to make guests feel welcome. There wasn't a doubt in my mind who'd bought those flowers or placed those magazines.

"Hey, Jasper." Knox Eden rounded the end of the couch, hand extended. The tattoos on his arm were visible today beneath the short sleeves of his Knuckles T-shirt.

"Knox." I stood, shaking his hand as tension crept into my shoulders.

Our first encounter at Eloise's old rental hadn't been great. The dinner at the ranch hadn't been much better. Their family was...different. Night and day to my own.

Last night, after Eloise had fallen asleep curled into my side, I'd thought long and hard about my family. About Samantha.

About those phone calls I'd been taking for years.

Was the reason I always answered because she was the only one to call? Because Sam was my only connection to anything that resembled family? Was that why I was so resistant to the Edens? Some lingering resentment for my own that I projected onto her family?

Maybe.

Maybe not.

They still didn't support her like she deserved. They still wanted to change her.

"Eloise said you guys are taking off for a wedding soon," Knox said. "Italy?"

I nodded. "The Amalfi Coast."

The trip would take twenty-two hours with the various stops and time changes. We'd be leaving early Thursday morning to arrive in Naples midday Friday.

"She's excited," Knox said.

"Me too," I lied.

The wedding would likely be a disaster. And though I was looking forward to a weekend away with Eloise, of hotels and time alone together, this trip marked the end.

Her laugh rang through the lobby, drawing my attention. That smile of hers was brighter than any light bulb. Any star. She beamed, entirely in her element.

"She loves this hotel," I told Knox.

"She does. Always has."

"This is her dream." Wading into the Eden family business wasn't really my place, but the whole point of our marriage was to ensure her future here was secure. For that, for her dream, I'd dive into the deep end. "She wants it more than anything."

"It's hers. Maybe not officially. Not yet. But Mom and Dad know it's hers."

I glanced back to her, to that breathtaking smile. "She's scared they'll take it from her."

"They won't."

"You're sure?" I asked Knox.

He gave me an apologetic smile, like the fact that I even had to ask was a failure on their family's part. "You don't know us very well. We look out for each other. Maybe timing hasn't been right in the past, but our parents know it's her dream too. They want that dream to come true for her."

"You're sure?" Same question, met with the same apologetic smile.

"One hundred percent." He believed it.

Wasn't this all I needed to hear? Knox's assurance meant this marriage hadn't fucked up Eloise's reputation. Her family still saw her as responsible. Now I could walk away.

Except something was happening here. Something I couldn't quite grasp. It was like my shoes were getting heavier. Like there were roots growing beneath my feet.

And they were pulling me toward the woman at the hotel's reception desk.

The idea of being tied to someone again made my stomach churn. But as my gaze drifted to Eloise again, to that smile, the roiling slowed. It didn't stop, but it calmed.

Knox followed my gaze, staring at his sister. "This hotel is the heart of Quincy. And Eloise is the heart of this hotel. Don't break it."

"I won't."

A fool's promise. But I made it anyway. Hurting Eloise wasn't an option.

If she wanted me to walk away, if she wanted her own freedom, I'd go.

But if she wanted me to stay...

It had happened last night, when I'd stood on the porch of the A-frame, watching my wife stand beneath the trees wearing only a towel, letting the rain soak her face.

Eloise was my wife.

There wasn't a damn thing fake about this marriage. Not anymore.

So we'd get through this wedding in Italy. Then we'd talk. Once she saw the world where I'd come from, she could decide.

If she still wanted to end it, I'd walk away.

With the final guest checked in, Eloise waited for them to collect their luggage and make their way toward the elevators. Then she hopped off her stool and walked over, her feet practically floating over the hardwood floors.

She moved with grace. With lightness. Like she had invisible wings.

"Hi, angel." I held out an arm, waiting until she slid into my side. Then I dropped a kiss to her hair.

"Hi." Her eyes sparkled as she looked up, probably glad I was putting on a show for her brother. Or maybe, if I was lucky enough, she was just as glad to see me as I was to see her. "What are you doing here?"

"Thought I'd see if you wanted to go to lunch since you didn't pack one."

"How did you know I didn't pack a lunch?"

Because there hadn't been a knife covered in peanut butter and jelly when I'd put my breakfast dishes in the dishwasher this morning. "Did you?"

"No." She smiled. "I was either going to get something from Lyla's or beg my favorite older brother to make me lunch."

Knox chuckled. "Griffin is your favorite older brother."

"Yes, but this is your chance to beat him out."

"That's what you said the last time I made you lunch."

"I did? Oh." She lifted a shoulder. "See? You're already the favorite. Congratulations. So about that lunch…"

Knox shook his head, his gaze shifting my direction. "You like ahi tuna?"

"Yeah." I nodded.

"Our delivery truck just got here. Let me help the crew get everything put away, then I'll make you lunch. I've been wanting to try something, but Memphis won't eat tuna right now, so you can be my test subjects. Give me thirty."

"Thank you." Eloise leaned her cheek against my chest. "I owe you and Memphis a night of babysitting."

"Deal." Knox winked at her, then headed toward Knuckles.

"Okay, let me check in with the housekeepers and get someone to come man the desk." Eloise untucked herself from my side.

"I'll hang out." I jerked my chin for her to go do her thing while I took the same seat on the couch, reading an online article about a man who completed 101 consecutive triathlons in 101 days.

If Foster wasn't fighting, maybe I could train for a race. An Ironman or something.

Working as a trainer had never been about the money. As a member of the Vale family, I had my own trust. That fortune, held in my name since birth, mostly sat untouched. I didn't need or want a flashy life.

But it gave me freedom. Freedom to buy an A-frame cabin

in Montana. Freedom to pay cash for a diamond ring from the local Quincy jeweler. Freedom to make sure that if the Edens ever did sell The Eloise Inn, I'd buy it in a heartbeat for Eloise.

And while I didn't need to work, I liked setting goals. Challenges. Maybe I could convince Foster to do a race. The two of us could train together. There was a Spartan race in Bigfork in May. We'd missed this year but maybe next.

If I was still in Montana.

Eloise appeared over my shoulder, dropping her forearms to the back of the couch. "Ready?"

"Yep." I nodded, tucked my phone away and followed her into the restaurant.

"Mondays are usually slow," she told me, waving at the waitress who motioned for us to take any table we wanted.

Eloise picked one in the center of the room, so I pulled out her chair, then took the seat beside hers.

"Why do you always take the seat beside me?" she asked.

"What do you mean?"

"You never sit opposite me when we're eating. You always sit beside me. Is that like an East Coast manners thing?"

No, I just didn't like having a whole table between us. The corner was enough. "Makes it easier to talk this way."

"Because you talk so much," she teased.

"I talk to you."

Her eyes softened. "I guess you do."

Last night's conversation seemed to hang over our heads. Or maybe just mine.

"Does Foster know about your ex?" she asked.

"No."

"Why'd you tell me?"

There was an eyelash on her cheek. I reached over to run my thumb across her skin, collecting the eyelash. With it on my finger, I held it out. "You asked me to try."

Eloise stared at the eyelash for a long moment, like she was making a wish, then she blew the eyelash away, sending it floating to the floor. She unrolled her silverware from her napkin before draping the white cloth on her lap. "Are you going to take that job?"

Only if she wanted me to leave Quincy. "I don't know. The guy seems nice enough. He's young. Which either means he's coachable or he thinks he already knows everything. I didn't spend enough time with him to find out."

"Why didn't you?"

I unrolled my own silverware, waiting for her to answer her own question.

"You missed me," she whispered, almost like she didn't think it was real.

The waitress came over with glasses of ice water, interrupting our conversation to say hello to Eloise and introduce herself to me. She didn't bother with our order since Knox had already told her he was making us lunch.

"So..." I said, leaning my forearms on the table as the waitress left. "Thought we could talk logistics about the wedding."

"All right." Eloise turned the rings on her left hand, spinning them clockwise.

"We'll get there the day before the wedding. Thought we'd need a little time to adjust to the time difference. Get some sleep."

"And explore?" She pinched her thumb and index finger together. "Just a tiny little bit. I'll sleep when we get home."

"And we can explore." We'd do whatever her heart desired. "The wedding is in the evening on Saturday. I thought we'd skip the actual ceremony. Just go to the reception."

"Fine by me." Eloise's gaze dropped to the table.

The ceremony would be boring as fuck. And I didn't feel like sitting beside my parents any longer than necessary.

"My parents will be there so you'll meet them."

"And they'll probably hate me because I'm not Sam." She sat taller, raising her chin. "Not that I care. After everything you told me last night, I already hate them too."

This woman. She was a warrior, fighting in my corner. Ready to go to battle.

That was going to be the hardest thing for her to grasp. There'd be no battle, not with my mom or dad. They didn't care enough to hate. To fight. At least, not for me.

Eloise would realize it soon enough. But for now, if she wanted to brace herself for some confrontation with Mom and Dad, I'd let her.

Chances were, she'd need that shield up for Samantha.

"I need you to remember something," I said.

"What?"

"It's all bullshit. What they think of me. The man I used to be. What they think really happened with Sam. None of it's real. Don't buy into anything. Just...trust me."

"Easy enough. I already do." She spoke the words effortlessly. As a woman who'd lived her life trusting.

The filth in the world would try and take advantage of her pure heart. That was fine. She didn't need to change. To worry. She wasn't the only warrior at this table.

She could prepare all she wanted, no one at this wedding was going to fuck with her.

Not my parents.

And certainly not Sam.

Or for the first time, I'd spill all of my ex-wife's dirty secrets.

Even if that meant spilling mine in the process.

CHAPTER 19

ELOISE

The days passed in a whirlwind. It had been too long since I'd taken a vacation from the hotel, and getting every shift covered, planning backups for our backups, had consumed my life.

Packing had been a chore. I owned exactly zero elegant gowns, but when I'd told Jasper that I was going to have to take a trip to Missoula to buy a dress when I didn't have *time* to take a trip to Missoula to buy a dress, he'd had ten overnighted to Quincy.

Ten dresses. All designer. I'd loved every single one, and when I hadn't been able to choose a favorite, he'd picked his.

That dress was currently hanging in our hotel suite's bathroom to let the wrinkles from travel loosen while I stood on our private balcony, soaking in the Amalfi Coast.

Italy. I was in Italy. With my husband.

If someone three months ago had told me I'd be here, I would never have believed it.

Jasper and I were staying in an eleventh-century hotel. There were only fifty rooms and suites, each occupied by a wedding guest. The charming building, with rounded windows and terra-cotta roof tiles, had been built into a hillside with terraced gardens stretching beneath our third-floor balcony. From this perch, the view was breathtaking.

The rocky coastline was teeming with lush greenery and cream buildings. Bridges with arched supports spanned across the jagged and steep gray cliffs. Narrow strips of sandy beaches were interspersed between the rocks. And beyond it all was the open ocean, stretching for miles and miles to the glowing horizon kissed by the setting sun.

I refused to blink, not wanting to miss a second of the dazzling view.

Twenty-plus hours of travel had wiped me out. By the time we'd finally landed in Naples yesterday, I'd been so exhausted that even the view hadn't been able to coax my eyes open. On the hour-long drive from the airport to the hotel, Jasper's shoulder had been my pillow.

When we'd checked into our room, he'd insisted I stay awake until after dinner, wanting me to adjust to the time difference and sleep at night. We'd explored for a few hours, walking around dead on our feet, and found a charming café for dinner. Then he'd whisked me to the room, where he'd kept me awake for another hour. After two orgasms, I'd crashed.

But the sleep had done wonders. When I'd woken up this morning, Jasper had already ordered room service. Breakfast had been waiting in our suite's sitting room, and after a delicious meal, as promised, we'd done more exploring before we'd had to return to the hotel to get ready for the wedding.

Jasper came up behind me, wearing only a towel from his shower. His naked chest pressed against my back as his arms wrapped around my shoulders.

I relaxed, leaning against him, and closed my eyes. It was

rare that he initiated a hug. If I had to choose between the view from our balcony or Jasper's embrace, I'd choose the latter every day and twice on Sundays.

"Everything good at The Eloise?" he asked.

While Jasper had jumped in the shower, I'd called to check in at the hotel. "Mateo told me that if I called one more time today, he was going to rearrange the furniture in the lobby and change all of my color coding on the schedule."

Jasper chuckled. "They're fine, El."

"Yeah." I sighed.

Mateo was covering all of my regular shifts. Mom had volunteered to come in and help with whatever needed to be done. Memphis would be tackling housekeeping over the weekend. And because his latest shifts had been as excruciating as the first, I'd given Blaze the weekend off, not wanting to saddle my family with that burden.

Though maybe I should have paired him with Mom. Then when I fired him after this trip, she'd understand why.

My family was fully capable of running my hotel, yet I was struggling to disconnect. During our exploring today, I'd called three times.

"It's just hard to let go," I said.

But maybe this trip was good practice. I'd have to let go of Jasper sooner rather than later.

We hadn't spoken about what was next, both choosing to concentrate on this trip. The conversation was inevitable, and every time it crossed my mind, my insides coiled.

"Did you have fun today?" Jasper asked.

"Yes." I twisted to meet his gaze. His face was smooth and freshly shaved, so I lifted up on my toes to kiss the underside of his jaw. "Thanks for taking me."

"Welcome." He pressed his lips to my temple, then turned to the view.

Jasper had been quiet today as we'd explored, not unusual. He'd indulged me, walking at my side as I'd wandered and snapped hundreds of pictures. The only sign that he'd been enjoying himself were the crinkles at his eyes.

Except those crinkles had faded with every passing hour. And by the time we'd made it back to the hotel to start getting ready, he was back to the stone-faced man I'd lived with for months.

Was he nervous to see Sam again? Would this be painful for him, seeing the woman he'd loved—*loves*—marry another man? The ceremony might be too hard for him to attend, but going to the reception wouldn't be much easier.

Last night, even tired, I'd noticed a shift in Jasper's mood. Sex had held an edge. A frantic pace. His entire body had been tense, every honed muscle straining.

Or maybe that tension had been my own.

Was I ready for this? Somewhere nearby, the ceremony would be starting soon. Sam and her fiancé would exchange vows and rings.

My hand slid along Jasper's, my fingers skating over the knuckles on his left hand. His bare left hand. The ring I'd bought him had disappeared. For all I knew, he'd thrown it in the trash.

He didn't wear rings. Fine. Part of me still hoped that maybe...maybe mine would be his exception.

Had he worn Samantha's ring? *Probably. Yes.* I knew the answer. I hated that answer.

That woman had taken everything. Every first. Every memory. From that very first night at the Clover Chapel, I hadn't even stood a chance, had I?

The ache in my chest made it hard to breathe, so I wiggled free, slipping from Jasper's arms. "I'd better get in the shower."

Before I could slip past him, he caught my elbow. Then he framed my face with his hands, dropping his lips to mine.

I rose on my toes, fluttering my tongue against his, needing to hear that low growl in his chest. The desire for me, not Sam. *Me*. Emotion clawed at my throat, so before I could cry, I broke the kiss, forcing a smile as I slipped into the bathroom. Then I channeled the turmoil in my heart toward looking my absolute best.

The gown Jasper had chosen was a pale lavender. The neckline left my shoulders exposed but its sleeves hit past my elbows. The bodice fit my slight curves, giving the illusion of an hourglass figure. A pleated gather at one hip created a sexy slit that ran to the top of my thigh.

I artfully applied my makeup, going heavier than normal with eye shadow. But my lips stayed pale. And my hair was straight, falling in sleek panels over my shoulders, where the ends tickled my waist.

When I emerged from the bathroom, I found Jasper in the sitting area, adjusting a silver cuff link.

The sight of him in a tux, the black jacket and slacks tailored perfectly to his broad frame, stole the air from my lungs.

This had been his life, hadn't it? Tuxedos. Elegant hotels. Money. He'd donned that suit and, with it, a power I hadn't noticed before. Wealth fit him. This was the other side of his life, the side he worked so hard to hide.

Cuff link secure, he glanced up. And froze.

Those dark eyes traveled down my body, head to toe, in a lazy inspection. His Adam's apple bobbed. And then, without hesitation or reserve, he adjusted the bulge swelling behind his slacks.

"You are magnificent." His gravelly voice sent a shiver down my spine. A curl of desire bloomed in my core. My hands itched to strip him out of that suit, but that would have to wait.

First, I had a job to do: make his ex-wife jealous. I'd gladly be the woman to rub what she'd lost in her face.

"Ready for this?" I asked.

"Are you?"

"Yeah." I was ready.

He walked over, bending to brush a kiss to my cheek. Then he held out an elbow, waiting for me to take his arm before he escorted me from the room and down the carpeted hallway to the elevator.

The ride to the first floor was quiet, but the moment the doors slid open, noise filled the lobby.

We strode toward the crowd gathered outside the ballroom, my heels clicking against the polished black and white marble floor. I clutched Jasper's arm while letting my eyes wander, taking in every detail from the crystal chandeliers to the ornately carved pillars that bracketed every hallway.

"This hotel…"

"Beautiful, isn't it?"

"It's a dream."

Jasper hummed. "I prefer a quaint little hotel in Quincy, Montana."

"Funny." I looked up, finding his gaze waiting. I'd expected to see some teasing there, but he was dead serious, wasn't he? He liked The Eloise better than this?

I loved Jasper for that.

I loved Jasper.

Somewhere along the way, I'd fallen in love with my husband.

That emotion came clawing back, but I swallowed it down, once more concentrating on the hotel's intricate details. "I'm taking notes tonight for our own wedding offerings."

"I would expect nothing less," he said as we fell in line with the other guests, inching our way into the reception.

A string quartet was staged in the corner, their music mingling with the hum of conversation and laughter.

The ballroom was bright, the walls cream, as they were throughout the hotel. Matching cloths covered the tables and chairs. The centerpieces were gold candelabras that held dripping white candles. Every table was teeming with pale peonies and pristine white roses. Crystal wall sconces and glimmering chandeliers bathed the room in golden light.

One wall was made of arched openings to an outside terrace. The scent of roses and tangy ocean salt carried across the air.

It was elegant. Mesmerizing. Samantha's tastes were similar to my own. That shouldn't have surprised me considering the man we'd both married, but seeing this venue brought the realization front and center. It left a sour taste in my mouth, but I refused to let any bitterness show. There was nothing but a carefree smile on my face.

If the worst thing people said about me tonight was that I was too smiley, I'd call it a win.

Women in designer dresses sipped from crystal champagne flutes. Men in tuxes, like Jasper's, held tumblers with amber whiskey or colorless cocktails.

The bride and groom were noticeably missing. *Thank God.* I was going to need a drink before that face-off.

As a waiter passed by with a tray of champagne, Jasper took

two glasses, handing me one.

Expensive bubbles burst on my tongue.

Jasper lifted his to his lips, taking a drink. His shoulders were pinned back, his posture poised, yet relaxed as he scanned the room.

I knew it the moment he spotted a familiar face. His frame locked tight, the muscles of his arm flexing. I followed his gaze to two older couples talking and laughing and locked in conversation.

One of the men had brown, almost black, hair with liberal streaks of gray. The woman at his side was slender, almost willowy, wearing a strapless black gown. She was beautiful and had Jasper's dark eyes. At her throat was an intricate—expensive—diamond necklace that caught the light every time she moved.

"Your parents?" I asked.

Jasper hummed.

I squared my shoulders, letting go of his arm to trail my hand down his sleeve before lacing our fingers together.

"You good?" he asked, glancing down.

I looked up at him, and the concern in his eyes melted my heart. I guess tonight, we'd worry about each other. "Yeah, babe. I'm good."

With a nod, he led the way, weaving past tables and clusters of wedding guests.

His father noticed us first, stopping the group's conversation. The couple they'd been talking to said a quick goodbye, then shifted to mingle with a different group while Jasper's father held out a hand, forcing Jasper to drop mine. "Hello, son."

"Dad." Jasper shook his father's hand, then stepped closer, moving in to kiss both of his mother's cheeks. "Hi, Mom."

"Hello, darling. Isn't this a lovely evening? We were just on the terrace and it couldn't have been more beautiful."

Seriously? This was a woman who hadn't seen her son in years, and she wanted to chitchat about the weather? And all his father had to say was *hello*? Not even a, "Good to see you, Jasper"?

My mother would have taken any one of her sons by the ear, hauled them into the hallway for a screaming lecture, then hugged them so tight they'd barely be able to shake her loose. And my dad, well...he wouldn't have allowed years to go by in the first place.

"It is quite lovely." Jasper placed his hand on the small of my back. "Let me introduce you to my wife. Eloise, these are my parents, Davis and Blair Vale."

"Such a pleasure." Davis's smile seemed genuine as he took my hand, patting it gingerly.

Then Blair moved in, pressing her cheek to each of mine, just like Jasper had done when he'd told her hello.

Keep smiling. Just keep smiling.

Both seemed sincere, yet at the same time, I was watching some rehearsed play. The lines and actions written were executed with precision. Except it lacked any semblance of emotion.

"How are things in Montana?" Davis asked Jasper.

Oh, so they did know where their son was living.

"They're going well, thank you," Jasper said. "How have you both been?"

"Excellent." Davis smiled and those same crinkles as Jasper's formed at his eyes, though Davis's were deeper.

"Well, not entirely excellent." Blair tsked. "I don't know if Samantha told you or not, I know you two keep up with each other, but we had to put down Lucky last month. It's been difficult."

"I'm sorry to hear that, Mom." Jasper took my hand again. "Lucky was Mom's Pomeranian."

"I'm sorry." Somehow, I'd been sucked into this weird vortex because I sounded as cold and detached as the rest of them. So I took a long sip of champagne. *Alcohol, save me.* Tonight, I was going to need it.

"The ceremony was breathtaking," Mom said. "Sam looks as beautiful as ever."

Maybe another woman would have infused that statement with some bite. A little malice for the new daughter-in-law to know she'd never live up to the previous one. Except it was just...a statement. No malice. No ill intent.

These fucking people.

I took another drink.

"Are you staying long?" Davis asked.

Jasper shook his head. "Not long."

"We'll be leaving after brunch tomorrow. We've got to get back. But you're welcome to join us in the morning."

That wasn't really an invitation. It was more like they'd made a reservation for too many people and had a couple of spots to fill.

"We'd love to," Jasper said.

No, we wouldn't.

His thumb traced along the length of mine. "We're going to find our seats."

Davis pointed across the room toward one of the tables close to an archway. "I believe we're at the same table."

Super. I smiled wider before a snarky comment could escape.

"We'll join you." Blair looped her arm through her husband's. "Eloise. What a beautiful name."

"Thanks." I almost told her I was named after my great-great-grandmother, but as I took in her pretty face, I realized that she wouldn't care. That detail would go in one diamond-adorned ear and out the other.

Blair had already moved on to the other people in the room, her gaze sweeping back and forth through the room. She smiled at someone, lifting a hand to wave.

A short, bald man approached and Davis stopped to shake his hand.

The way both he and Blair shifted, turning their backs to Jasper because someone better had come along, made me scoff.

I gulped my champagne this time.

Jasper just kept on walking, leading me to our table, where he pulled out my seat before taking his own.

When I downed the rest of my champagne, he traded my empty glass for his nearly full one.

I drank it as I stared at his parents. We'd already been forgotten, hadn't we? Jasper had already been dismissed. Rage vibrated through every cell in my body as I watched Davis and Blair laugh with that bald man.

"I didn't understand," I whispered.

"I know, angel." Jasper draped his arm around the back of my chair. When he'd taken his seat, he'd moved in so close that our thighs were touching.

So I leaned into him, my gaze locked on his parents as I struggled to comprehend what I was seeing.

"That's their on switch," I said, more to myself than Jasper.

He hummed his agreement.

And Jasper and I had gotten the off switch. Sure, they'd

spoken the right words. They'd used the correct mannerisms. But that entire encounter had been utterly shallow. Devoid of any actual love for their son.

When it came to Jasper, they were detached. *Disinterested.* That was the word he'd used. It fit perfectly. They saved their energy for everyone else.

It was more abrupt than I could have ever expected. More obvious.

My lip curled. My hands balled into fists. "I hate them."

A waiter appeared, his tray loaded with champagne. "Another glass, sir?" he asked, his English heavily accented.

"Yes," I answered for Jasper. "Actually, no. If I get drunk, I'll say something mean. But I guess they probably wouldn't even care, so why not get drunk? I doubt they'll even remember my name by morning."

The guy looked to Jasper, his eyes wide.

"Yes, please." Jasper gestured for him to set down two fresh flutes.

With our empty glasses swept off the table, the waiter vanished into the growing crowd.

Davis and Blair continued to visit, more people joining them and the bald man.

No wonder Jasper was so closed off. How many times had he been gently rejected like that? How many times had he witnessed his parents fawn and fuss over *anyone* but him?

Fuck you, Davis and Blair. Fuck you very much.

I tore my gaze away, turning to Jasper.

His eyes were waiting. "Hi."

"Hi." God, I wanted to cry. I wanted to scream.

He was so wonderful. So special. And his parents...

They didn't even care.

My nose started to sting. A lump in my throat began to choke me. But I refused to cry, not here. Not tonight.

So I leaned in, pressing my lips to his, hoping he could feel my love. Wishing it would seep into his heart so that when he looked in the mirror, he saw a man who deserved it.

When I pulled away, his eyes searched mine. His hand came to my hair, taking a lock and letting it slip through his fingers. "Good?"

Not even a little bit. "Good." I took hold of his arm, hugging it as my head fell to his shoulder.

Then I glanced around the ballroom, looking everywhere but at his parents.

The swish of a white gown caught my eye. The room erupted in cheers and clapping as the bride and groom swept into the room.

My heart lurched.

Samantha.

She was gorgeous. Her hair was about as long as mine, curled in perfect waves of honey and wheat. She was tall and slim with curvy breasts. Of course she'd be the most beautiful woman in any room, especially this one. I'd expected nothing less, but the fact that she was flawless burned. Oh God, it burned.

Jasper and Samantha would have looked perfect together. His dark to her light.

Be tough.

I'd promised myself weeks ago that no matter what happened here tonight, I'd be tough. That I wouldn't let my feelings show, not in front of these people.

So I smiled, feigning happiness for the newlywed couple.

Jasper's hand came to my leg, squeezing my knee.

So like I did with his parents, I dismissed the bride and

concentrated wholly on my husband, pressing a kiss to his cheek.

And this time when I faced the room, I was met with a pair of jealous hazel eyes.

Maybe she was beautiful.

But my blue eyes were jewels compared to her muddy irises.

My cheeks were beginning to hurt from this saccharine smile, but I didn't falter as I met her icy glare.

Fuck you too, Samantha.

CHAPTER 20

JASPER

Over the course of two hours, Eloise had shifted in her chair. Gone was her perfect posture aimed at her place setting. Now she was sitting sideways, one of her legs tucked under her rear while the other was draped across my lap. Inch by inch, she'd effectively blocked out my father, seated on her other side, to give me her undivided attention. She was close to crawling into my lap.

And the best damn part? I doubted she even realized she'd done it.

Through the first course, she'd faced her plate, eating and sipping her champagne, listening to the conversation at the table while everyone in the room had taken their seats.

When Mom and Dad had begun talking politics with the others at our table, Eloise had made her first shift. It had been just a little turn, her knee pressed tight against my own.

During the main course, she'd crossed her legs and her calf had brushed against my shin.

Through the toasts, she'd twisted further, her torso perpendicular to the back of the chair, her eyes locked on me instead of the head table.

After another flute of champagne, she'd tucked that leg into the seat while the other draped across my thighs.

My thumb traced circles on the inside of her knee as I listened to her chatter.

The Eloise who'd captivated me in Vegas, the woman who voiced whatever thought was in her head, had reappeared. Her cheeks were flushed, her lips pink. She was breathtaking. The most beautiful woman in the room—in any room.

"I wish we had an outdoor space for weddings at the hotel." Her eyes shifted over my shoulder toward the archway and terraces at my back.

Darkness had fallen outside, the gardens now lit with twinkling lights. It was too noisy in the ballroom to hear the ocean waves, but tonight, we'd sleep with the balcony doors open to enjoy the sound.

"Maybe we could turn the roof into a garden," she said. "I'm putting that on my wish list right above the fountain."

"You want a fountain?" I asked.

"Yep. But not as much as I want a rooftop garden."

I grinned, drowning in those sparkling blue eyes. If she wanted a rooftop garden, then she'd have a rooftop garden.

She tried to shift again, to move closer, but she was as close as she could get while staying in her own chair.

So I fixed the problem for her. With a quick lift beneath her ribs, I pulled her off her own seat and plopped her onto my lap.

She smiled, like she'd been waiting for me to do that all night.

One of the other table guests, a woman with spiked gray hair, shot us a sideways glance.

Eloise gave the woman a finger wave and a blinding smile. She might as well have flipped her off.

I fought a laugh, reaching for my champagne flute.

That woman was the only one to have paid us any attention since the cake had been cut. My parents were locked in conversation with another couple, and as much as Eloise had shifted, blocking out Dad, well...he'd done the same to her.

I doubted he'd done it intentionally either. He just didn't care.

So much for my parents getting to know my wife.

It had gone exactly as I'd anticipated. There'd only been one shock to my system tonight—seeing Sam.

I'd expected to feel something. Anything. Pain from old wounds. Envy at seeing her with a new husband. Longing for what we'd once been.

Nothing. Not a damn thing. She might as well have been a stranger. It was...odd. Though not nearly as odd as the fact that I was actually enjoying this party.

Thanks solely to the angel in my arms.

"Are you drunk?" she asked.

"No."

"I am." She blew out a long breath. "Just a little bit."

"Really," I deadpanned. "I had no idea."

She rolled her eyes.

I chuckled and kissed her cheek, then lifted my glass. "Want more champagne?"

"No, I don't want to be hungover tomorrow. Can we do a helicopter tour?"

"Yes."

"Or should we do a boat tour?"

"Whatever you want."

"But what do *you* want?"

You. Just you. "Helicopter."

"Okay, good." She beamed. "I was hoping you'd say that."

We were spending another day in Italy before we flew home on Monday. I regretted planning such a short trip now. Watching her soak in the sights, watching her stunning smile as she took it all in, was like seeing the world from a new pair of eyes.

"Good evening, ladies and gentlemen," the lead singer said into the microphone. The string quartet that had played through dinner had since packed up their instruments and left. In their place was a live band—three guitarists and a drummer.

I recognized them from a relatively famous band that toured around the DC area. They hadn't made it big, but for the crowd I'd once run with, they were the popular band to have perform at your wedding.

The lead singer welcomed Sam and her husband to the floor for their first dance.

Every eye was on them as they spun around the floor.

I studied Sam, waiting for that familiar heartache and resentment to flood my veins. Instead, more nothing.

It should have felt different, seeing her again after all this time. How many years had I spent fixated on that woman? How many hours had I dwelled on the past? Countless. Every one of them pointless.

Something unlocked in my chest. Something that felt a lot like...freedom. Relief.

This wedding had been a test. A chance for me to see if I was still that man from a decade ago.

I wasn't.

And I wasn't the man Samantha thought she knew. Not anymore.

Done. I was done with Sam. It wouldn't be hard to ignore that next phone call. My attention swung from the dance floor to my parents. I was done with them too.

Having loving, attentive parents hadn't been in the cards I'd been dealt. Like seeing Sam, maybe that should have bothered me. But tonight, I just didn't fucking care.

The only person in this room deserving of my affection was in a lavender dress.

"You okay?" Eloise whispered.

Yeah, I was okay. Better than. I kissed her forehead. "Yes."

The first dance ended and the energy in the ballroom shifted as the lead singer welcomed others to the floor. The event staff came flooding through the doors, carrying replenished trays of cocktails and wineglasses. Others had snacks they'd likely be passing out until the party died.

My father stood from his chair, holding out a hand to help my mother to her feet. Then he escorted her to the dance floor, twirling her in his arms.

"Do they love each other?" Eloise asked.

"Yes, I think so."

She scoffed. "Then that only makes it worse. I really, *really* hate them."

I chuckled, kissing her forehead again. "You don't have to hate them."

"Too late."

Fierce loyalty. A precious heart. My Eloise. "Thank you for coming with me tonight."

She narrowed her eyes at mine. "Promise you're okay?"

"Promise."

Her hand lifted, her fingertips threading through the hair at my temples. "Don't cut your hair until...later, okay?"

"Okay."

Later. She was still expecting me to leave, but soon enough, she'd realize she could dictate all my trips to the barber. Hell, she could cut it herself if she wanted.

She propped her chin on my shoulder, her gaze drifting outside. "The rooftop garden has to have twinkle lights."

"Agreed."

I relaxed deeper into my chair, content to act as Eloise's. Then I watched my parents dance for a few moments until a familiar gaze snared me from across the room.

Samantha stared at me from her seat at the head table. She held a glass of champagne in one hand. The other was in her husband's.

That guy had been a prick in high school. Hell, we'd all been that way, hadn't we? He'd been at the same parties. More often than not, he'd been the guy to bring the cocaine.

At the moment, he was leaned in close, talking to the bridesmaid at his side, one of Sam's sorority sisters.

From the way they spoke, too close and too intimately for friends, I suspected that Sam had gotten everything she'd wanted: a rich husband who didn't give a damn if she slept with someone else. He'd be partaking in that open relationship. Because before this trip was over, I'd bet my inheritance he'd be fucking that bridesmaid.

More relief washed over my shoulders. That used to be my life. That used to be my reality. Thank fuck, I'd escaped.

If not for Dan, maybe I would have stayed. If not for Foster, maybe I would have returned.

If not for Eloise, I wouldn't have even known what I'd been missing.

"I have to pee." She groaned, sitting straight. "But I don't want to risk a bathroom run-in."

"What's a bathroom run-in?"

"You know, where I go to the bathroom and while I'm in the stall, these other women, probably your ex or her bridesmaids, come in and I overhear them saying something nasty about my dress or my hair."

"What could anyone possibly say about your dress or your hair?" She was the most breathtaking woman in the room, more stunning than even the bride.

"I don't know." She shrugged. "Girls are mean. But I also don't want to bump into your ex at the sink so she can tell me while we're washing our hands that you'll never love anyone the way you loved her and blah, blah, blah, blah, blah. It happened to my friend at junior prom. Drama with a capital *d*."

The corner of my mouth turned up. "A bathroom run-in. Best to avoid those."

"Exactly."

That sensation I'd had at The Eloise before we'd left Montana hit me again. Those roots kept tugging. I'd thought they had something to do with Montana, with my growing connection to Quincy. But it had always been her.

"What?" She cocked her head to the side. "You're looking at me funny. I'm drunk and talking too much, huh?"

"No, El. You're perfect." I shifted to dig out one of the key cards from my pocket. "We have a room at this hotel. No bathroom run-ins necessary."

"Oh, yeah. Duh." She giggled, then with a quick peck on the cheek, slid off my lap. "Be right back."

Eloise stuck close to the edge of the room, passing the archways on her way to the doors. Her dress swished as her hips swayed.

A man checked out her ass as she passed. I clenched my jaw, about to stand and head upstairs with her, when someone touched my shoulder.

I didn't need to turn to sense Samantha at my back.

Her hand lingered on my jacket, long enough to make my skin crawl, so I stood, keeping the chair between us.

"Hi, Sam."

"Jasper."

"Congratulations. This is a beautiful wedding."

"Yes, it is." She glanced to Eloise's empty seat. "Where's your wife? I was hoping to meet her tonight."

I chuckled. Oh, yeah. There would have definitely been a bathroom run-in.

"What's funny?" Sam asked.

"Nothing." I waved it off.

"She's very...beautiful."

"She is. Inside and out," I said. "Eloise just ran upstairs for something. She'll be back."

Sam's gaze narrowed as she studied my face. "You look... different."

"Happy," I corrected.

There were only a few times when I could remember shocking Samantha. The most notable was when I'd told her I wanted a divorce. She'd been totally unprepared for me to take issue with us fucking other people.

But tonight, she looked arguably as surprised.

Maybe because she'd never made me this happy and was realizing how much our relationship had lacked. Well, that was her problem. With any luck, tonight would be the last time I saw Samantha.

"I'm going to go check on Eloise. Enjoy your celebration."

Before she could say another word, I turned, following the same path Eloise had taken out of the ballroom.

My shoes clicked on the marble as I hustled to the elevator, stepping in with another gentleman on his way to the third floor. Then I strode down the carpeted hallway, pulling the other key from my pocket, glad I'd snagged both on the way out tonight.

Eloise was in the bathroom smoothing her hair, and when I appeared in the mirror, she gasped, slapping a hand to her heart. "You scared me. Warn a girl."

"Sorry." I closed the distance between us, spinning her from the mirror to haul her into my arms. Then I slammed my mouth onto hers.

She moaned as I slid my tongue inside, stealing that sweet taste. Then she put her hands on my chest, gently pulling away. "You're going to ruin my makeup."

"Can't have that." I picked her up at the waist, setting her on the counter.

The travel-sized plastic bottles of toiletries she'd lined up beside the sink scattered, two rolling to the floor as my hand skated up that sexy as fuck slit in her dress, pushing the fabric aside.

"Jas." Her breath hitched as I stroked along the gusset of her lace panties.

"Shimmy out of these," I ordered, tugging at the fabric.

She shifted from side to side as I pulled the panties down. Then she pulled the skirt of her gown away, until she was bared to me, her ass perched on the edge of the counter as she spread wide.

My cock throbbed, aching behind the zipper of my slacks. I freed myself, fisted the shaft and dragged the tip through her entrance, spreading that first pearl drop through her slit.

Eloise hummed, her head lolling to the side. Her legs spread wider as her hands came to my shoulders.

I hooked a hand under her knee, holding it high, stretching that toned leg until I felt resistance. Then I slid into her tight sheath with a single thrust.

"Yes," she hissed. "I missed you."

She'd had me three times last night and once this morning. But sex since we'd come here had held an edge. Her nerves. Mine.

They were gone now. All that was left was us.

I rocked us together, slowly, keeping that leg pinned, her knee pressed up toward her chest.

"Oh God." She whimpered when I drove to the hilt.

"So fucking deep." I looked down to where we were connected, a surge of lust spiking as her body stretched around mine. "Look at us, angel."

Eloise dropped her gaze, her bottom lip caught between her teeth. Then she met my gaze, her cheeks flushed.

Did she see how perfect we were together? Did she realize that it didn't matter if I wore a ring? If she had my last name?

Eloise Eden was mine.

And I was hers.

Until the end.

Her makeup was flawless. But since she looked as beautiful with it as she did without, I crushed my lips to hers, my tongue delving inside as I moved. Faster and faster I pistoned my hips. When her thigh muscles trembled, I eased her leg down, letting it dangle off the counter like the other.

Then I gripped her by the hips, holding her tight, as the sound of our sex echoed off the bathroom walls.

Eloise tore her mouth away, panting for breath. Her hands fumbled with the hem of my tux shirt, hauling it up high enough so she could drag her palms up my abs. Then she slid her hands around my back, dipping them lower until she had my ass in her grip.

Her nails dug into my flesh, her fingertips pressing hard into my muscles. The bite only spurred me on.

"I love how you fuck me." She clawed her nails harder.

"You'd better love it." As far as I was concerned, my cock was the only one she'd be getting from here on out.

Her inner walls began to pulse, her limbs shaking. Her grip on my ass never let up, so neither did I.

This woman got everything I had—heart, body and soul.

"Jas." She held me tighter.

"Come, El."

That was all it took. One command and she shattered.

On a roar, I followed her over the edge, lost in this woman.

Lost in what we might become.

If she'd have me.

As the climax faded, we leaned on each other, our skin sticky where we were still connected, our breaths mingled as our hearts raced. Until slowly we pulled apart. I tucked myself into my boxers and ran a cloth under warm water to clean Eloise.

"You don't need to do that," she whispered.

"Let me do it anyway." I kissed her cheek.

She twisted, taking in her face in the mirror. A giggle burst from her lips. "I look like I was just thoroughly fucked."

I met her gaze in the glass.

This was my chance. A chance to tell her I wanted more. To stay in Montana. To see if we could make this fake marriage into something real. But the words clogged in my throat.

It would be better to wait until we were home, right? To talk about this after the wedding when we were home at the

A-frame?

"Want to skip the rest of the party?" I asked.

"No way. I want more champagne, and those snacks they were carrying around looked yummy."

I took her hand, helping her off the counter. Returning to that wedding was the last place on earth I wanted to be, but if she wanted a snack, I'd be her escort. "Then let's get you some food."

"And cake," she said, smoothing down her dress. "I didn't get cake. I need to test it and make sure it's not as good as Lyla's. Do you eat cake?"

"Sometimes." I nuzzled my nose against her throat, drawing in that perfect scent. "But I'm going to eat something else for dessert later."

My wife.

CHAPTER 21

ELOISE

"You're a good dancer," I told Jasper as he led me around the floor. "We should dance more. Do you know the two-step? Or the jitterbug?"

"No," he said, twirling us in a circle.

"Oh. Want to learn? I just know the girl part, but Griffin or Knox or Mateo could teach you. They're all good dancers. We could all go dancing at Willie's one night."

Jasper spun us again, his low hum the only acknowledgment of my idea.

"Was that a yes?"

He chuckled.

"I'm taking that as a yes." I smiled, following his footsteps.

His cheek was pressed against my temple. One hand held mine while the other cupped my ass, unabashedly feeling me up. Jasper's grip was a not-so-subtle reminder of the claw marks I'd left on his own delicious behind.

From the moment we'd returned to the wedding reception, there'd been a bubble around us. Jasper and I had been in our own world, ignored by the other guests. Ignoring the other guests.

We'd found fresh flutes of champagne. We'd raided the food trays, sampling the post-dinner fare. And even Jasper had indulged in the cake—definitely not as good as Lyla's—before he'd swept me onto the dance floor.

I'd been in his arms ever since. My head was perfectly buzzed from the champagne. I was still riding the high from sex upstairs earlier. My limbs felt loose. And even though his icky parents and his infuriatingly beautiful ex-wife were in the room, somehow, I'd managed to block them out.

No one had better try to pop my happy bubble.

"Where did you learn to dance?" I asked.

"High school. One year of ballroom dancing was required to graduate."

I'd peppered him with questions all night. If my time with him was running out, I wanted to know everything and anything.

Jasper had indulged me, sharing without hesitation. Maybe the champagne had gone to his head too.

"Did you like your high school?"

He shook his head. "Not especially."

"I loved mine," I said. "For the most part. It's not like there wasn't the normal girl drama and whatever, but I always liked that it was the school where my brothers and sisters had gone. And it was the school where my parents went too."

"A legacy."

"Yeah." That seemed like too fancy a word for Quincy High. "I like dancing with you."

He turned his cheek, pressing his lips to my temple, then kept moving us around the floor.

"Do you like Montana?"

"This winter was fucking cold. But otherwise, yeah."

"Too many years in the desert?" I teased.

"Probably."

"You just need warmer clothes." If he'd stay, I'd find him the best winter wardrobe around. "Favorite part about Quincy? And you can't say Foster because I already know he's your favorite. And you can't say sex with me every night either because obviously that's amazing. You have to pick a favorite thing or a place or something like that."

Jasper opened his mouth. "The—"

"And you can't say the A-frame."

He stopped dancing. "Do you want to just tell me what my favorite is then?"

"The Eloise Inn?"

Jasper chuckled, shaking his head. "That's your favorite."

"I'll share it. You have to admit it's pretty fantastic."

"It's pretty fantastic."

"See? I knew it was your favorite."

He flashed me those straight, white teeth as his eyes crinkled at the sides.

"You're so handsome when you smile." I traced my finger across his bottom lip. "I like it when you smile."

"I like it when you smile too." He resumed our dance, matching our steps to the beat of the band's slow melody. "Next question?"

"How did you know I was going to ask another question?"

"Your name is Eloise Eden."

I giggled. "How many times have you been to Italy?"

"Three."

"Are you having fun on this trip?"

"Yes."

Score. "Me too. I didn't expect to have fun, especially tonight."

"Neither did I, angel," he murmured.

Take that, Samantha.

It had been too easy to pretend tonight, to fall into this illusion of a happily married couple. And it felt so real that my hopes were soaring beyond the limits of my control. Tomorrow, when reality came crashing back, it was going to be as miserable as the champagne hangover I'd undoubtedly have.

But...it wasn't tomorrow yet.

"How many—"

A woman appeared at our side, cutting my question short.

Her blond hair was swept into a chignon. On her wrist was a delicate rose corsage. The resemblance to Samantha was uncanny. This had to be her mother.

"Ashley." Jasper stopped our dance, shifting me until I was tucked against his side, his body slightly in front of mine. Like a shield.

"Hello, Jasper." Ashley smiled, offering her cheek.

He kissed it but his arm banded around my hip stayed firm. "Congratulations."

"Thank you." She kept her entire focus on him, her gaze not even flicking my direction. Apparently I wasn't worth acknowledging.

Or introducing.

Jasper didn't give me a nod either.

Gee thanks.

"Charming wedding," he said. "Though I expected nothing less."

"Since I didn't get to partake in yours, I inserted myself fully into this one. Much to Samantha's dismay."

Jasper's smile was tight. Cold. "We appreciate the invitation."

"Honestly, I didn't think you'd come." Ashley's attention

shifted to me. The sneer on her face, the open disdain, was something this woman had clearly practiced for decades.

And here I was thinking we'd escaped the drama. *Damn.*

I smiled wider, leaning into Jasper and putting my hand on his stomach. *Don't say something rude. Don't say something rude.* By some miracle, I managed to keep my mouth shut.

This was the welcome I'd expected from his parents, the confrontation I'd prepared for. The nasty glares. The hostility. We'd been so close to avoiding it tonight.

"Jasper." A man clapped him on the shoulder, holding out his hand. "Good to see you. I meant to come say hello earlier but it's been a busy night."

"John." Jasper dipped his chin. "Congratulations."

"Thank you." John didn't ignore me and his stare was more cautious than callous.

"This is my wife, Eloise." Jasper loosened his grip so I could shake John's hand.

"Pleasure," I lied.

"Mine as well." John kept ahold of my hand. "I haven't gotten to dance all evening. May I cut in?"

Oh, no. I opened my mouth to protest, but John was already crowding Jasper out of the way, tugging me into his arms.

Jasper's jaw flexed but he didn't steal me away. Instead, when Ashley moved in to steal my place, arms raised for him to take the lead, he danced with her.

Well, shit.

This was awkward.

"Beautiful evening," I said. How much longer was this song?

"It is," John said. "Weddings are always a great excuse to bring people together. It's been too long since we've seen Jasper."

"He's just so busy. It's hard for him to get away."

John's eyes, the same muddy color as his daughter's, narrowed. "From Montana."

"Yes. That's where we live."

"And you work at a motel?"

Did I want to know how he knew about me? Nope. "I manage my family's hotel."

"Hospitality is a necessary industry." Spoken like a true douchebag who snubbed those he considered beneath his station.

"Jasper mentioned you're in politics, is that right?"

He gave me a curt nod, almost like he was offended that I'd switched the topic of conversation while he was trying to run me down.

A few feet away, whatever Ashley was saying to Jasper couldn't have been good, given that angry muscle in his jaw was flexing.

"It's not easy to see Jasper with another woman."

My gaze whipped to John's, but I bit my tongue, holding back a snarky retort. Or an education about his cheating daughter.

"They have an unbreakable bond," he said.

"Yet it broke." About the time she'd taken another man's cock. I smiled sweetly. "So I'll have to disagree with your opinion."

"It's a fact, my dear. One known by every person in this room."

"Even your new son-in-law? Yikes. Poor guy. He must feel very welcome in your home."

John's nostrils flared. "He, unlike you, isn't blind to reality."

My gaze drifted around us, and for the first time tonight, I saw a pointed stare. A woman turned away too fast when she met my gaze. Had people been staring at me all night? Pitying me?

Did they see me as some pathetic stand-in? The woman who could never compete for Jasper's heart? Not when it had belonged to the woman in a white gown.

The woman he'd loved his entire life.

"There's a reason you're in Italy." John bent lower to speak directly in my ear. "Jasper will never let go of Samantha. He might pretend to care. He might even be fooling himself. But at some point, he'll realize it's fake. And then you'll disappear. I have no delusions Samantha's marriage will last. And once it fizzles, they'll find their way back to each other."

Fake. Jasper and I were fake. And oh, how I hated that word.

It took everything I had to hide a reaction. To keep it hidden that he'd fired a shot and hit me straight in the heart. *Be tough.* "Like I said, I'll have to disagree with your opinions."

"You're a stupid girl to believe you're anything other than a fleeting distraction," he whispered.

A stupid girl Jasper had married on a drunken whim.

A mistake.

"Thanks for the dance." With one purposeful step, I pulled away.

Jasper's arms were waiting.

He swept me away from John and Ashley, the pair exchanging a look like they'd planned that interruption all night.

"What did he say?" Jasper asked.

"Nothing nice," I admitted, struggling to breathe.

"I'm sorry."

I shrugged, swallowing the lump in my throat. *Don't cry.* "It was bound to happen. You warned me about it, right?"

My mistake had been thinking we'd get that attitude from his own parents, not Samantha's. No bathroom run-in tonight. Just an ambush on the dance floor.

As Jasper led us around, I scanned the room again. People *were* staring. Whispering.

Damn, I was an idiot. How could I have let myself believe this was real?

Stupid Eloise.

Maybe Samantha had broken his heart, had betrayed his trust, but he'd loved her for years. We were at her wedding, weren't we? Maybe John was right.

Maybe Jasper wouldn't ever really let her go.

My chest ached, and the swelling of emotions made it hard to breathe. Goddamn it. *Don't cry.* I would not cry tonight.

"Ask me another question, El."

"I'm all out of questions." My voice cracked.

"Ask me." His lips caressed my forehead as he spoke. "Please."

It was the please that made tears flood my eyes. But I blinked them away, refusing to let the assholes in this room win. "What's your favorite city in the world?"

"Paris."

It was on my bucket list.

"Have you been?" he asked.

I shook my head. "Someday."

Someday I'd visit all the pretty cities. I'd add more stamps to my passport. Maybe, if I was lucky, the man who came with me on those trips would be free to love me too.

"Come on." Jasper broke the dance, clasped my hand and led me from the ballroom. His strides were so long that I had to skip every couple steps to keep up.

He walked straight for the elevator and hit the button for our floor, digging a key card from his pocket the moment we reached level three. As he headed down the hallway, he pulled out his phone from his jacket, quickly typing in something before pressing it to his ear.

"Who are you calling?" I asked, rushing to keep up.

He kept moving, unlocking our room's door. "Yes, I need a chartered flight from Naples to Paris. Tonight. Departing in two hours."

I gasped.

Jasper looked down at me, something serious in his gaze. Then the crinkles appeared. His hand cupped my cheek, his thumb stroking my skin, before he waved me into the room. "Go pack. Hurry."

Pack. For Paris.

At the moment, being anywhere other than Italy, than this hotel, seemed like a brilliant idea.

I flew into action, racing around the room to sweep up everything I'd scattered around in the past couple of days.

Jasper did the same as he talked on the phone, giving our details to whoever was on the other end of that call.

How much did it cost to fly from Naples to Paris on a whim?

At the moment, I really didn't care. France sounded like the perfect escape.

Jasper ended the call, his suitcase and carry-on bag both packed and zipped shut on the bed. He came to the bathroom, standing at my side to help collect my toiletries from the counter where we'd scattered them earlier, shoving them into my travel case.

"Are we really going to Paris?" I asked.

He met my gaze in the mirror. "We're really going to Paris."

...

The City of Light.

Paris at dawn was magical.

The streets were quiet. Only a few cars traveled along the sleepy roads. A woman walking her dog passed by, but other than the murmured French she spoke into her phone, the city was still tucked in from last night.

Jasper and I stood on the Pont d'Iéna, the Seine flowing beneath the bridge's arched feet. His gaze was on the river. Mine was locked on the Eiffel Tower, catching the early sun's rays.

The jet he'd chartered last night had touched down in Paris five hours after we'd rushed from the hotel in Italy. He'd hailed us an Uber to a hotel, but only so that we could drop off our luggage before the same car had brought us here. Just in time to watch the sunrise.

"Thank you for bringing me here," I whispered.

Jasper's chin was on my head, his arms around my shoulders. "Dream come true?"

"And then some."

Because we were together. Because I'd let myself fall into the illusion again.

Someday, I'd go back to Italy. I'd visit Rome and Tuscany. I'd eat my weight in pasta and gelato. But I doubted I'd ever come to Paris again.

This was a memory I didn't want covered with another.

The breeze caught a tendril of hair, whipping it into my face. I was still in my dress from the wedding. Jasper was in his tux, though he'd draped the jacket over my shoulders to keep me warm.

A yawn tugged at my mouth.

But I refused to move from this spot or admit I was exhausted.

If this was my morning in Paris, I wouldn't waste it. So we stood together, locked together, as the city began to stir. Tourists and Parisians crossed the bridge. Cars clamored along the roads. Only when the gates to the tower opened did Jasper and I finally abandon our spot on the bridge. Then we spent the day exploring.

From the Louvre to the Notre-Dame Cathedral to the charming, crowded streets of Montmartre, we barely skimmed the surface of all there was to see, bouncing from one place to the next. In another life, each spot would get an entire day of its own, but since we only had one, I made the most of it.

Until the sun had completed its journey across the sky and ducked beyond the horizon. Until we were back in the same place we'd been this morning. On the bridge over the Seine, standing at the base of the Eiffel Tower once more to watch its shimmering lights against the darkened sky.

"Ready to go back to the hotel?" he asked.

"Not yet."

My feet ached. My bones were weary. It was getting harder and harder to keep my eyes open.

"This is a dream," I murmured, yawning for the hundredth time. I leaned on Jasper, my arms around his waist, feeling like I could sleep standing up.

I took one last look at the tower, then closed my eyes, committing it to memory.

Committing this place and Jasper, tucking the image away in the deepest corners of my mind, to the place where I vowed never to forget.

If there was ever a place to share before our final farewell, it was here.

"Where to next?" he asked.

"Quincy, Montana."

It was time to go home.

CHAPTER 22

JASPER

"Can I get you anything, sir?" the flight attendant asked.

"No." I shook my head, keeping my voice low.

She looked to Eloise, curled into a ball and asleep on my lap, and smiled. Then she went to the row behind ours, moving on to the next passenger in the first-class cabin.

I relaxed my head against the seat. We were on the final leg of the trip home, and sleep had been sporadic since we'd left Italy.

I'd managed to catch a few hours at the hotel in Paris, but because we'd changed our flight to depart from France rather than Italy, we'd had to be at the airport early this morning. Eloise had slept some on the flight across the Atlantic, but I'd never been great about sleep on airplanes.

Just a few more hours, then we'd be home. Another hour of flying, the two-hour drive from Missoula to Quincy, then I'd crash in my own damn bed.

We could both use a solid night's sleep.

Eloise had fallen asleep not long after we'd taken off on this final flight, but she'd kept jolting herself awake, until finally, she'd climbed over the console between us and curled up in my lap. She'd been dead to the world ever since.

I yawned. Exhaustion should have won out—it had been a damn long few days—but I couldn't seem to shut off my mind. I couldn't stop replaying what Ashley had told me at the wedding during that short dance.

It had been a load of bullshit about how Samantha would always love me. How it wasn't too late for us.

I almost felt bad for Sam's new husband.

Almost.

Clearly, Sam hadn't married for love.

Did she even know what love was? Did I? What Sam and I'd shared had seemed like love. A bond. Attention. When stacked side by side with my parents, what Sam had given me, especially in the beginning, had resembled love. Once, long ago, I'd been so damn sure that what I'd felt for Samantha was love.

Now...

I wasn't sure. I'd learned more about love from the woman drooling on my shoulder in months than I had from years with Samantha.

With the arm not trapped beneath Eloise, I plucked my phone from the cup. We'd loaded Wi-Fi onto both our phones in case we wanted to watch a movie, but nothing had held my interest, so I checked to see if there were any missed texts or emails.

No surprise, there was nothing from my parents. No text asking if we were still meeting for brunch. They'd probably arrived at the restaurant and completely forgotten they'd even invited Eloise and me to tag along.

Or maybe they'd been relieved when we hadn't shown up.

It stung. Would it always? Would there ever come a time when I could see them and not hope that they'd care? Not even meeting my wife could spark their interest. They'd been happier talking to their friends last night than their son and new daughter-in-law.

It was one thing for them to dismiss me. But Eloise?

She looked so young today, her face without makeup and her hair pulled up. She was in a pair of gray sweats and a matching sweatshirt with sleeves that fell to her fingertips.

Maybe this anger toward my parents had nothing to do with me. Maybe it was for Eloise.

She deserved better than they'd offered.

We both did.

I pressed a kiss to her forehead, then went back to my phone, scrolling to the email that I'd been ignoring since Friday.

It was from the fighter I'd met with in Vegas. He needed an answer about the job offer.

So with one hand, I typed out my reply.

Eloise stirred the moment I hit send, like she'd felt the weight of that decision. "Hi." Her eyelids were too heavy to open. So she let them fall closed and snuggled deeper, curling her hands beneath her chin. "How much longer?"

"Not long."

She sighed and, this time, opened her eyes for good, sitting up straight and climbing off my lap.

I shook out the arm that had been behind her. It had fallen asleep five minutes after she had.

On a yawn, Eloise snagged her phone from the backpack at her feet. Whatever she read on the screen made her gasp.

"What's wrong?"

"Oh my God." She answered by handing it over.

There was a text open from Taylor. I hadn't met her but Eloise had talked about the girl enough I knew she worked at the hotel desk.

I'm so sorry to bother you on vacation but Blaze came in to the hotel today even though he wasn't scheduled to work. He would hardly leave the front desk and every time I told him I was working and couldn't talk, he'd just ignore me.

"Who is Blaze?" I asked.

"My mom's college roommate moved to Quincy. Her name is Lydia. Blaze is her seventeen-year-old son. Mom asked if I'd give him a job. I guess he was struggling and Lydia thought a job might do him some good."

So Anne had asked for a favor. "That's the kid you were training last weekend?"

Eloise nodded, pinching the bridge of her nose.

She'd gone to work all weekend to train a new housekeeper, but I hadn't asked for details. When she'd come home, she'd been exhausted. I'd assumed it was because she'd been working so hard to get ready for the trip.

Taylor's text was broken into two so I kept on scrolling, reading the second message.

While he was talking, a bird hit one of the front windows. He went out to get it and even though it wasn't dead he brought it inside anyway. When it tried to fly away, he broke its neck. I started crying and called my mom. She said that if he keeps working at the hotel, then I'll have to find a different job. Blaze finally left when Mateo came in but I wanted you to know. I'm sorry.

"What the hell?" Blaze had killed a bird? In front of a teenage girl? "That's fucked up."

"Yep." Eloise took the phone, typing out a reply to Taylor. She hit send, then tucked it in her backpack. "He's fired. I hate firing people but I don't think I'll mind this time."

"I don't want you doing it alone."

"I'll be fine. I'll take care of it."

"Look at me," I ordered, waiting until I had those blues. "Not alone, Eloise. Call me. Call your dad. Call one of your brothers. But you don't talk to this kid alone. Please."

She sighed. "I'll have to change the schedule. I don't want Taylor at the front desk alone anymore."

"I don't want you there alone either."

"Well, that's not an option," she muttered. "I never should have hired him. What a mess."

"Your mother's mess. She put you in this position."

"I know. But I could have told her no."

"And how would that have gone over?"

Eloise fiddled with her fingers in her lap. "She probably would have been upset."

"Exactly." My molars ground together. "Your parents get mad because you're too close to your employees. Yet your mom pressures you to hire her friend's kid. How is this different?"

"Well, hopefully this time we won't get sued."

I huffed. "Make your mother fire him."

"She didn't hire him. I did. Ultimately, it's my responsibility. So I'll deal with it."

"But you shouldn't have to. She shouldn't have asked you to do this in the first place."

"I know, Jasper." She wrapped her arms around her waist, her shoulders curling forward.

The seat belt light turned on above us, followed by a chime that filled the plane's cabin. Then the pilot came on the intercom, announcing we'd be starting our descent.

There was more to say about her parents, about this situation with Blaze, but I bit my tongue, waiting until we were off the plane and leaving the airport to drive home.

The moment we were on the highway, I stretched a hand across the console, covering her knee. "When I said I don't want you to fire Blaze alone, it's not because I don't think you can do it. I don't trust that kid."

"It's not that." She waved it off. "It's my parents. You're so quick to criticize Mom."

My jaw clenched. "You agreed. Your mother shouldn't have asked you to hire this kid, especially if she knew he had problems."

"I don't think she knew. Trust me, when she finds out about this, she's going to be ten times more upset than I am. And like I said, I could have—should have—told her no."

I pulled my hand away, wrapping it around the steering wheel so I had something to squeeze. "But you didn't. Because you didn't want to cause trouble, right? Because they hold that hotel over your head like a goddamn string and you're their puppet."

Eloise flinched. "Jasper."

"Tell me I'm wrong."

The heavy silence that filled the cab was answer enough.

"Your dream is that hotel," I said. "You work your ass off. They want you to be this hard-ass person instead of who you really are. You give it everything you have, and it's still not good enough for your parents."

"That's not fair."

"Isn't it?" I scoffed. "We stayed married because you were terrified they'd take it away from you. That they'd think less of you. Because deep down, they have made you afraid that they'll give that hotel to someone else."

Eloise shook her head. "You're twisting this around. They

support me."

"They have a strange fucking way of showing it," I muttered. "Have they ever said congratulations after we got married?"

"Is this why you were acting so strange at the ranch? Why you avoid them? Because you think they don't support me or that they aren't happy for me?"

"I'm not going to pretend I like your parents."

"Jasper." Her mouth parted. "Don't say that."

I shot her a flat look. "So you can say you hate my parents but I can't take issue with yours?"

Eloise winced. Then her eyes flooded with tears.

Fuck. Too far. I'd taken it too far.

She had every right to dislike my parents. Hell, I disliked my parents. But she loved hers. And I'd just put her in the position to choose.

Her family. Or me.

Tension settled thick and sweltering in the cab. The whirl of the tires on pavement was the only sound for miles. Eloise kept her gaze pointed out the passenger window as I focused on the road.

It should have been a relief to see the A-frame. It wasn't.

"You're right," she whispered as I parked. "All of it. But I love my parents anyway."

That was who she was.

Eloise loved.

Without conditions. Without hesitation. Even when some people might not deserve it. Like me. Did I deserve it?

"Their hearts are in the right place," she said.

"Are they?" Fuck, I was being a dick. Why couldn't I just drop this subject?

"You said it was okay if my family hated you." Her chin

quivered. "That it would be easier that way. But what you really meant was it was okay if *you* hated them. That it would be easier for you."

The nail drove straight through my chest.

Yes, it would be easier.

To walk away. To cut ties.

Eloise sniffled, wiping under her eyes before a tear could fall. "That, right there, is the reason I hate your parents. Why I hate Samantha, despite how much you claim to love her. You don't get to tell me I'm scared, Jasper. Not when you're just as afraid. You've built a fortress around yourself because you're so scared that you'll love someone and they'll leave you. You push everyone away before they even have the chance to get close."

My chest twisted.

"El—"

She shoved out of the car, then hauled out her bags, taking them inside before I could help.

I dragged a hand through my hair, tipping my head to the Yukon's roof. "Fuck."

She was right. So damn right. But between the wedding, seeing Sam, the trip to Paris, I was coming apart at the seams. Eloise and I needed to talk, except at the moment, I didn't trust myself to articulate my feelings. To say it right. So I shut it all down, focusing on a single task.

Getting the mail.

I shoved out of the Yukon and walked down the driveway. The clean, mountain air didn't do a damn thing to loosen the pressure in my chest. Every step felt heavier and heavier. But I kept on walking. By the time I returned to the cabin, maybe I'd have a clue about what to say.

To fix this.

Yesterday in Paris had been incredible. A day I'd never forget. I didn't want to ruin this trip with a fight.

Inside the mailbox were two magazines, both for Eloise, and a white envelope so large it had been curled in half to fit. I tucked the magazines under an arm, then inspected the envelope.

It was addressed to Eloise from Misner Family Law. Her attorney.

My stomach dropped.

I slid my finger beneath the envelope's seal, prying it open. Eloise was already mad. She could add invasion of privacy to her list.

With a careful tug, I eased the documents from the envelope enough to read the top page.

Not that I needed to. I already knew what I'd find inside.

Divorce papers.

CHAPTER 23

ELOISE

Jasper stood on the deck, coffee cup in hand. He was in jeans and a T-shirt, his feet bare. He stared at the trees.

I stared at him.

In the past two days, I'd seen more of his back than I had in all of our time together.

Whenever I came into the room, he left. At night, he'd sleep facing one wall while I stared at the other.

My entire body felt heavy. My muscles were nearly as weary as my heart. Never in my life had I felt this tired. Two sleepless nights. Two days spent fighting tears, and the battle had drained me entirely.

Jasper lifted his mug, taking a sip of coffee. He didn't so much as glance into the house.

Was this how it would end? In silence?

The lump in my throat was as hard as a rock, but I swallowed it down. It landed in my empty stomach like a sledgehammer. With my purse slung over a shoulder, I swiped my keys from the kitchen counter and walked out of the A-frame.

My fake marriage was falling apart.

But at least I had The Eloise. My marriage to that hotel was as real as the morning sun, and for yet another day, she'd be my salvation. So I climbed in my car and drove into town.

My mental to-do list had exploded the past two days with nothing but yuck.

Search for a new rental.

Call my lawyer.

And at the top of the list, *Fire Blaze.*

I hated my to-do list. Couldn't I rewind time a couple days?

On Sunday, Jasper and I had been exploring Paris. It had been, without contest, the best day of my life. As we'd walked, hand in hand, I'd actually convinced myself he cared. That he might love me.

Maybe he did. At least, maybe he loved a part of me.

Except, for better or worse, my family was the other part. My parents, my brothers and sisters, were a piece of my heart. The Edens came as a packaged deal.

Jasper couldn't care for me and despise them.

He'd made his point on the drive home. It wasn't fair for me to voice my dislike for his parents and expect him to keep quiet. And he'd made another point about Mom and Dad supporting me.

Yes, I was scared to lose the hotel.

But at the end of the day, I trusted them. I had faith that they loved me, that they wanted the best for my life. If they decided that I didn't have what it took to own The Eloise Inn, I knew that decision would be painful for them to make. They'd only do it because it was the best decision. Because they knew, if that hotel failed under my control, it would be devastating.

It wasn't a black-and-white situation. But I didn't know how to explain that to Jasper. Not when his parents had been so... cold.

The only way Jasper was going to see the beauty of my family was by living it. By putting up with my brothers. By getting to know my sisters. By seeing the love my parents gave us unconditionally.

How was I ever going to show him what a family should look like when he locked them out? When he walked away?

It was over, wasn't it?

We'd end on this horrible, heart-wrenching fight. And I hadn't even had the chance to show Jasper why he was so wonderful. Why he deserved love.

My eyes flooded. I brushed the skin beneath my lashes. It was practically raw from how many tears I'd swept away in the past two days. Then I pulled into the alley behind The Eloise, parking beside Knox's truck, and headed inside.

The morning was a blur of activity. Not only was I playing catch-up from being gone, but we were prepping for one of the busiest holiday weekends of the year.

Independence Day weekend in Quincy was a roller coaster, a carnival of amusement and chaos. Tourists flocked to enjoy the local festivities—a parade along Main and the county rodeo. Fireworks at dark. Dancing and ruckuses at the local bars.

The hotel was booked solid.

It would be all hands on deck this weekend for every Eden business. Talia would take the weekend off from the hospital to help Lyla at the coffee shop. Griffin and Dad would be on call to run errands to the hardware store or the grocery store for whatever anyone needed. Mom would likely bounce between Eden Coffee or Knuckles to help Knox.

And whoever wasn't busy would be helping at the hotel.

But no matter how busy we were, we all made it a point to congregate at the fairgrounds to watch the rodeo. It was tradition.

Had Jasper ever been to a rodeo?

He'd shown me Paris, the city of my dreams. And all I wanted was to sit beside him, drink a beer and teach him the difference between saddle and bareback bronc riding.

Would he even stick around until then? Or was he packing up the A-frame? Had he accepted that job in Vegas?

The thought of Jasper leaving made my entire body ache, so I shoved it aside and focused on work, biding my time until an angry kid with black hair and thick glasses walked through the front doors.

Blaze crossed the lobby, his eyes on the floor and his shoulders curled in. He was in those awful jeans again. The *Fuck You Mom*s had been touched up at the thighs and knees.

This kid. He needed more than a job.

"Hi, Blaze."

He blinked.

"Thanks for coming in today," I said. "Give me one minute."

Mateo had come in earlier to help out. He'd been installing a shelf I'd bought for the break room, so I shot him a text, asking if he could watch the front desk for a few minutes.

He came striding down the hallway minutes later, giving Blaze a flat look.

"We'll be in the office," I told him.

"Take your time." The look he sent Blaze was full of warning.

Jasper wasn't the only man in my life not keen on this kid and me being alone.

But despite everyone else's opinions, this was my mess. Not my mother's, mine. I should have told her no. Since I hadn't, then I'd fix this mistake.

So I escorted Blaze to my office, taking the chair behind the desk I rarely sat at while he sat on the opposite side. My heart thumped as I faced him, my palms clammy. God, I hated firing people, even strange kids who creeped out my desk clerks. But I kept my shoulders straight, my chin held high. And I crisply delivered the lines I'd practiced over and over last night when I hadn't been able to sleep.

"Blaze, I'm going to have to let you go. I appreciate your time here. Unfortunately, this hasn't been a fit for our housekeeping department." I held my breath, waiting for his reaction.

There was no outburst or argument. Blaze simply shrugged. "Fine. This was my mom's fucking idea anyway. When do I get my money?"

"Your final paycheck will be sent to your address on record when we process payroll on the first."

He stood from the chair and let himself out of the office.

Huh. That's it? Well, at least one thing had gone right today.

I stood from my own chair, then flipped off the light as I left the room, rejoining Mateo at the desk.

"How'd that go?" he asked.

I lifted a shoulder. "Could have been worse."

Mateo glanced past me toward the fireplace.

Blaze stood staring up at the hearth's column of stone that towered to the rafters.

I did a double take. *Damn it.* "He's still here?"

Just when I'd thought this had been easy.

I sucked in a fortifying breath, then walked toward the couches. "Blaze, was there something else you needed?"

He kept his gaze fixed to the ceiling. "Taylor is working today, right?"

"Um…" How the hell did he know that? I'd just called her

a couple hours ago to see if she wanted a few more hours. She'd agreed to sit at the desk while I finished the next schedule and documented Blaze's termination. How did he know she was coming in? "Did she tell you that?"

Maybe they were friends?

"I saw her walking. She was in her work clothes."

The hairs on the back of my neck stood up.

Taylor drove her Honda Civic to work because her family lived out of town a few miles. Sure, she could have come downtown early. Maybe she'd stopped by the coffee shop or another store on Main and that's when he'd spotted her. But regardless, when she walked through these doors, I didn't want him here to greet her.

"Why do you need to see Taylor?"

He dropped his chin, and for the first time, he looked me in the eyes.

A chill raced down my spine.

Yeah, this kid had to go.

"I want to tell her I got fired," he said.

Because he thought it was her fault? I couldn't tell with that flat tone.

"I'll be sure to let her know." I held a hand out toward the door. "Thanks again for coming in today. I'm sure I'll see you around town."

He cocked his head to the side and a swoop of that black hair fell into his face. But otherwise, he didn't move.

"Blaze, you need to leave. You can't stay here."

"Why not?"

"Because I said so." And apparently, I'd just become my mother.

And it was the wrong thing to say. If Blaze's gaze had been

cold before, it was arctic now.

Goose bumps broke out on my forearms, and suddenly, I saw the kid who'd brought an injured bird inside this building and broken its neck.

"I want to talk to Taylor," he said.

"Well, she won't be here today after all." I pulled my phone from my pocket and sent her a quick text.

Change of plan. Don't come to the hotel. I'll call you later.

If Blaze had an unhealthy obsession with Taylor, the last place I wanted her was in this lobby.

With my phone tucked away, I crossed my arms over my chest. "Time to go home, Blaze."

He stared at me. Unmoving.

Ugh. I didn't have time for teenagers today.

The lobby door opened.

Shit. Taylor. My heart climbed into my throat as we both looked toward the door.

But it was Jasper.

He strode into the lobby, dressed like he'd come from the gym. His black shorts accentuated the strength in his thighs and displayed the definition in his calves. That white T-shirt stretched across his broad chest and hugged his roped arms.

A body refined to perfection. A body honed from time spent throwing punches and kicks.

Jasper's hair was trapped beneath a faded baseball hat. Combined with that clench of his jaw, it gave him a menacing, intimidating edge.

Any normal kid probably would have cowered with Jasper stalking his way, stopping behind the nearest couch, arms crossed.

Not Blaze. Though his glare withered, just enough.

"Blaze," I snapped. "Goodbye."

His lip curled. "Bitch."

"Watch it," Jasper rumbled. "That's my wife."

For a fraction of a second, I let myself believe that statement. I let it lighten the weight on my shoulders.

That's my wife.

Then the sadness came whirling in like a winter storm, coating everything with ice. The heaviness in my bones returned.

No, I wasn't his wife. Not the way it mattered.

That sting in my nose threatened tears I couldn't cry, not yet. I'd save them for later, after I ushered this kid out of my hotel.

"This is public property," Blaze sneered. "I can be here."

"Correction," I said. "We're open to the public, but make no mistake, this is my building. And I get to say who stays and who goes. Consider yourself no longer welcome."

"Fuck you, lady."

I pointed to the door. "Now you've got a tagline for your next pair of jeans."

He glanced back and forth between Jasper and me for a long moment. Then finally, Blaze huffed and stormed for the door, ripping it open as he walked outside. He lifted a hand, flipping us off as he crossed the front windows. Then he rounded the corner and disappeared.

"Well, that went great." The air rushed from my lungs. "He's going to egg my hotel, isn't he? Do kids even egg buildings anymore? Or do they go straight for the spray paint?"

I was joking. Sort of. Right now, with Jasper staring at me, I needed to make a joke, even if neither of us laughed.

Jasper planted his hands on his hips. "What did I say about meeting with that kid alone?"

I pinched the bridge of my nose. "I know."

"Hey." Mateo's hand landed on my shoulder. When had he walked over? "You okay?"

"I need to talk to Taylor and call her mother. And then call Mom and tell her to talk to Lydia." Though I doubted Blaze's mother had much control over that boy.

I pulled my phone from my pocket. Taylor had replied *okay*. "Would you make sure he's really gone?" I asked Mateo.

He nodded. "You did good."

"Thanks." My eyes flooded. Pride from my brother shouldn't have been the tipping point, but it was all too much. There were no empty spaces to absorb it. No extra strength to carry it.

Mateo squeezed my shoulder, then walked outside, following Blaze's path past the windows.

Closing my eyes, I dragged in a calming breath. It didn't help. Not even a little.

The heat from Jasper's body, his warmth, hit me at the same time as his scent. Then his knuckles grazed my cheek. "You okay?"

"Great," I lied, opening my eyes.

It was the look on his face that broke me. The concern. The fear.

The tears spilled over my cheeks.

"You're not okay."

More tears welled, so fast he became a blur. "It's jet lag."

"Eloise."

"Don't." A sob broke free. "Don't say my name like that."

"Like what?"

"Like I'm your wife." My voice cracked with my heart. Too much. It was just too much.

The tides of battle had turned, and I was about to get

slaughtered by my own goddamn emotions.

So I buried my face in my hands to muffle the cries, to catch the tears, as the breakdown I'd been fighting for two days finally won its war.

"Hey." Jasper hauled me against his chest, his arms wrapping me tight.

There wasn't enough strength in my heart to push him away, so I burrowed deep, soaking his shirt with my tears and letting the words in my heart flow free.

"I know this is the end. I just didn't expect it to feel like this. And I don't want to end it fighting."

I didn't want it to end. Period.

"It's not the end."

I wanted this so badly, I could have sworn he'd said it wasn't the end. My imagination was just plain mean some days and it only made me cry harder.

"Eloise, look at me." Jasper unwrapped his arms, taking my face in his hands. He gave me a moment to get myself together and listen. "I got the divorce papers."

Ouch. Damn it, this hurt. "I didn't realize your attorney was sending them."

"Not mine, angel. Yours."

"Oh." Guess that item was off my to-do list.

"I threw them in the trash."

My brain was too fogged to keep up. "Wait. You did? Because there was something wrong with them or—"

"It's not the end."

"It's not?"

"No." He shook his head, his eyes searching mine. "You *are* my wife."

"But you won't even wear your ring," I blurted, then a rush

of emotion hit again. Confusion. Joy.

Too much. So I buried my face in Jasper's shirt and let him hold me while I cried. Hard.

Was this happening? When the tears slowed, when the sobs turned to hiccups, I drew in a long inhale of his cologne and unburied my face from his chest. "Are you sure?"

"That you're my wife?" His lips pressed against my hair. "I'm sure."

The relief nearly sent me to my knees. But I clung to his shirt, fisting it in my hands like I was wrapping my fingers around his heart. If he ever tried to leave, I'd drag his ass back to Quincy.

Back to me.

"It's not the end," I repeated.

"It's not the end."

A laugh bubbled free. I unpeeled myself from his chest, searching those dark eyes.

They had the crinkles at the sides.

He kissed me, dragging his tongue across my bottom lip, slow and savoring. It only lasted a moment before he slanted his mouth over mine and delved, claiming every corner of my mouth.

I let that kiss sink into my weary soul, to calm some of the storm.

His shirt was soaked and wrinkled when I finally let it go.

"Sorry."

Jasper cupped my jaw, wiping my damp cheeks with his thumbs. "You good with this?"

I nodded. *Very good.*

"In the car, when we were fighting, you said something."

"I don't want to talk about that." Not today. Not after this.

"This, we have to talk about. Now." He gave me a sad smile. "You said that I love Samantha."

"Oh." That was what he wanted to talk about? Really? Today?

I'd said a lot on Monday that I really didn't want to relive. It had all been true, brutal honesty. But I still didn't want to rehash it. There was no fight left in my bones.

"I don't love Samantha." He framed my face again, making sure my eyes were locked on his. "I don't know if I ever really loved her. Not the way it should be."

My breath hitched.

Did that mean...

Before I could even finish that thought, the lobby door opened and Mateo walked inside.

"Blaze is sitting on the hood of his car parked out front."

Ugh. Major mood killer.

"Okay." I sighed. "Hopefully he'll give up and leave."

"I don't like that kid," Jasper said, letting go of my face to haul me against his chest again. "No complaining when I'm your shadow for the next few days."

"Sir, yes, sir." My arms were trapped so I couldn't give him my usual mock salute.

His chest shook with a quiet laugh.

I smiled, sagging against him. Then, because I was happy, I started crying again. "Sorry. I'm just...overwhelmed."

"I got you," he murmured, holding me tighter. "What do you need?"

You. "A nap."

Jasper let me go, snagging my hand. Then he led me to a couch, sitting against one armrest before smacking his thigh. "Come on."

"I need to work."

"Take five," Mateo said. "I've got the desk."

"Are you sure?"

He winked, then left Jasper and me alone.

I stared down at Jasper, at that lap I loved to curl into so much. Five minutes wouldn't hurt, right? So I sat down, snuggling into his chest, letting the warmth from his body wrap around me like a blanket.

"Five minutes."

He kissed my forehead. "Five minutes."

I was asleep in seconds.

He held me for an hour instead, knowing I needed more than minutes. When I woke, Mateo was still at the desk.

And Blaze was nowhere to be found.

CHAPTER 24

JASPER

Eloise popped the lid on her to-go cup of coffee and swept her purse from the counter. Then, like she did most mornings, she turned in a full circle. Two circles, actually. One spin to the right. One spin to the left.

"I'm forgetting something," she said.

"Whatever it is, I'll bring it to you later."

"Okay." She gave me a soft smile, her gaze trailing down my naked chest.

While she'd taken a shower and dressed for the day, I'd climbed out of bed and made coffee, only bothering to pull on a pair of sweats.

Her gaze lingered on my abs for a moment before her eyes shifted to my hands splayed on the island, those blues locking on my left. Her smile dimmed.

She was searching for the ring, wasn't she?

Eloise had been paying my ring finger more attention this past week, ever since that day in the hotel lobby a week ago when she'd fired Blaze. The day I'd told her the divorce papers had landed in the trash. When she'd mentioned the ring in the heat of the moment.

Had she been searching for it all this time? I hadn't noticed her staring at my hand, but maybe she'd hidden it better before Italy. Or maybe I'd just been oblivious.

But it was out there now, plaguing us both.

"You're going to the gym?" she asked, her gaze dropping to her coffee cup. When she looked up again, her smile was back in its beautiful glory.

"Yeah. Foster and I are meeting in half an hour."

"See you after?"

I nodded. "Want me to bring you lunch?"

"Yes, please." She rounded the corner, rising up on her toes for a kiss.

I bent, sweeping her into my arms and sealing my mouth over hers. Our tongues tangled in a lazy, slow dance, kissing until she had a pretty flush to her cheeks and my cock stretched my sweats.

Another morning, I'd peel away those black slacks and fuck her while she was bent over the counter. But she'd had a hectic week, and I knew she wanted to get to work. So I eased away, holding her for just another minute to bury my face in her hair and draw in my favorite scent.

She clung to me with her arms banded around my ribs and locked behind my back. "I'd better go."

"Yeah," I murmured, loosening my hold. With a kiss on her forehead, I followed her outside, standing on the porch to watch as she climbed in her car and waved before driving down the lane.

The morning air was warm and the forecast was calling for another hot July day. The scent of pinesap filled my nose. The river rushed in the distance and birds chirped as they swept through the trees. Sunbeams streamed through branches, casting everything in a yellow morning glow.

It should have snared my focus. This little corner of Montana, my little corner, had become a source of peace. Instead, I looked to my hand and sighed.

If Eloise had refused to wear the ring I'd bought her, it would have bothered me. Especially now, after all we'd gone through together.

The ring she'd given me was simple. Classic. A titanium band with polished edges and a matte center.

What the fuck were the odds that she'd pick the exact style ring that Sam had given me years ago?

When she'd given it to me, I'd almost thought it was a joke. Not that Eloise would ever know that it was the same, but they were identical.

The ring Eloise had bought had spent some time in my drawer upstairs, buried beneath my socks. I just hadn't been ready to wear a ring again. Especially when it had been so damn familiar.

I'd worn Samantha's ring.

And it had meant fuck all.

Didn't it mean more to Eloise that I was here? That she had me wrapped around her own ring finger?

Eloise Eden owned me.

I loved that woman.

I loved her in a way I hadn't even known existed. A soul-deep, undying love.

Wasn't it more important that I showed her how I felt? Every day. Every night. From the food I cooked, to the way I worshiped her body.

For fuck's sake, I cuddled. I let her sleep on top of me every goddamn night, didn't I?

It was just a ring.

With or without it, I was hers.

But she needed the ring, didn't she? She needed that symbol. So today, I'd drop it at the jewelry store to get resized. It was a little too tight.

Leaving the porch, I went inside to swap out my sweats for shorts and a clean T-shirt. Then I drove across town to Foster's gym.

"Hey." Foster sat in the center of the ring, stretching his hamstrings.

"Hi." I jerked up my chin, toeing off my shoes before joining him.

Stepping through the ropes always centered me. MMA fights were held in a cage but Foster had always preferred his daily training in a boxing ring, even when we'd lived in Vegas. I felt the same.

Something about the ring, the four corners, the smaller size, grounded me. It allowed me to shut out everything and everyone beyond these imaginary walls.

"How's it going?" he asked as I took a seat across from him, beginning the regular stretch routine.

"Good. You?"

"It's good. But I got an interesting call this morning. From that new kid making a name for himself in Vegas." Foster didn't need to clarify. We both knew it was the kid who'd tried to hire me. "He told me he approached you about a job. That you turned him down. I think he thought you were staying because of me. He must not know about Eloise."

When I'd gone to Vegas for that interview, I'd let Foster believe that I'd talked to the kid before Eloise and I had gotten married. That my trip to Vegas was more a courtesy than a serious inquiry.

"I told him I'd train him. He just had to relocate."

Foster grinned. "I'm glad you're staying. If you and Eloise had decided to move to Vegas, the Edens might have set up a roadblock on the highway."

I chuckled.

Maybe someday, if Eloise was all right with it, I'd tell him the whole story. I'd tell him about Vegas. About how Eloise and I had agreed to fake it.

Or maybe not.

Part of me liked that this secret was just ours.

"I need a job," I told Foster. Not for the money. I could live comfortably off my inheritance for the rest of my life. But I needed something to keep myself occupied.

"You have a job."

I gave him a flat look. "You're retired."

"So?" He shrugged, shoving up to his feet. Then he smacked his stomach. "Talia likes my abs. You can help me keep them."

I hopped up, reaching out a hand. "How about we just train as friends?"

"Not friends." He clasped my hand. "Brothers."

"Brothers." We were brothers, weren't we? Foster and I had been brothers long before I'd married Eloise. But damn, I liked that it was official. "All right. Let's get to work. Keep your woman happy." And mine too. Eloise liked the definition at my hips.

We spent the next two hours in the ring, sparring and doing drills. Neither of us needed an event, a championship fight, to push ourselves. We trained because it was the outlet we'd both come to rely upon. And when sweat drenched my shirt, when my legs were warm and my muscles loose, Foster and I returned to the mats to stretch and cool down.

"So what kind of job do you want?" he asked.

"Hell if I know." I wasn't even sure what kind of opportunities there were in Quincy. "For now, Eloise needs some help at the hotel."

The Fourth of July had been hectic this past week. The rodeo last weekend had been a unique experience, something I hadn't thought I'd enjoy. But we'd ended up having a great time. Eloise's excitement had been contagious. Even with her family there, I'd had fun—probably because I'd sat toward the end of our row with Foster on one side and Eloise on the other.

Even after the celebrations, Quincy was crawling with tourists. The hotel was swamped and that six-hour window between check-out and check-in was pure insanity.

Eloise had given me a crash course in housekeeping and running their industrial washers and dryers so I could contribute. It had been the right decision for her to fire Blaze, especially since she'd told me he caused more work than he actually accomplished. But she still had a part-time hole in her staff, which I had tried to help fill.

"It's good of you to help her," Foster said. "Talia said this was the busiest she's ever seen Quincy or the hotel."

"Happy to." It was the truth. I'd never been a man who needed the spotlight. At the moment, I was content to do whatever it took for Eloise to shine.

Was that my calling? I'd never felt like I had some grand purpose in life. I was a man content to help someone else achieve their dreams. First Foster. Then Eloise.

That sounded like a good plan for now.

"Speaking of the hotel," I said, shoving up to my feet. "I'd better head home and take a shower. Then get downtown to see what's happening."

"I think we're heading that way later." Foster stood too, following me out of the ring. "Talia wants to eat at Knuckles tonight. You guys want to join us?"

My first reaction was to say no. Cooking Eloise dinner before stealing her away to bed had become the highlight of my day. But maybe she'd like a date. "Yeah. Maybe. Let me talk to Eloise."

Foster nodded and lifted a hand, waving as I headed outside.

I drove home, hurried through a shower and threw on a pair of jeans and a black T-shirt. Then I snagged the ring from the drawer, shoving it in a pocket before I headed to the kitchen to pack a lunch for Eloise and me.

I was about to leave but something stopped me. I turned around in the space, taking in the counters. Had I forgotten something too?

"Huh." Strange. There was an odd twist in my gut, almost like a sense of dread.

I let the still house sink in. I listened for anything amiss— running water or an uncommon electrical buzz. But the A-frame was quiet. Normal.

Eloise's forgetfulness must have rubbed off. So I shook away the feeling and headed into town.

The only open parking spaces downtown were two in the alley behind The Eloise. I parked the Yukon and instead of going inside the hotel, I crossed the street, swinging by the jewelry store before heading next door to get in line at Eden Coffee.

Lyla looked as swamped as she had been all week, but her smile never wavered. Eloise did that too. If a visitor had a bad experience at the hotel, it wouldn't be because of my wife.

"Hey." Lyla let out a deep breath when it was my turn in line. "Oh my God, this day has been nonstop."

"Need anything?"

"No." She shook her head. "But thanks for asking. What can I get for you?"

"An iced coffee for Eloise."

"Coming right up." She smiled, then got to work. The moment Lyla slid the plastic to-go cup across the counter, she greeted her next customer.

I made my way across Main, glancing down the busy sidewalks.

Twenty feet from the hotel, that same strange feeling I'd felt at home hit. A niggle. A pit forming in my gut. I glanced around, feeling eyes on me, but there were people everywhere. And not a familiar face in the bunch.

It was that goddamn kid. Blaze. It wasn't only Eloise's busy workload that had kept me close to the hotel. It was that kid.

No one had seen him since the day Eloise had fired him last week. According to Anne, Blaze's mother had been mortified that he'd gotten fired and had grounded him for life.

Still, I didn't trust Blaze. I didn't like his obsession with Taylor. And I sure as fuck didn't like the look he'd given my wife.

Eloise was sitting at the desk when I walked into the lobby. Her fingers flew across her keyboard, her eyes narrowed in concentration. But when she looked up and saw me, that smile she gave me chased away any of the worry.

One look and I was instantly okay.

"You got me a coffee." She pressed her hand to her heart. "Best husband ever."

I chuckled, setting it and lunch beside the empty cup on her desk. Then I leaned in to drop a kiss to her cheek. "How was your morning?"

"Fine. How was Foster?"

"Good."

She looked me up and down. "No blood? No bruises?"

"Not today."

"Then Foster gets to live."

Only Eloise would take on Foster Madden, the Iron Fist, because he'd dared punch her husband.

Fuck, but I loved her. More and more each day.

"How about dinner tonight?" I asked.

"Don't we eat dinner every night?"

"Smart ass." I tickled her ribs, earning a yelp. "How about we go out to dinner?"

Eloise's jaw dropped. "Jasper Vale, are you asking me out on a date?"

"Well, you are my wife. Maybe it's time we went on a date."

Her eyes softened. "Say it again."

"Will you go out to dinner with me?"

"Not that. Call me your wife again."

"Wife."

Eloise put her hand on my cheek, leaning in for another kiss. "About this dinner."

"Knuckles?"

"Or...my parents invited us to the ranch." She tensed, probably expecting an instant rejection.

It was there, on the tip of my tongue, but I didn't want to hurt her feelings, so I held it back.

"We haven't talked about...you know," she said. The fight. "I've been thinking about everything you said. You made a lot of valid points. And I heard you. But, babe, your parents suck.

Mine don't."

I arched an eyebrow. She was right about my parents. Her own?

"They aren't perfect." Eloise held up her hands, probably because she knew exactly what I was thinking. "They don't claim to be. But they love me."

The Edens and I had that in common.

Son of a bitch. I was going to have to figure out how to live with them, wasn't I? No way I'd make her choose between us.

"Would it be so hard?" She placed her hand on my chest. "Unlocking your heart for my family?"

This woman.

She really didn't understand, did she?

This imaginary lock to my heart? I didn't have the key.

I'd handed it to her weeks ago.

"Okay. We'll go to dinner at the ra—"

Eloise launched herself into my arms, moving so fast I almost didn't catch her.

Almost.

"Thank you," she murmured against my neck.

"Say it like you mean it, El."

She giggled, catching my drift. Her lips found mine, and I got the thank you I wanted.

I was sucking on her lower lip when some outside awareness made me pull away. That same feeling crept beneath my skin, raising the hair on the back of my neck.

"What?" she asked, following my gaze toward the windows.

There was nothing but sunshine and smiles beyond the glass.

"Nothing." I shook the feeling away, then kissed the corner of her mouth. "Put me to work."

She gave me that adorable mock salute. "Sir, yes, sir."

CHAPTER 25

ELOISE

Jasper was asleep on his stomach, one knee raised as he hugged his pillow. Exactly how he'd looked when I'd slipped out of bed this morning to take a shower. The covers barely covered his ass, revealing those dimples above his cheeks and the rippled muscles of his back.

Warmth spread through my chest as I watched him sleep. It was still hard to believe this was really happening. That he was mine.

As much as I wanted to strip off my clothes and curl up against his naked body, work was waiting. So I padded across the bedroom, my feet sinking into the rug beneath the bed. Then I brushed the hair from his forehead.

"Bye, babe," I whispered.

His eyes stayed closed but he stretched out an arm, blindly reaching for me. When his hand skimmed my shirt, he fisted it, drawing me closer. A silent request for a kiss.

I was learning to read Jasper. To hear him even when he didn't speak.

So I kissed his stubbled cheek.

I love you.

Every day it got harder and harder not to say it aloud. Last night, after dinner at the ranch, I'd been so proud of how hard he'd tried that I'd almost said it on the way home.

Why hadn't I? Why was I holding back? Because I wanted Jasper to say it first? Because he still wouldn't wear a stupid wedding ring?

How many people had told Jasper they loved him?

Not enough. Shame on me for waiting.

"I love you."

Jasper's eyes popped open. A myriad of emotions flew through those dark irises. Happiness. Hesitation. Regret.

He wasn't ready to say it back. If the only person he'd said *I love you* to had been Samantha, then I didn't blame him for being scared.

That was okay. I'd wait.

For Jasper Vale, I'd wait until the end of my days.

I brushed that hair off his forehead again, then kissed his temple. "I gotta go. See you later."

"El, I..." He swallowed hard, his Adam's apple bobbing. His fist in my shirt tightened.

"I know, Jas."

I knew his parents had never taught him about love. I knew that Samantha's version of love had come with conditions and manipulations and limits.

Mine did not. He'd realize that. If I told him enough, he'd learn what true love looked like.

So I stood, crossing the bedroom, giving him the time to let those words sink in. To feel them. If I said them enough, he'd realize they weren't all that terrifying.

A lightness settled into my bones as I left the A-frame. My mental to-do list reshuffled as I drove into town, making room for a new item at the top.

Change my last name.

"Eloise Vale."

Yeah, I liked the sound of that.

As I eased into a parking space behind the hotel, Knox pulled up beside me.

"Morning," he said, climbing out of his truck.

"Hi." I fell in step beside my brother, following him inside. Normally, Knox was in before dawn to start on kitchen prep. "Late start today?"

"The boys had a bad night."

"Sorry."

"Don't be. I'm not." He threw his arm around my shoulders. Knox would skip sleep for a decade if it meant time with Memphis and his sons. "Dinner was fun last night."

"Yeah." Fun might be a stretch, but it had been exponentially better than Jasper's first trip to the ranch.

Not everyone had been able to come to Mom and Dad's last night. Griffin and Winn had stayed home because Emma hadn't been feeling well. Lyla had been exhausted from a slog of long hours and hadn't wanted to drive out. And Foster and Talia had gone on a date together, so it had just been my parents, Mateo and Knox's family.

It had been quieter, but Jasper had engaged in the conversation. He'd talked to Memphis mostly, both of them trading stories about growing up on the East Coast. When Dad had asked how he'd met Foster, he'd shared their whole story, including how he'd gotten into martial arts in high school. To my mother, he'd been polite, even though I knew he was still irritated about the Blaze situation.

Jasper had mostly spoken when spoken to. But that was just

who he was. Different than any of the guys I'd brought home or dated before. My family would learn that about him. Like me, they'd learn to read his silent cues.

Knox and I walked inside the hotel, and when we reached the doors for Knuckles, he retreated to his kitchen while I headed for the desk to relieve my night clerk.

The morning went by in a blur of check-outs and housekeeping assignments. By eleven o'clock, I felt like I'd run three miles.

I'd just finished checking out a couple from California when the lobby doors opened and Jasper strode inside.

My mouth watered.

He was wearing that baseball hat again along with a white T-shirt and a pair of cargo shorts. The ends of his hair beneath the cap were curled and damp because he'd probably gone to the gym before heading home for a shower.

"Wow," I whispered. Seriously, my husband was freaking hot.

The corner of his mouth turned up as he rounded the desk. "Hi, angel."

"I really like you in that hat."

He bent, brushing his lips to my forehead. "I'll wear it for you later." *And nothing else.*

The unspoken promise caused a shiver to roll down my spine. "Yes, please."

Jasper leaned against the desk, glancing around the lobby.

Maybe it should have been awkward after this morning, but it wasn't. Probably because I didn't regret telling him how I felt.

"How's the morning going?" he asked.

"Busy." I slumped in my seat. "But everyone is checked out, so I can catch my breath."

"What can I help with?"

"The lobby is a mess." There was a crumpled napkin on the table by the fireplace. The magazines were scattered everywhere and the chairs were askew because a couple this morning had repositioned them while they'd been visiting.

"I'll take care of it," he said.

"You don't have to."

He shrugged. "I'm not doing anything else."

"You never told me what you decided with that fighter in Vegas. What did you decide?"

For weeks, I'd been terrified to ask him about that interview. So I'd just blocked it out and let my hectic schedule overshadow my fears. But so much had changed this past week. And after this morning, asking wasn't so terrifying anymore, not when I had a fairly good idea of his answer.

"I told him that I'd train him."

Wait. What? Well, that wasn't the answer I'd expected. He'd really taken that job? Did that mean he'd be spending part of his time in Nevada? "Oh."

"But he'd have to move to Montana."

The air rushed from my lungs as he smirked.

"Jerk." I poked his rib with a finger.

Jasper grinned. "I'll have to find something to do eventually. For now, I'll help around here. You good with that?"

"Very." I nodded. "Thank you."

"Welcome." He kissed my cheek, then rounded the desk, going to straighten up the lobby.

My computer chimed with an incoming email, but I ignored it, content to watch Jasper for a minute.

The lobby door opened, forcing my gaze away from Jasper's ass.

Winn walked inside, waving to Jasper before she came around the desk for a hug. "Hi."

"Hey. What are you up to?"

"Lunch with Pops."

Her grandfather, Covie, was the former mayor of Quincy and a regular at Knuckles.

"Working today?" I asked, taking in the badge and gun holstered on her hip.

"Yes. Catch-up from the Fourth."

"Same," I said as the elevator doors slid open and two guests made their way over.

"I'll let you get back to work," Winn said, shifting out of the way.

The guests needed a recommendation for a hiking trail, so I plucked one of the area maps from the drawer where I kept them, spreading it out on the counter and circling a few of my most recommended spots.

With the map in hand, they headed outside into the summer sunshine.

Covie had come in while I'd been talking with the guests. He and Winn were chatting with a local man who'd also probably come in for lunch too.

A woman in a floppy hat was talking on the phone on the opposite end of the room. This was her first stay at The Eloise, but she'd already booked a room for next summer.

My fingertips skimmed the desk as I took it all in, breathing in the scent of the lobby. Of the sunshine and fresh air that wafted inside every time the door opened.

No matter whose name was on the deed, this hotel would always be mine. Like the man tossing an empty to-go coffee cup in the trash.

Maybe the reason I'd stayed married to Jasper hadn't been because of this hotel. It hadn't been to go to that wedding in Italy. Maybe I'd stayed with Jasper because, deep down, I'd glimpsed something in him in Vegas.

Something that had resonated in my heart, and even though I hadn't been able to see it yet, I also hadn't been able to let him go.

Winn and Covie walked toward Jasper, Winn making introductions.

The doors opened and Frannie Jones and Clarissa Fitzgerald walked inside, two local girls I'd known for ages. They were a year younger than Mateo and both had crushed on him endlessly in high school.

Other than in passing, I hadn't seen them much these past couple years. But now that news of Mateo's return had spread, they'd probably be stopping by The Eloise more often, hoping to snag his notice, just like in high school.

Clarissa scanned the lobby, searching for my brother, but when her eyes landed on Jasper, she did a double take. Her cheeks flushed and she leaned in to whisper something in Fran's ear.

Then Fran's gaze shot straight to Jasper too.

I rolled my eyes and rounded the counter as they neared.

"Hey, Eloise." Fran pulled me into a hug.

Clarissa was still staring at Jasper as he talked to Winn and Covie.

"Hey," I said. "What are you guys up to today?"

"Lunch at Knuckles."

"Fun. Hey, Clarissa."

She tore her eyes from Jasper's face. "Hi. Um, who is that?"

"My husband."

She blinked, and as my statement settled in, her eyes widened. "Oh. I heard you got married. I just... I haven't seen you guys around town."

"Yep, that's him."

Clarissa gave me an exaggerated frown. "Busted. Sorry."

"It's fine." I laughed, waving it off. "I check him out all the time too."

"Well, before I embarrass myself even more, we're going to lunch." Clarissa looped her arm with Fran's and together, they headed for the restaurant.

I shifted past the desk, about to go and say hello to Covie myself, but when I looked over, Jasper was shoving past Winn.

His face was hard, his eyes...frantic.

I froze.

Time slowed.

Jasper ran, his body an explosion as he sprinted across the lobby.

Behind him, Winn was reaching for her gun.

Why was she reaching for her gun?

My heart jumped, my eyes tracking in the same direction as hers.

And there, by the front door, was Blaze.

Everything clicked at once.

Jasper's fear.

Winn's shout to drop it.

The pistol Blaze had lifted and aimed my way.

One moment, I was standing on my own two feet.

The next, chaos.

My body slammed into the floor, the wind knocked entirely out of my lungs.

Gunfire filled the lobby, the noise so loud it drowned out

the screams and shouts.

Then…quiet.

A silence so eerie it chilled me to the core.

Jasper's body covered mine. He'd slammed into me so hard that we'd flown behind the counter, skidding to a stop.

Warmth spread against my shoulder. Wet warmth.

Blood.

"Jasper," I whispered, ice flooding my veins.

He didn't move. His body was hard and so heavy against mine it was hard to breathe.

Beyond the counter, people were crying. Footsteps pounded on the floor. But I blocked it all out, shifting back and forth, trying to dislodge Jasper. Why wasn't he moving?

"Jasper." My voice was panicked. I leaned up as far as my neck would stretch, trying to see where he was hurt. Red spread through the white cotton of his shirt, all across his shoulder. "Jasper."

He didn't move. He didn't breathe.

My gaze caught on his hand, pressed against the floor at our sides.

His left hand.

And on his finger, the wedding band I'd given him weeks ago.

CHAPTER 26

JASPER

Five shots.

I'd heard five shots go off as I'd tackled Eloise to the floor. Then...nothing. For a long moment, not a sound.

But beyond the counter, people were moving now. Footsteps. Crying. Screaming. The doors had opened and people were shouting outside, calling for help.

"Jasper." Eloise shook me, squirming beneath me.

I didn't budge.

Was Blaze still out there? How long until he rounded the counter to come for Eloise? Part of me wanted to risk it. To look around and see if there was a way to get her the hell out of this hotel. But I stayed huddled on top of her, hoping that my body would be enough to shield hers.

"Jasper," she screamed in my ear.

I was crushing her. But I didn't move.

"Winn!" Eloise shouted.

My hold on her only tightened, my frame molding around hers like I was trying to tuck her into my pocket.

At my movement, Eloise stilled. "Jas? Oh my God. You're bleeding. You have to move. You have to get up. I need to get you help."

Bleeding? The pain registered a moment later. The burning in my shoulder. The blood, soaking my shirt.

Fuck.

That motherfucker had tried to kill Eloise.

I shoved up, ignoring the screaming in my shoulder. The world tipped upside down, spinning until it had righted itself again.

"Are you hurt?" Safe behind the counter, I used my good arm to start checking every inch of her body.

Eloise scrambled to her knees, her hands going to the blood. Her blue eyes flooded. "Oh my God. Your shoulder. Winn!"

A moment later, Winn rounded the counter, her gun gripped in her hands.

"Blaze?" I asked.

Winn shook her head, her expression hard but grim. A cop doing what she'd been trained to do. To lock it down. To help others.

"Put pressure on it, Eloise." Winn's voice was calm. Firm. "Until an ambulance gets here, just keep pressure on it."

Eloise nodded, the tears beginning to streak down her face as she pressed her hands to the hole in my shoulder. One side where the bullet had gone in. And the other where the bullet had come out.

I hissed, the pain beginning to blur the edges of my mind. "Are you okay?"

"He shot you." Her voice trembled. "He shot you."

But he hadn't shot her.

I sagged against the counter, the crash coming.

Eloise was okay. She was okay.

If I had lost her today, if I hadn't been fast enough…

Fuck, I could have lost her.

"I love you," I whispered.

A sob escaped her mouth. Her hands clamped my shoulder so hard I winced, but with the tears streaming down her face, she didn't notice. "Why did you do that?"

I tried to lift my arm but it wouldn't work.

Why wouldn't it work?

Oh, yeah. That motherfucker had shot me. Was Blaze dead?

"Jasper, look at me." Eloise moved so close to my face that my eyes crossed. "Stay with me."

"Where else would I be?"

She pressed her forehead to mine, then kissed my mouth, her salty tears lingering on my lips. "I love you. Don't close your eyes."

"Okay," I murmured and closed my eyes. My body was going into shock. The adrenaline. The blood. "Love you, El."

The world faded in and out. EMTs. An ambulance. Talia wearing her hospital scrubs. Pain. Getting shot hurt like a bitch. It all faded in and out with a blur.

Everything but Eloise.

Until I was in a hospital bed and she finally let me close my eyes.

When I woke up, minutes or hours later, darkness had settled beyond the windows. And asleep beside me in the narrow bed, my wife.

Cuddling.

I closed my eyes.

And pulled her closer.

CHAPTER 27

JASPER

Eloise held up a hand, stopping me from crossing the loft. Her gaze darted between me and my target.

The bed.

"Don't you dare."

"I'm fine." I took a step, ready to rumple the covers she'd so crisply made while I'd been in the shower.

"Jasper," she warned. "You're not fine. You got shot."

"Two weeks ago."

Her mouth pursed in a thin line.

I took another step.

"I mean it. I'm not having sex with you. You're hurt."

"I'm not hurt."

Our glares locked in the same standoff we'd been having for the past two days.

At my checkup earlier this week, Talia had given me the all clear for light activity. But apparently, Eloise considered sex too strenuous.

So far, I'd let her thwart my advances. But enough was enough. My body ached and it had nothing to do with my shoulder.

With two long strides, I closed the distance between us, wrapping my good arm around her shoulders, trapping her before she could get away.

Her mouth was open, her protest ready.

I stopped it by slamming my lips on hers, sliding my tongue inside. One lick and she melted.

She sank into the kiss, fluttering her tongue against my own before her arms wrapped around my waist.

Fucking finally. I kissed her until her lips were swollen. Until she had that pretty flush to her cheeks. Then I let her go, dropping my forehead to hers.

"See? I'm okay."

"You got shot."

"But you didn't."

She sagged against me, burrowing into my chest as she drew in a long inhale.

"I miss fucking my wife."

"I miss you too. But…we'll be late."

I growled. "We'll be fast." After two weeks of not having her, there was no chance I'd last.

"Tonight," she promised. "When we get back, you can have your way with me. As long as you promise to take it easy."

"Fine by me. You can do all the work."

It had been two excruciating weeks, and I was desperate for sex with Eloise. I needed that physical connection. A reminder that we were good. Alive.

I dropped my forehead to hers, the image of Blaze flashing in my mind. His face was one I'd never forget. I'd been seeing him in my nightmares for two weeks. In those dreams, I hadn't made it in time. I'd wake up, panicked. Then I'd feel her against me, sleeping soundly, cuddled close.

Maybe one of these days I'd tell Foster about the dreams. Confess them to someone. As much as Eloise had become my safe haven, this was one story I'd keep from her. She had her own demons to fight from the shooting.

"I love you," she murmured.

"Love you too."

It was still new, hearing it. Saying it. But every time, those words sank a little deeper. Lingered a little longer. By the time we were old and gray, they'd be tattooed on my bones.

We stood together in the middle of the loft, holding tight for a few moments. Then she eased away. "We'd better go."

"All right." I kissed her hair, then followed her downstairs.

Eloise snagged her keys and the veggie tray we'd made earlier from the kitchen, then we headed outside, climbing in her car.

In the past two weeks, she hadn't been out of my sight for more than minutes at a time. Otherwise, we'd been inseparable.

And since she wanted to go to dinner at the ranch tonight, I was riding shotgun. Not that I minded.

Over the past two weeks, the Edens had closed ranks.

Talia had required I stay at the hospital for a few days after the shooting, giving my wound a jumpstart on healing and to monitor it for any sign of infection. Eloise had stayed the entire time, setting up camp in my room. Her parents had been the ones to bring us clean clothes, food and whatever else we'd needed.

Since we'd come home to the A-frame, Anne had visited every day. She'd assigned herself chores, laundry, cleaning and cooking. Eloise had insisted her mom hadn't needed to help, but Anne hadn't listened. Personally, I was grateful for the cooking. No way Eloise would have let me in the kitchen and

I'd never liked peanut butter and jelly.

Harrison had tagged along with Anne yesterday, bringing along enough split firewood to last us five years. Then he'd stacked it outside by the shop.

Eloise's siblings had, well…bombarded us.

I'd thought their steady stream of visits would stop once we left the hospital. If anything, it had gotten worse.

Today was the first time we hadn't had a guest. And that was just because we were all congregating at the ranch.

Knox and Lyla had brought us enough food to last a month. Talia and Foster came at least twice a day. Griffin stopped by each morning and Winn swung over each evening. Mateo had been our least frequent visitor, but that was because he'd taken over at the hotel. Instead of stopping by, he called Eloise every two hours, asking questions and keeping her involved.

We hadn't been to the hotel since the shooting.

That would come. Later.

Eloise wasn't ready. Neither was I.

For now, it was in good hands and when Eloise was ready to return, I'd be right by her side.

If she decided to return.

There was a chance that Blaze had stolen her happiness from that building. He'd fired off three shots that day. Two had missed wide. The third had gone through my shoulder.

The fourth and fifth shots I'd heard had been Winn. She'd shot Blaze straight through the heart.

Not a day would go by that I wasn't grateful for Winslow Eden. She'd saved lives. She'd saved Eloise. Had she not been there, well…there wasn't a doubt in my mind that Blaze had come with the intention to murder.

The week after the shooting, Winn had come over to tell us

about what had happened that day. The whole story.

The investigation was technically ongoing, but Winn had shared it was only documentation at this point. They'd searched Blaze's computer to find some hidden video accounts. He'd recorded himself killing animals. His neighbor's puppy. His own cat.

Winn had told us there'd been countless videos on his phone with rants about how he hated his mother. How he blamed her for divorcing his father. How his father should have hit her harder.

None of us had realized that Lydia had been abused by her ex. But I suspected that abuse had also translated to Blaze. Maybe physically. Definitely mentally and emotionally.

Combined with that at home, he'd been bullied at his old school in Missoula. In other videos, he'd made lists of people he'd be killing one day. He'd talked about how he'd take guns into the school. Which kids he'd shoot first.

Then there'd been the videos from Quincy. There was one of the A-frame dated the day before the shooting. Another of Eloise and me in the hotel lobby. Three of Eloise walking into work and one of me taking her a coffee. I hadn't needed to see them. Just the mention had made my blood run cold.

No one would ever know exactly what had transpired, but that day two weeks ago, Blaze had killed his mother. They'd found Lydia in her kitchen, shot in the back of the head. From there, it was assumed that Blaze had come to the hotel.

I shuddered, knowing just how close I'd been to losing Eloise.

"Hey." She reached her hand across the console.

I took it, lacing our fingers together. "Hey."

Her thumb touched my ring, then she focused on the road.

We'd found this uncanny ability to know when the other person was thinking about that day. So we'd touch each other, remind each other that we were here. Together. Living.

It was a strange feeling, being grateful that a troubled kid was dead. Even stranger, I was grateful that he'd come into The Eloise. That he'd shot me instead of a school full of children in Missoula.

I still wasn't sure how to line up those emotions. Yesterday, when Eloise had lain down for a nap, I'd started researching therapists.

We hadn't talked much about the shooting either. Another conversation shelved for later. But when we were ready, we'd need help. I wouldn't let this fester. I wouldn't let this trauma come between us.

"Do you think Winn is okay?" I asked as we hit the highway, heading for the ranch.

"I think this will weigh on her." Eloise gave me a sad smile. "But she knows she didn't have another choice. And she has Griffin."

She had me too. If she needed anything, I'd be there in a heartbeat.

I owed Winn my life. Eloise's life.

They were one and the same.

While everyone had come together after the shooting, crowding around us at the A-frame, the ordeal had rattled the Edens. Tonight's dinner was just another excuse to pull together.

It was still strange, being a part of their family.

But they were growing on me.

The drive to the ranch was quiet, but the moment we parked, her parents flew out of the house.

Harrison opened my car door before I could even touch the

handle. "Hey, Jasper. Thanks for coming out."

"Glad to be here." It was the truth.

I looked past his shoulder to see Griffin and Winn on the porch. Winn was holding their daughter on her hip while Griff carried their son.

Closing ranks. Sticking close.

The Edens waded through thick and thin together, didn't they?

I liked that.

Anne collected the veggie tray from the back seat, tucking it in one arm while the other tugged Eloise into a hug. As she pulled away, Anne had tears in her eyes. So did Eloise.

"Come on inside," Anne said, leading the way to the wraparound porch.

I was about to follow when Harrison stepped in front of me.

He extended his hand, but when I shook it, he pulled me into a hug. A hug so fierce it pinched my shoulder, but I didn't let the pain show. "Thank you. Realized today I hadn't said that yet."

Today. He hadn't said that to me yet, *today*.

It was the hundredth time he'd thanked me in the past two weeks. I suspected it wouldn't be the last either.

But for his daughter, for my wife, I'd take every bullet in the world.

He let me go, taking me in head to toe. His eyes were misty, much like his wife's. He swallowed hard, then nodded for me to follow him inside, where everyone had already congregated in the kitchen and dining room.

Foster and Talia were at the island, sharing their list of baby names.

Knox was in the kitchen with Drake seated on the counter

as his helper while Memphis paced the room, rocking their baby, who slept in her arms.

Griffin and Harrison launched into a discussion about the ranch—something about the corral design.

Mateo stole Emma from Winn, tossing his niece in the air. Her giggle carried above the rest of the conversation.

The house was insanity. Seven different conversations were happening at once. It had been like this the first time I'd come out here too, the noise shocking, but to everyone else, it just seemed…normal.

Anne and Eloise huddled around the fridge, pulling out drinks and offering beers and glasses of wine.

Lyla appeared at my side, standing with me in the periphery to take everyone in. "Think you can handle this family?"

"Honestly? No." I chuckled. This was a far cry from the household where I'd been raised.

But as I looked to Eloise, as I saw the kids, the growing family, I wouldn't want anything else for her.

For whatever family we might have one day.

"You'll figure it out," Lyla said. "You're stuck with us now."

"I am. You good with that?"

"Definitely. I think it was divine intervention that I never worked up the courage to ask you on a date."

"Why do you say that?"

She smirked. "You would have always fallen in love with my sister. And I hate love triangles."

I laughed, my own noise mixing with the rest. Oddly enough, it fit, didn't it?

CHAPTER 28

ELOISE

A couple walked into the hotel, stealing my attention from my computer.

For the past month, every time the lobby doors opened, I held my breath. Tension crept into my shoulders, drawing them toward my ears.

Jasper, seated in the chair beside mine, reached over and covered my hand with his.

The tension ebbed. I released the air in my lungs.

The smile I gave the couple wasn't as forced as my smiles from yesterday. Or the day before that. Or the day before that.

It had been over a month since the shooting. When I looked at the floor beneath this counter, I could still see Jasper's blood. I could still hear the boom of guns firing. The terrified screams. The bullet holes in the wall behind me had been patched, but if I looked carefully enough, I could still find them.

But day by day, it was getting easier. Therapy had helped. That, and Jasper hadn't left my side.

The day I'd decided it was time to come back to work, he'd come along. I'd assumed he'd leave once I was settled. Instead, he'd found his own chair, the matching partner to the one I'd sat on for years. It had been in the closet of my neglected office. He'd hauled it out and had been sitting in it ever since.

At times, he'd help with hotel work, like scheduling or payroll. Mostly, he read while I worked.

Who knew a man reading could be so sexy? Considering everything Jasper did was attractive, I shouldn't have been surprised. This winter, if we had a string of quiet days, I hoped I could convince him to read aloud to me. But the reading would have to wait. At the moment, we were still swamped.

The shooting had rocked Quincy. It was something our small town wouldn't soon forget.

I'd thought traffic at the hotel would slow down. That people would fear this lobby. The first week had been slower. There'd been some cancelations. But then it had ramped up like nothing had happened.

Plus we'd had an influx of local traffic, people who'd come in to gawk and see if they could spot the bullet holes. Those visits annoyed the shit out of me—and Jasper. But mostly, people would come in to give me their best and meet our local hero.

My handsome husband. The man who'd leapt in front of a bullet for his wife.

There weren't many people in Quincy who didn't know the name Jasper Vale. Not anymore. Much to his dismay, he was a celebrity now. Everywhere we went, he'd be approached.

Eventually, that spotlight would fade, but it would take time. Sitting at the desk certainly wasn't helping him blend into the background. Yet he sat here all the same. Not just for my sake. But his too.

We were finding our way through this together.

The doors opened again, but with his hand over mine, I didn't have the same knee-jerk reaction. Instead I looked up and smiled as my parents walked inside.

"Hey, guys." I hopped off my chair, rounding the desk to hug Mom and Dad. "What are you up to today?"

"Errands." Dad went to Jasper, clapping him on the shoulder. "I tried those stretch bands this morning. Worked great. My shoulder already feels better."

Jasper dipped his chin. "Glad it worked."

Apparently, Dad had tweaked his shoulder trying to lift an old tractor tire by himself. When he'd complained, Jasper had given him some elastic bands and shown him some stretches to do that might relieve the ache.

Of all the people in my family I'd thought would warm to Jasper first, Dad would have been my very last guess.

Then again, Jasper had taken a bullet for me. Dad would do just about anything, including faking an injury so he could have an excuse to spend time with his son-in-law. To get to know the man I loved.

"Do you have a minute to talk?" I asked. There was something I'd wanted to visit with them about all week. "Maybe we could get some lunch?"

"I could eat." Dad patted his stomach.

"Me too." My stomach had been growling for almost an hour. I blamed that on Jasper. We'd had a rushed breakfast because we'd gotten distracted by sex on the dining room table.

If our sex life had been invigorating before, now that we weren't faking anything, we were insatiable. He teased that since he was here at the hotel instead of working out with Foster, it was my job to make sure he stayed in shape.

I took my job seriously.

"Let me just find someone to sit here for me," I said, picking up the phone to call a housekeeper.

The minute the desk was covered, I took Jasper's hand, the two of us following my parents into Knuckles.

The restaurant was bustling with activity. Knox was probably scrambling in the kitchen, working fast to feed the Friday lunch crowd. The hostess seated us at a booth in the back, one reserved solely for my family, and handed over the lunch menus.

"Should we eat first? Or talk?" Dad asked.

"Talk." Hungry as I was, it was time to have this conversation. Maybe I should have been nervous, but this discussion had been a long time coming. And no matter the outcome, I'd have Jasper.

"What's up?" Mom asked.

"The hotel."

My parents shared a look. Dad's grin faded as he leaned his forearms on the table. It was the serious posture he'd assume whenever he had bad news. "It's been a hard summer."

I nodded. "Yes, it has been."

"Your mother and I would understand if you wanted to try something different. If you wanted to leave the hotel."

After the shooting, I'd considered it. Especially those first few days back at work when I'd hated every second, forcing smiles and pretending like the world was only sunshine and rainbows. When I'd had to stare at the spot where a kid had died.

The kid who would have murdered me because I'd fired him from a part-time job.

The Eloise was…mine. Good and bad, this hotel was still my dream. And I wouldn't let anyone steal that from me.

"I want the hotel." I squared my shoulders, sitting taller. Beneath the table, Jasper's hand squeezed my thigh. "I understand why you weren't ready to give it to me a few years ago, but a lot has changed. We're flourishing. I've proved myself time and time again. It's time to take the next step. If you're not ready for that or if you've changed your mind about giving it to me, then I'm going to step down as manager. Effective immediately."

Mom and Dad sat back, both a little surprised. Even I was a little surprised. I couldn't remember a time in recent years when I'd demanded anything from my parents. Certainly not a hotel.

But I'd spent the past few weeks thinking a lot about this situation. About my family. Mom and Dad hadn't made Griffin or Knox jump through hoop after hoop to inherit their businesses. So I was done jumping to earn mine.

It would break my heart if they said no. But if that was their decision, I had a husband who'd help me glue the pieces together.

Dad relaxed, then grinned at Jasper.

Mom shifted, pulling out a folder from her purse. Then she unfolded the top flap, pulling out a stack of crisp, white papers. She smiled as she slid them across the table. "We've had these drawn up for a while, but with the shooting, we wanted to give you time."

Wait. This was it? Already? I'd planned for this to get awkward and uncomfortable. Not to just…get a hotel.

"Read through the document," Dad said. "Let us know if you have any questions. Our lawyer drafted it up, similar to how we transferred the ranch to Griffin. But if you want to hire your own attorney to review it, that will be fine. If you're good with everything, we've already signed it. You just need to sign it too."

I turned to Jasper.

He was smiling.

"You knew."

"Yeah."

Mom and Dad slid out of the booth. "We'll leave you two alone to talk."

"What about lunch?" I asked.

Mom took Dad's hand. "We'll go bug Knox in the kitchen."

"We're proud of you," Dad said before they walked away.

"Did that just happen?" I whispered to Jasper.

"Yeah, angel."

"I didn't expect it *today*." I looked at the papers. I skimmed the top sheet with a fingertip. Maybe part of me hadn't expected it at all. "What if I fail?"

"You won't." His confidence was unwavering.

"What if I do?"

His hand cupped my cheek, forcing my gaze to his. "Do you think I'd let you fail?"

"No." I leaned into his touch.

From the moment we'd started this adventure, standing beside that fountain, he'd been by my side. The ups and downs. The good and bad.

Husband and wife.

"I own a hotel."

He chuckled. "You own a hotel."

"Oh my God, I own a hotel. My hotel."

Jasper tucked a lock of hair behind my ear. "Dream come true?"

Only because he was here. "And then some."

EPILOGUE

ELOISE

ONE MONTH LATER...

"I'm staging an intervention."

"Huh?" Lyla asked from across the counter at Eden Coffee.

"I'm kicking you out."

She blinked.

"Of here. Right now. You have to leave."

Lyla studied my face, then looked to Jasper at my side. "Is she drunk?"

"I'm staying out of this. Good luck, Lyla." He bent to kiss my hair, then walked to a table against the wall, taking a seat.

Jasper didn't approve of this idea I'd concocted at breakfast. Mostly because it was supposed to be our day off, and instead of being at the coffee shop, he wanted to spend it celebrating.

But he'd let me drag him downtown anyway. Probably because he knew that I was still coming to terms with everything that had happened last night.

After missing my period, I'd taken a pregnancy test after dinner. He'd almost cried when I'd handed him that positive stick. Or maybe I'd just imagined the sheen of tears in his eyes. I couldn't exactly be sure. I'd been a hot mess, bouncing between panicked hysterics and joyous laughter, crying enough for us both.

I was still utterly freaked. Neither Jasper nor I had planned on this, and my birth control's epic failure had instantly changed our plans. The idea of motherhood—when I'd just taken over the hotel, when Jasper and I had finally settled into our marriage—was terrifying. Exciting.

My emotions were volleying between happy and scared like a ping-pong ball, so instead of dealing with my fears, I was here, harassing Lyla instead.

"You've worked one hundred days in a row," I told her. "Yes, I counted. You haven't taken a day off since that Sunday in April when you went to Missoula to get your hair cut."

She scoffed. "I've taken other days off since then."

I arched an eyebrow. "Oh, really? When?"

She thought about it for a moment, then huffed. "What are you, the work police? Who are you to talk, anyway? You're always at the hotel. Go away. I'm busy."

"Nope." I planted my hands on my hips. "One afternoon. That's all I'm asking for. You leave here for one afternoon and do something non work related."

"Why?"

I gave her a sad smile. "Because I'm worried about you. I don't want you to burn yourself out."

"I won't."

"But you might." I clasped my hands together. "Please? Just take the rest of the day off so I can stop worrying."

"I can't just leave, Eloise."

"Why not?" I waved to Crystal, Lyla's barista, as she came

out of the kitchen carrying a fresh tray of scones. "Crystal is here. Jasper and I will hang out and help close."

Now that the summer rush was behind us, Wednesdays were slow in downtown Quincy. If there was ever a day for Lyla to cut out early, it was now.

"Go home," I said. "Relax."

"I can't go home," Lyla said. "If I do, I'll think of everything that needs to get done and I'll come right back."

Not all that long ago, when I'd lived in my rental a couple blocks away, I'd been the same way with the hotel. It had taken Jasper to solve that problem. Every night, I looked forward to going home. And while there were always things on my mind, it was easier to ignore them, to save them for the next day. Another in the endless string of perks that came with a sexy husband who kept my mind occupied.

"You could go to a movie," I suggested.

"I don't feel like popcorn. Last time I was there I ate too much and it gave me a stomachache."

"Then don't get popcorn."

"Then what's the fun in going to a movie?"

The movie. I rolled my eyes. "You're exhausting. Go for a hike then. You love hiking, and I know you hardly went this summer. It's a beautiful day. Get some fresh air. Disconnect. Do anything. Just leave this building until tomorrow morning."

"Why?" she whined. "I like it here. Let me stay. I'll make you something yummy. Chocolate croissants?"

"Tempting. But no." I shook my head. "This job is becoming your personality."

She scrunched up her nose. "Harsh."

"You came into the hotel on Monday and asked if you could get me anything else. In my building. You serve and wait on people every day. Just...for one afternoon, do something for you."

Lyla groaned. "You're not going to leave me alone until I agree, are you?"

"Nope."

"Fine. I'll go for a hike or whatever."

"Yay. Thank you." I clasped my hands in front of me to keep from clapping. "Maybe you'll meet your dream guy while you're out hiking."

"I'm starting to think my dream guy doesn't exist." She untied her apron. "You'll call me if something goes wrong."

"Yes."

"There's plenty of food in the kitchen, but if for any reason cooking is required—"

I held up my hand. "I promise not to go anywhere near an oven. That's why I brought Jasper. Or I'll ask Crystal."

She glanced around, almost like she expected the coffee shop's walls to rescue her. Until she must have realized that, just maybe, I was right. "All right. You win. I'll go. Happy now?"

"Yep." I waited until she disappeared to the kitchen before I fist pumped.

"Thank you," Crystal mouthed, checking over her shoulder to make sure Lyla was gone. Then she leaned in closer. "You guys don't need to stick around. I'm just fine on my own."

"Oh, we don't mind." I shrugged. If it would make Lyla feel better that we were here to help close and clean up for the day, we'd stay. "But we might wander around for a while if you don't mind."

"Fine by me."

It had been months since I'd walked aimlessly up and down Quincy's sidewalks. Not since before the summer rush.

So I waited to shoo Lyla out the back door, lingering on the threshold to make sure she actually got in her car and drove away. Then I found Jasper at his table. "Feel like taking a walk?"

"Sure." He stood and took my hand, leading me out of the coffee shop.

Like I'd told Lyla, it was a beautiful day. The air was beginning to cool. The leaves were just barely tinted with yellow. Fall was never a long season in Montana. Maybe that was why I liked it so much. You had to appreciate it while it lasted.

"You okay?" Jasper asked as we settled into an easy stroll.

"I don't know. We're having a baby. Are you?"

Jasper clasped my hand tighter, leaning down to kiss my hair. "I'm good, angel."

"Then I'll be good too."

We walked for a while, holding hands, staring into windows and smiling at the people we passed. When we reached the end of the block, Jasper turned us around and we meandered back toward Eden Coffee.

"Will you marry me?"

Wait. What? I stopped, forcing him to stop too. No way I'd heard that right. "Say that again."

"Will you marry me?"

I reached up and felt his forehead with the back of my hand. "Are you sick?"

Jasper chuckled, his eyes crinkling at the sides. "Are you going to answer me?"

"I already married you."

"But do you want a wedding? A real wedding. Have a party. Invite your family. Have your dad walk you down the aisle. All that?"

Oh. Would I marry him? Did I want the fancy ceremony

and lavish party?

I'd thought so. Once. But if we had a wedding, it would overshadow our night at the Clover Chapel. A night that was as imperfect as it was beautiful. The idea of erasing it made my heart sink.

"Do you?" I asked Jasper.

Maybe he wanted a wedding. A new memory to conceal the old. A wedding not tainted by his ugly ex-wife.

"No." He shook his head. "I don't want a wedding. But if you want to wear a white gown, if you want me in a tux, just say the word."

We didn't need a gown or a tux.

Our love story wasn't typical. It certainly wasn't what I'd imagined as a little girl. But it was ours.

"No wedding. But I'd take a honeymoon."

"Deal." Jasper clasped my hand again, holding it tight. Holding it the way Dad held Mom's. Then he started us down the sidewalk again. "Where do you want to go?"

A thousand places came to mind. They were all from that list I'd created as a kid with Mom, places that our hotel guests called home.

Where did I want to go? Anywhere. I'd go anywhere with Jasper.

I lifted our clasped hands, bringing his knuckles to my mouth for a kiss. "Surprise me."

. . .

Four months later, with our daughter growing inside me, my husband took me back to Paris.

EXCLUSIVE BONUS CONTENT

JASPER

Christmas was my favorite season at The Eloise Inn. Winter could go fuck itself. But Christmas I liked.

That first subzero day was always a miserable shock. On the drive into town, the thermometer had shown minus two. But the cold, my frigid mood, disappeared the moment I stepped through the lobby doors.

It wasn't all that different than the feeling I got from walking inside the A-frame. A feeling that had everything to do with the woman at the counter talking on the phone.

Where Eloise was, I was home.

When she spotted me, she held up a finger, mouthing, "One sec."

I jerked my chin to the fireplace and carried the car seat over, setting it down on the table to unbuckle our baby girl.

Ophelia was bundled in a pink snowsuit. The color was almost identical to the rosy shade of her cheeks. Her big, brown eyes seemed to take it all in, from the garland over the fireplace to the massive tree adorned with ornaments and red velvet bows. The sparkle from the white twinkle lights in the windows lit up her precious face.

The scent of vanilla and pine filled the air. Beneath it was the undercurrent of smoke from the fire crackling in the hearth. Above it, hung on the towering stone column, was the wreath I'd painstakingly hung with Mateo the day after Thanksgiving.

Everyone else in America called it Black Friday. Not Eloise. She'd dubbed it Decoration Day. Attendance was mandatory.

Anything the Edens considered an official holiday was mandatory. New Year's. Easter. Thanksgiving. Mandatory, and spent at the ranch.

Next week for Christmas Eve and Christmas Day, we'd all crowd into Anne and Harrison's house, eating and laughing and exchanging gifts. We'd watch football and play games. We'd take the kids sledding if there was enough snow.

I was praying for a fluke heat wave so we could skip the sledding.

Whatever we did, we did together. I'd never known a Christmas like that before. Hell, I'd never known family like that before.

But my daughter would.

Ophelia cooed, her eyes aimed over my shoulder.

"Is that Mommy?" I kissed her chubby cheek, taking a seat on the couch so she could use my knees as a springboard to jump up and down. I plucked the beanie from her head, her short, dark hair full of static as it stuck up in every direction.

She'd had a rough day. Both her naps had been too short and she'd been fussy since morning. Maybe she was dreading this dinner too.

For the first time ever, my parents were visiting Quincy.

They'd arrived earlier today and were staying at the hotel. One night only. Tonight, we'd meet for dinner at Knuckles. Tomorrow, they'd fly home on their private jet.

We hadn't invited them to the A-frame, nor had they asked to see our home. Christmas was in three days and they were likely rushing back to Maryland for an event or function.

But they'd wanted to meet their granddaughter.

Ophelia was six months old. They could have come at any time this fall, but they'd waited until Christmas, the second busiest time of year at the hotel besides summer.

Eloise was right. They did suck.

We'd had a rocky start, but Anne and Harrison had been the ones who'd taught me what parents were supposed to be like.

The distance between me and Mom and Dad had only grown. I hadn't seen them since Samantha's wedding in Italy. That had also been the last time I'd spoken to my ex-wife.

She'd called, not long after the shooting. When I'd seen her number on the screen, I'd hit decline. Then I'd blocked her number.

When Mom had called to announce this visit, she'd mentioned Sam was getting divorced. For her sake, I hoped Samantha found the right man. One who'd love her entirely.

It just hadn't been me.

I'd been waiting for a brunette with brilliant blue eyes.

"Hi, babe." Eloise plopped down in the seat beside me, reaching for our daughter. "How was your day?"

Ophelia answered with a whimper.

"She's tired," I said, draping my arm across the back of the couch.

"That makes two of us." Eloise yawned, leaning into my side.

Last night had been a long one with Eloise and me both up and down with the baby. At three, I'd taken Ophelia downstairs in an effort to let Eloise sleep before work. But there wasn't a corner of the A-frame that could hide from our daughter's cry.

Eventually, we'd need a bigger house. We'd need a home with more individual rooms. But neither of us was ready to move out of the house where we'd started. So for now, we'd deal with the lack of sleep. We'd traipse up and down that circular staircase and use the tiny office we'd converted into a nursery.

By baby number two, either we'd move. Or add on.

Neither of us wanted Ophelia to be an only child. I'd lived that childhood. But we were soaking her in right now. Marveling at this little miracle who had us entirely wrapped around her finger.

When she cried, I came running.

"How did check-in go?" I asked.

Her lip curled. "Fine."

Meaning my parents were exactly the same as they'd always been. Polite. Disconnected. Why were they here again?

Unless something had drastically changed, the only grandparents Ophelia would know were Anne and Harrison. I'd made peace with that. Eloise was still struggling.

She'd expected Mom and Dad to change after we'd had a baby.

A part of me had hoped that too.

The day Eloise had come home and told me she was pregnant, I'd made a vow. To her. To myself. My family would come first. Always.

I didn't need or want to get a job just for the sake of working. So I stayed home with my daughter. I worked at the hotel when Eloise needed a hand. And Foster and I had partnered on a couple business ventures around the state, opportunities to put our money to work while we remained silent investors. But otherwise, my life centered around the two ladies on this couch.

Eloise yawned again, sinking deeper into my side. "I need a nap."

I patted my thigh. "Five minutes."

Without a word of protest, she crawled into my lap, settling Ophelia against her chest while she snuggled into mine.

Eloise fell asleep first. Three breaths and she was out. Ophelia's eyelids drooped, her mouth parting. Then she drifted off too.

Those roots beneath my feet had burrowed deep, like an oak tree, immovable against any storm.

My parents. Dan. Samantha. Even Foster. They'd all pushed me in a different direction. Every bit of pain, every bit of disappointment, every win, every loss, had led me here. So I could be in exactly the right place at exactly the right time.

In Montana.

On a couch.

With my family asleep in my arms.

ELOISE

"**W**elcome to The Eloise Inn," I said to the couple standing on the other side of the hotel's front desk. "Checking in?"

"Yes. Beau and Sabrina Holt," the man said. He was so tall I had to crane my neck to meet his gaze. While he fished a wallet out of his jeans pocket, sliding his driver's license across the counter, his wife glanced around the lobby.

She had stars in her pretty eyes as she spun in a slow circle.

It never got old, watching people fall in love with my hotel.

My fingers flew across the keyboard as I pulled up their reservation. "Where are you visiting from?"

"Prescott," Sabrina said, leaning her head on Beau's arm. "This is just a weekend getaway from the kids. We've never been to Quincy."

Before I could prattle off a list of places they should visit, the door to Knuckles opened and Jasper walked out carrying two to-go containers. My stomach growled, starving for lunch.

He nodded to the guests as he walked behind me, setting our food aside until I finished.

"If you need any recommendations for activities in the area, just let me know," I told them as I programmed their key cards.

The man looked at his wife, a grin toying on his lips. "I think we've got plenty to do."

Meaning they'd be calling for room service for most meals, and I probably wouldn't see them until they surfaced to check out Monday morning. Good for them.

"Enjoy your stay." I waved as they walked toward the elevators, then I rose up on my toes to kiss the corner of Jasper's mouth. "Thanks, babe. I'm starving."

"Burger or chicken sandwich?"

"Halfsies?"

"Sure. I'll go get a knife."

"Or you can just eat half, I'll eat half, and then we'll swap."

He kissed my forehead, then retreated to Knuckles again for a knife.

That man's mouth had been on every inch of my body. Mine had explored every centimeter of his. But when it came to sharing food, he cut it in half first.

It probably had nothing to do with swapping saliva and everything to do with my appetite lately. There was a good chance that if he didn't divide it, I'd eat both meals. God, I was hungry.

My hand splayed across my pregnant belly as the lobby door opened and Mom walked into the hotel.

"Hi." She came around the counter with a plastic container stuffed with cookies.

"For me?" I smiled. If she walked those into the restaurant for Knox, there was a very good chance I'd cry.

"Yes, for you." She kissed my cheek, then popped the top of the container.

The scents of cinnamon and vanilla and sugar wafted from

inside. I snatched the largest and took a huge bite, moaning as the snickerdoodle melted in my mouth. "Thanks, Mom. I've been so hungry lately."

"I was that way too. As soon as I hit the six-month mark, I'd start eating everything in sight."

I took another bite as Jasper emerged with a roll of silverware tucked under his arm and a glass of ice water in each hand.

"Hey, Anne."

"Hi, Jasper." Mom stole the container of cookies from me and gave them to my husband. "For you."

"Hey!" A crumb came flying out of my mouth as I chewed. "I thought those were for me."

"Changed my mind. I'm sure he'll share."

Jas gave me a smirk. "If she's lucky."

I rolled my eyes. "Can I eat my burger now?"

He chuckled as he divided everything in half, then slid over my lunch.

"Want to sit, Anne?" he asked.

"No, I can't stay. Just dropping off cookies and this." She took a small envelope out of her coat pocket.

"Is that for Jasper too?" I teased even though my name was written on the letter's face.

"Smart-ass." She kissed my cheek, then waved at Jasper.

I shoved three french fries in my mouth, then tore into the envelope.

Dear Eloise,

When Griffin got married, I started this tradition of writing letters to each of you on your wedding days. But since you and Jasper got married in Vegas, I didn't get to write you a letter. I know, I know. You got married ages ago. To be honest, I'm not very good at writing letters and I've been waiting to figure out exactly what to say.

I remembered a story this morning, one that I don't think I've ever shared with you kids.

When your dad and I got engaged, we didn't have much money. He was working on the ranch, and I had just finished college. The plan was to pay off my student loans and save up as much as we could to build a house on the ranch. We didn't want to spend a bunch on a fancy honeymoon, but we decided to use whatever money we got as gifts to go on a trip.

The morning after the wedding, we were at my parents' house, opening presents. We had a basket of cards to open. He started on them first but noticed the envelopes had been opened already. We realized pretty quickly that someone had taken that basket during the wedding reception and rifled through the cards. All the cash people had gifted us was gone. My parents had given us five hundred dollars. That was a fortune for them.

We never found out who did it. No one remembered seeing that basket disappear from the gift table.

It was such a violation. I cried on your dad's shoulder for hours, mostly feeling sorry for myself. But he promised me it would be okay. He promised me we'd still have a honeymoon.

There were a few checks in the cards. We used that money to buy groceries, a case of beer and a new tent.

And for our honeymoon, we went camping. It was one of the best weeks of my life.

I doubt you and Jasper will ever want for much. Maybe that's why I thought you'd appreciate this story the most. I see the way you lean on each other. I see the way you hold each other up. I have that with your father. I'm happy you have that with Jasper too.

I love you. I'm proud of you. And I'm happy for you.

xoxo
Mom

I looked up from the paper to the lobby's door. Mom was gone, well on her way home to the ranch by now. I grabbed my phone from the desk, pulling up her name.

"Yes, those cookies really are for you," she answered. "But don't hog them, okay? Share with Jasper."

"Okay." I smiled. "I love you, Mom."

"I love you too, Eloise."

Jas's eyes were waiting as I ended the call. "Love you, El."

"Love you, Jas." I leaned in to kiss his cheek. Then I stole an onion ring from his lunch.

ACKNOWLEDGMENTS

Thank you for reading *Jasper Vale*!

A massive thanks to my amazing team. My editor, Elizabeth Nover. My proofreaders, Julie Deaton, Judy Zweifel and Kaitlyn Moodie. My cover designer, Sarah Hansen. My publicist, Nina. To Logan and to Vicki, thanks for all you do.

Thanks to all the influencers who read and promote my books. To my family, every book reminds me of your unending love and support. Thank you! And lastly, another thanks to you for reading. I am so grateful that with all the books in the world, you chose to get lost within the pages of mine.

Don't miss the rest of the Edens!

Don't miss the exciting new books
Entangled has to offer.

Follow us!

 @EntangledPublishing

 @Entangled_Publishing

 @EntangledPub